The Gideon Files, Book Two

White Jade

Ande Li

ROOM 808 PRESS
Publishing Imprint for Authors Maurice X. Alvarez & Ande Li

Copyright 2019 Ande Li at Room 808 Press

ISBN-13: 978-1-951575-00-7
ISBN-13: 978-1-951575-01-4

Source: Digital copy

Cover image: popovartem.com, Stock photo ID: 345710582, Dec 1, 2015. Photograph. Shutterstock. Web.

Acknowledgements

For the readers, who continue to support and encourage their storytellers. We may supply the words, but your imagination helps to bring our worlds to life.

Chapter 1

The pretty young woman, with her auburn hair curled and tucked into an elegant chignon, placed one hand on her generous, lace-adorned chest. "What you said last night was beautiful," she sighed. "It really touched me," she say, stroking Jonah Gideon's arm with her free hand.

He responded with a tepid smile and tried not to recoil from Ellie's touch, by reminding himself of their better days together, when he had been blissfully unaware of her habitual infidelity. "Thank you. We appreciate you coming today."

"I meant what I said last night," she whispered. "If you need *anything* at all, I'm here for you."

"Thanks, I'll remember that," Jonah said, more out of politeness than actual interest. He struggled to keep his focus on Ellie, to better avoid her wandering hands, but he continued to see wispy figures passing through the funeral parlor rooms.

One of his souvenirs from his recent trip to New York had been his awakened sensitivity to the presence of ghosts and spirits. At least, he could clearly distinguish between the ethereal vestiges of the dead and the physical forms of the living, but both were equally visible to him, and suddenly, Boston seemed much more crowded than it had been when he left over a month ago.

"I like this new look," Ellie smiled, brushing the dark scruff of a beard on Jonah's jaw. "You seem so much more serious since you've been back, so mature."

Jonah looked across the viewing room of the funeral parlor, to make sure that his cousin Malcolm's parents— Jonah's Uncle Teddy and Aunt Connie—were not overextending themselves. They had all been there since the parlor opened at seven that morning, and Jonah didn't think that he had seen either his uncle or aunt leave the room yet, and very rarely during the viewing sessions the day before.

Jonah's old girlfriend Ellie seemed unaware of anyone but him, and she stayed next to him, even as he approached the circle of his older relatives, few of whom knew Ellie or her significance—or lack thereof.

"Oh, who's this, then?" asked Connie, her blue eyes clear and sharp behind her reading glasses, under her halo of pepper-gray hair.

"I'm Ellie," she introduced herself, flashing the same coquettish smile that she undoubtedly had used on the various men with whom she had cheated on Jonah.

"What a pretty girl you are," Connie beamed, and glanced at Jonah. "My nephew doesn't need pretty. He needs good and kind. Are you?" she asked pointedly.

Avoiding a glance at Ellie to see her reaction, Jonah stepped forward and took Connie's hand. "Can I get you or Uncle Teddy some water, or anything else?"

"No, thank you, dear," she said, stroking his hand, as she got to her feet. "But I need to get up and stretch my legs a little bit, so you can walk with me." He held his elbow out to her automatically, and she wrapped her thin hand around the crook. Once out of earshot, she whispered, "You looked like you needed rescuing. You shouldn't let women take advantage of you like that."

"I'm trying, Aunt Connie." Jonah walked his aunt out of the viewing room into the hallway, expectantly darting his eyes to the doors, even though he knew that the chances were slim to none that Adam or Mina would be coming to the burial services, especially since he had exchanged messages with Mina late the night before.

How r u? she had written, well after midnight.
OK. Up late?

Can't sleep, she had replied. *Burial at 11?*

Yes. Gave eulogy tonight. Should have had whisky first, he had joked, punctuating with a smile emoji.

She had replied with a smile and wink to their private joke, knowing that he had to abstain from stimulants of any kind. *Good luck tomorrow. Talk soon.*

He had fought the impulse to reply with something flirtatious or romantic and had just played it safe with: *Thanks. Good night.*

Now, thinking back, he could've been a little more charming, but he was too tired to think of anything good, and he was always better in person than in texts, anyway.

He was distracted by his aunt's voice, and her fingers tightening on his arm. "Well, this is a surprise. I didn't expect her to come all this way."

Jonah followed his aunt's eyes to the elegant Chinese woman on the arm of a younger, equally elegant man, both outfitted in trim black suits. He did a double-take, as he recognized Adam immediately and was expecting to see Mina with him, but then Jonah recognized the middle-aged woman's serene, proud carriage.

Adam and Mina's mother, Selina Xing, whispered something to her son, as her eyes made contact with Jonah's, and the two of them approached Jonah and his aunt. Selina's attention and gentle smile were focused on Malcolm's mother, but Jonah sensed her acute awareness of him, just as she seemed to be aware of most of the people in the room, stranger or not.

"Thank you for coming, Selina," Connie said. "It's been so long."

"It's good to see you." Selina gripped Connie's hands in hers, and her demeanor was as calmly assuring and collected as a professional funeral director: respectfully courteous, but inured to grief on a personal

3

level. "Of course, I had to come. My husband would be here, too, but he's overseas on business."

Connie pulled Selina alongside her. "Teddy will be so glad to see you, too," she said, then turned her keen blue eyes to Adam. "I haven't forgotten about you, young man," she teased. "I'll be back for you in a moment."

"I'll be right here, Aunt Connie," Adam said, as he and Jonah watched the women disappear into the parlor.

Before Jonah could ask whether Mina had come with them, he saw her by the door, as stealthy, sleek and graceful as a black cat. She didn't want to make a scene with her entrance, so she had slipped in discreetly, probably while the attention had been on Adam and Selina. She was dressed in a simple black sheath dress and tailored jacket, with her long hair braided and coiled and her rings on the gold chain around her neck.

"Mina didn't mention that you'd be coming," Jonah said.

"It was a last-minute decision. We caught the six o'clock shuttle out of Newark this morning, so everything was a little rushed. Mom arrived after midnight and bought our tickets for us at the terminal— she spent the night in the airport lounge."

"Shit, if you'd texted me, I would've sent a car or something."

Adam waved his offer aside. "No, you have enough on your mind," he said. "And on your face, too. What the hell is that?" he cracked, referring to the beard. "You only left New York four days ago."

"I got tired of shaving," Jonah said, brushing at his short whiskers. "You're just jealous because you'll never be able to grow anything so luxuriant."

"Thank goodness," Adam cracked. More soberly, he asked, "Did they do a good job with Malcolm?"

"Yeah, they did." Jonah followed Adam's line of sight, to the mannequin-like figure of Malcolm in the

4

coffin, with Mina kneeling in front of it silently and stoically. "She didn't really need to come. She and Malcolm said everything they needed to say back in New York," he said in a hush. "His spirit's not even here anymore."

"Funerals are less for the deceased than they are for their survivors," Adam said quietly. "We didn't come for him; we came for you, and our mom was adamant about being here for Malcolm's parents."

Mina stood behind Selina's seat and set her hand on her mother's shoulder, then leaned over to listen to her whispers. There was a similar, tranquil energy that seemed to drift between Mina and Selina and passed into those around them. With a look of surprise, Connie pointed to the wedding and engagement rings that dangled from the fine gold chain around Mina's neck, and Mina nodded without comment.

Jonah had never noticed how much Mina resembled her mother, with the same fine-boned grace and dark almond eyes, but perhaps it was more than the appearance. The last time he had seen the two women together, Mina had been a starry-eyed ingenue marrying her supposed true love, and Selina had been the reserved, watchful mother who wasn't as charmed by Malcolm as her daughter was. Since that time, Mina had become more worldly and world-weary, and Selina seemed less suspicious and aloof.

"Adam?" called a husky woman's voice behind Jonah and Adam. Jonah suppressed a cringe, but Adam caught his meaningful blink and grinned. "God, I thought that was you!"

Adam turned to greet Ellie, who seemed to have forgotten again that they were in a funeral parlor. Thankfully, Adam was more decorous. "Hi, Ellie," he said, taking her hands before she could throw her arms around him. "It's been a while."

"Wow, you look great," she gushed, looking him over. "I don't know how I never noticed how hot you were."

Jonah covered his mouth, as Adam looked clearly uncomfortable with the unwanted and inappropriate attention he was getting, now from other mourners who had been drawn by Ellie's party-girl brashness.

"Hey," Mina said quietly, laying her hand on Adam's elbow and flashing Jonah a fleeting smile, "can I steal you for a second?"

Adam jumped at the chance to make his escape. "I'm sorry. Mina needs me," he said, and let his sister lead him towards where Selina and the Gideon elders were sitting, along with the spirits of some of their ancestors who had arrived. Jonah caught the eye of his paternal grandfather, who had passed three years ago, and exchanged a smile and nod with his "Pop-Pop."

"Is she looking for more money, I wonder," Ellie said, assessing Mina. "She took poor Malcolm for millions, I hear."

Understanding the situation better now, after his recent discussions with his late cousin, Jonah replied, "Actually, he was very happy with the divorce settlement." He also knew the extent of Malcolm's continued generosity towards Mina in his will, as he had worked with Malcolm and their estate lawyer months ago, but he hadn't said anything to Mina. He certainly wasn't going to tell Ellie at Malcolm's funeral.

"She probably bewitched him," Ellie said cattily. "I hear she works as a psychic for hire now, so she must know a thing or two about fleecing people."

Jonah had a hard time remembering how he and Ellie had lasted over a year, except that maybe he had been feeling his mortality shortly after his thirtieth birthday and didn't want to be alone. That was a few years ago, anyway—he was over his premature mid-life crisis, while she had never stopped sowing her wild oats, even while they were together.

"Excuse me for a minute," he said. "I must be allergic to something in here." *I'm allergic to crazy, that's for sure.* He exited the parlor and went outside, all the way down the steps and to the sidewalk, for some fresh air, both the literal and the figurative kind.

Jonah closed his eyes and savored the bracing autumn air. He could smell the briny air from the harbor a mile away, flushing the odors of embalming fluid, stale smoke, and the dozens of floral arrangements, out of his lungs. The funeral home had been in business for well over a hundred years, and it smelled like it. He had been there before for other services, but this was his first visit since his olfactory and visual senses were altered; he could sense layers of scent and colors that he had never noticed before, and the intensity was overwhelming and sometimes nauseating.

In his next breath, he smelled orange oil and tea, and he opened his eyes at the familiar perfumes, but it was Selina who had trailed him and was standing an arm's length away.

"Missus Xing," he greeted with a slight, reverent bow of the head. "Thank you for coming," he said. Remembering his manners, he asked, hastily, "Have you eaten, or had anything to drink?"

Selina gave him a wry smile. "I'm fine, Jonah. Thank you." She looked over her shoulder at the crowd spilling out the door. "Your family is well-loved and close-knit. Even your Pop-Pop has come to keep your family company."

Jonah was surprised by her mention of his grandfather, who leaned against the frame of the double front doors and gave him a jaunty wave, but then realized that it would be stranger if Selina didn't see spirits, when both her children did.

7

"It meant a great deal to my aunt and uncle that Mina and Adam came, too," Jonah said. "Aunt Connie didn't know that Mina still wears the engagement ring and wedding band."

Selina straightened her stance. "It was kinder not to tell Connie the real reason that Mina still keeps them. Most of your family members have fonder memories of Malcolm than Mina or I do."

"So, you knew?" Jonah said in a whisper. "About how Malcolm treated Mina? She didn't even tell Adam, and I only found out a week ago."

Selina met his gaze directly, with her own brown eyes dark and fathomless. "I know my daughter better than anyone. She's defiant and willful, but she keeps no secrets from me." She shrugged her slender shoulders. "I've told Mina to lose the rings; they're like shackles, reminders of her pain, weighing her down and keeping her in her past."

"Even Malcolm wants her to move on," Jonah said. "He wants her to be happy."

"I forgot that you see ghosts, too," she said. "You can tell, then, that your family, past and present, seem to consider her the closest thing to your cousin's widow."

"She is, actually. He never dated anyone seriously, after they divorced," Jonah said. "Or before they got married, either, come to think of it." He looked sharply at Selina. "Not that it excuses his behavior any. Mina deserves better."

"She does, but she must give herself permission to seek it," Selina said, as the funeral director waved to Jonah from the door. "They're finishing up inside, it seems. Go, be with your family."

Mina sat in the back of the rental car next to Selina, as Adam drove from the funeral parlor to the cemetery. She saw her mother's hand resting on the armrest between them and covered it with hers, drawing her attention.

"Thank you for coming with us, *ma-ma*," she said, automatically slipping into her Chinese intonations, as she and Adam always did when speaking with their parents. "It was harder than I thought it would be."

Selina placed her other hand on top of Mina's. "I've buried enough friends and enemies to know that the emotions are always stronger than you expect. And Connie is burying her child, so as a mother, it was my duty to be here."

Mina stared out the window. "Is Dad really on a business trip?"

Selina smiled. "Your father is always brokering or closing a deal, Min-Min. In this instance, I asked him to stay in Malaysia to finish his work; he's not very good at funerals, anyway. He'll come with me next time, to meet Adam's special new friend," she said, glancing over the driver side headrest at the back of her son's head. "Adam tells me that she's very nice."

"She is. Xani's very loyal and family-oriented," Mina said, "but she can be very plain-spoken, when the situation requires it."

"That simplifies things, then," Selina said. "I look forward to meeting her. I also spoke to Malcolm's cousin, Jonah, earlier. He likes you."

Mina bowed her head. "Yes, *ma-ma*, it appears so. What do you think of him?"

"I recalled Jonah from your wedding. He seems dutiful and even asked me if I had eaten," Selina said. "Did one of you give him pointers?"

Mina smiled. "No, he probably just heard me say that too many times during the weeks he was living with me," she said, and Adam coughed over her. "It's okay, *ge-ge*. I told Mom about Jonah, as soon as I realized who my dog really was."

"So, he's observant and willing to learn," Selina said. "That's an important quality in a friend."

"And Adam gets along with him," Mina said.

"Adam gets along with everyone," Selina returned. "Your brother is like your father, in that way. You, on the other hand, are prickly and distant, like me, and need someone who can sense and accommodate your moods."

Adam made the last turn onto the last stretch the cemetery road, and Mina automatically peered ahead to see if she could catch a glimpse of Jonah getting out of one of the funereal cars. She caught her mother's stare and felt her face redden. She was always defenseless against Selina Xing's signature gaze: analytical and cynical, in equal measures.

"Will you heed my advice, Mina?" Selina asked quietly.

"Yes, *ma-ma*." She expected words of caution about letting her guard down or sharing too much about herself too soon, as Selina had advised with Malcolm, and Mina steeled herself for a stern reminder.

Instead, Selina looked out at the peaceful rolling lawn of the cemetery. "It's dangerous for you here. It's best that you not linger any longer than you must."

"Dangerous," Mina echoed. "Do you know something? Or sense something?"

"I know this isn't your territory," Selina said, "and the others who hold this region are suspicious of your presence. Their eyes seem to be everywhere. Do the witches here not make allowances for truces during mourning?"

"Considering that Miranda was the one responsible for Malcolm's death, I wouldn't expect one," Mina said. "I was hoping to slip in and out undetected, but I guess I have no such luck."

"You must've dishonored them, for them to watch you so guardedly."

"If I dishonored them, it was because they were dishonorable first," Mina said curtly. "They were disrespectful and cruel, and I did what was necessary to protect my friends."

"I'm not scolding you, Min-Min," Selina said. "But you know the beings that your enemies use and serve, so their arrogance should be expected, and any actions you take against them would have consequences."

Mina sighed tiredly. "Any tips for dealing with witches like Miranda?"

"Keep your head, and she will lose hers, in time," Selina said. "She may be older and stronger than you, but remember who and what you are," she said, stroking Mina's cheek.

"It won't matter in a few hours, anyway," Mina said. "Our flight is at five, so once I'm gone from here, things can go back to normal."

Selina Xing once had a different name and a different face, when she had lived on the other side of the world. She had once been named *Jin Mudan*, or the Gold Peony, but that was centuries ago, before her land was pillaged and exploited by enemies from other lands, as well as from within.

From the time she left her family, she had lived a solitary life in the green expanses of China's countryside, traveling freely but favoring the waterways, especially in the southern regions. She still remembered exploring the lush, misty mountains of Guilin, and further east in the Fujian province, catching fish in the Min River and frogs and field crabs in the rice paddies fed by its tributaries.

Then, the European colonials came, bringing new religions and opium, followed by waves of other invaders, then revolutionaries, until war and industrialization had transformed her home and restricted her range. She had been long gone by the dawn of the

20th century, but she still missed her old lands. She would no longer hunt there as she once did: the rivers were polluted with waste and death, the fertile paddies were drained to make way for new roadways and buildings, and even her mountains were blasted and quarried for the sake of human progress and expansion.

It had been her exhaustion and desperate hunger that had finally betrayed her, when she was too young to know better. She had followed the smell of chicken feathers to a farm, intending to hunt the rats that grew fat on grain feed, but she had ventured too close and too carelessly and was caught in a trap. Thankfully, it was a wire trap, and not a bone-crushing claw trap, but it had made little difference to her. Her days as a free spirit had come to an end.

Now, as Selina regarded the plate of cold cuts, deviled eggs and eggplant rollatini that Adam had brought her from the catered table set up in the Gideons' living room, she had a momentary sense of nostalgia for the old days, when she could recognize her food before smelling or tasting it, or at least take part in mercifully killing her prey, honoring its sacrifice by consuming most of it.

"Do you want something else, Mom?" Adam asked, noticing her slight frown, as he set her drink down at the dining room table, near Connie and Teddy Gideon's seats. "There are sandwiches, potatoes..."

"No, I'll be fine," she said patiently. "If I want something, I won't be shy about getting it myself. Besides, it's a repass, not an all-you-can-eat buffet."

"Okay." Adam took a deep breath, reminded that she was an adult with all of her faculties intact. "I'll be right back."

"Don't rush," she said. "You are here for your friends, so *be* here for them." She watched Adam join a group of college friends, who had all attended school together with Malcolm. Even in the Gideons' family room, nearly filled to capacity with over of dozen of Malcolm's old schoolmates, the noise level was respectfully subdued.

"Mom," called Mina quietly over her shoulder. Selina held out her hand and grasped Mina's firmly.

"You look tired, Min-Min." Even though her daughter was a couple of inches taller than her, Selina's higher heels allowed her to look Mina directly in the eye. "Have you eaten anything since this morning?" she asked, gesturing to her own full dish.

Mina shook her head. "It's a lot of comfort food: sweets and starches. I'll feel awful on the plane ride home, if I have anything now."

"It's a short ride, and you need to eat," Selina said, picking up one of the deviled eggs in the napkin and handing it to Mina.

"Thanks, Mom." Mina finished the egg in a couple of bites. "I think you're right. Something here does feel wrong," she said. "But there are too many unfamiliar faces here, I don't know what to look for."

Selina heard the ire in her daughter's voice, so she decided to give her a little help. Plus, any humble affirmation from Mina always put Selina in a more generous mood, and from Mina's small entreating smile, she was well aware of it.

"The guests all came directly from the cemetery, which sits on consecrated ground," Selina observed, scanning the faces. "The caterers came here directly."

Mina looked at the dishes and the spread in the other room with alarm. "If the witches are pretending to be caterers, they wouldn't try to poison anyone, would they?"

"Not unless they're incredibly stupid," Selina said, then glanced at Mina. "From what you've told me of your enemies, they prefer to operate more strategically, and there are too many guests for them to tamper with the food or drink."

"That's true. They would look for specific targets," Mina said, her gaze riveting on one of the uniformed servers, a slender young woman with her straight blond hair in a ponytail. "She looks familiar."

Sure enough, the blond server returned Mina's stare and held it longer than one would for a passing or curious glance. Selina took a seat and glanced up at Mina. "I won't interfere unless you want me to. I'll be here, if you need me."

"Thanks, Mom," Mina said. Selina offered her another egg, and Mina shook her head. "I'm good, thanks."

As Selina tried to keep Mina in sight, she noticed Jonah passing through the room to make sure that everyone was situated and had helped themselves to something. He and his younger cousins were seeing to the needs of the guests, so that the elders could gather and converse uninterrupted and unbothered by the logistical details of the repass.

Seeing her sitting by herself, Jonah started to detour to join her, then noticed the direction of Selina's eyes and turned subtly to avoid blocking her view. "Is everything alright?" he asked quietly.

"Hard to say when my daughter's involved," she said lightly, cutting off a piece of rollatini with her plastic fork, then uncoiling the breaded vegetable from around the cheese filling before tasting it. "What are your intentions towards her?" she asked bluntly.

Jonah's blue eyes widened. "My intentions? I haven't thought that through just yet. I've been busy this week." At Selina's expectant stare, he managed, "We haven't spent a great deal of time together, but I do care about her. I don't want to crowd her or rush her into anything, so I'm keeping my distance. I'll let her decide what she wants, first."

Selina nodded, hearing his sincerity through his overwrought response. He seemed slightly intimidated by her, which she liked. It meant he understood the dynamics of their family, at least on a rudimentary level. "Good. She doesn't need more distractions."

"Excuse me?" he frowned.

Selina had no time to explain, as she needed to focus her attention on keeping track of the creatures that were suddenly emerging from the shadowy corners of the room, inky and phantasmal forms that stalked the guests, undetected. Well, *almost* undetected.

"What the fuck are those things?" Jonah muttered, seeing them converge on Malcolm's parents in the living room. "Shit, they're going towards my aunt and uncle!"

Selina looked over at Mina and grabbed Jonah's arm. "Wait," she whispered. "You don't want to turn their house into a war zone, do you? Besides, there are too many to try to fight, so you'll just do more harm than good. Look," she said, nodding subtly towards Mina.

The blond server had engaged Mina in deep conversation, smiling confidently as she gestured to the shadow creatures positioned around them. Selina recognized Mina's deliberate stillness, her daughter's meditative method of breathing whenever Mina wanted to avoid hitting someone or cursing them out.

Mina nodded to the server, and the shadows rescinded into the dark corners, except for one who remained behind Connie Gideon, looming behind her as she chatted with the guests, unaware of any potential danger. The server, looking pleased, passed a business card to Mina before returning to bussing plates and glasses from the repass guests.

Adam joined Mina and invited her to say hello to some of the guests in the family room, his voice seemingly light and unconcerned, but Selina noticed her son's subtle glance into the living room at where Malcolm's parents were, still watched by the uninvited specter. Adam led his sister into the other room but returned to the dining table shortly.

"We should leave soon," Selina said, getting to her feet.

"Mina said she's not allowed to leave with us," Adam said quietly. "The shadow stalker guarding Connie will stay until you and I are gone, but if Mina tries to escape, or if anyone tries to intervene with Connie…"

It was as Selina had feared. "They want to keep Mina here, cut off from us."

"Mina said it was her idea, for us to leave safely, in exchange for her agreeing to meet them, on their own grounds."

Selina recalled the business card that the server had given Mina. "What was on the card?"

"It's an address for a building near Peterborough and Jersey," Adam said.

"That's near Fenway Park," Jonah said. "There are more parking lots and storage lockers around there than anything else."

"Mina hasn't been told when they want her there," Adam said. "But it won't be until tomorrow, so she has to stay overnight. And that thing," Adam glanced at the stalker in the living room, "will stay to ensure that Mina doesn't leave Boston prematurely."

Selina recalled what Mina packed in her small sling bag. Her daughter had been planning to be gone for less than a day, and with having to endure airport security screening, she hadn't brought any of her work supplies or equipment along in her overnight satchel, just some basic personal items and a pair of comfortable shoes. "I have a few things I can leave with her," Selina frowned, "but she'll be alone."

"I'll stay with her," Jonah offered.

"It's too dangerous for you to be involved," Selina said.

"Respectfully, Missus Xing, you wouldn't be in Boston at all, if not for me and my family, so I feel some responsibility for Mina's safety," he said.

16

Jonah was brave, she had to admit. Hopefully, he was competent too, otherwise he would be more of a liability to Mina than an asset. "Where is she now?" she asked Adam.

"Talking with some of our old college friends," he said.

"Keep watch over Connie, but walk the rooms, and make sure there's only the one stalker we have to worry about," Selina said to Adam and Jonah, following Mina's voice to the family room, where she was surrounded by Adam and Malcolm's old classmates and listening to their funny anecdotes about her abusive ex-husband. They were as unaware as most of Malcolm's friends and family members had been, of his violence towards Mina during their brief relationship, and Mina chose to maintain her silence, but Selina recognized the tightness of her daughter's smile.

Selina beckoned to Mina from the doorway, out of the caterers' sight, and Mina joined her promptly. "Do you want me to stay? Or, leave and come back?"

Mina shook her head. "I'll handle it. You and Adam should leave as soon as you can. I need him to be in New York for me, to keep an eye on things."

Selina smiled indulgently. "And where should I be?"

"Somewhere safe, *ma-ma*," she said readily. "*Ba-ba* would never forgive me, if anything happened to you."

"Your father loves you and can never stay mad at you," Selina said, tapping Mina's nose playfully. "Watch yourself, and stay focused."

"I will, Mom," Mina whispered, her voice barely above a breath. "I'll be home, soon."

"Don't be quick; be thorough," Selina cautioned sternly. "You can't afford to be careless, so don't let your feelings distract you."

17

"I know," Mina said, as she gripped Selina's hand. At Selina's questioning glance, she said, more emphatically, "I won't."

Mina's expression hardened, and her grasp tightened, as her eyes drifted towards something behind Selina. "What is it?"

"One of the shadow stalkers is coming behind you." Mina said quietly. "There should only be one here; I already told Miranda's agent that I would stay."

"Honor is part of your code, not theirs." Selina felt its chill at her back and a prickle at her neck. "I'd expected as much. It's an extra incentive for you to cooperate, and it is curious about who I am."

Adam joined them, and he was careful not to stare at the stalker behind Selina. "We should start heading out, in case there's traffic around Logan." He gave Mina a hug and a kiss on the forehead. "I'll text you later."

Selina was gratified and warmed by the closeness of her children, and a little saddened by how fast they had grown into adulthood, in their experiences, as well as in their years. Adam, especially, had undergone significant changes since she had last seen him, months ago, and seemed more grounded. Mina was still as serious as she had been as a child, but she was quicker to smile nowadays, even if it was usually a dark smirk.

There was no trace of that on Mina's face now, as she finally released Selina's hand. "I'm starting to think that it was a mistake for you to come."

"Fear is no excuse for shirking duty, Min-Min," Selina said. "Focus on your tasks, and let me manage mine."

Chapter 2

Mina stayed till the last of the guests had gone, except for Jonah and some of Malcolm's other cousins, and together, they cleaned up the house so that Connie and Teddy could rest after their exhausting day—their exhausting week, really. The stalker, having done its part to ensure that Mina didn't leave with her family, slipped away with the other guests, but Mina remained on guard for its reappearance, just in case it was hiding.

Jonah and Mina watched the caterers pack up their supplies into their truck, and Mina noticed that the blond who had spoken to her earlier was not amongst them. As the catering truck left, Jonah helped Mina with clearing the last of the dishes in the dining room.

"I asked the caterers, and there's no one on their staff matching that description," Jonah said. "If she was here, she wasn't part of their company."

"I know I didn't imagine it," Mina said curtly. "Those stalkers were brought by someone."

"I'm not doubting you," Jonah said, taking a stack of cups from Mina's hands. "I'm just repeating what the site manager told me."

"I'm sorry," Mina said. "I didn't mean to snap at you. I know it's been a difficult enough week for you, as it is, without you having to deal with this shit."

His hands full, Jonah bumped his elbow gently against Mina's. "Hey, you've helped me deal with mine, so I'm happy to return the favor. My dad taught me to always settle my debts."

Mina had noticed Jonah's calm and steadiness throughout the services, and wondered whether he was accustomed to that kind of profound loss, more so than some other members of the family. At the mention of his father, she then also realized that she had never met either of his parents.

"You don't talk about your parents often," she said delicately, and she suspected she knew why.

"They've been gone for well over twenty years," he answered. "They died in a car crash when I was twelve. Connie and Teddy took me in after that, so I moved to Boston and lived with them for a few years until I left for college."

Mina thought his accent was subdued for a New Englander. "Where did you grow up?"

"All over," he said. "Chicago, DC, Seattle... even Soho for a little while. My dad didn't like to stay in any one place for very long."

"When you say Soho..." Mina prompted.

"New York, not London," he clarified, then looked around. "What's to keep you from leaving and going home now? There's no one watching you."

"There's always someone watching, trust me," she said. "I'm not leaving you to deal with Miranda and her followers by yourself, anyway. I'll go when the threat is gone."

Jonah looked at her uncertainly. "That can take a long while."

"It won't," Mina said, wiping some spilled tomato sauce off her jacket and lobbing the crumpled paper napkin into the nearby garbage. "She's expecting that I'll go down quick, but I still have a few tricks up my sleeve."

"That reminds me. Your mom left me something, to give to you," he said, as he heard Connie's voice calling him from the sitting room. "I'll be right back. Don't go anywhere."

Adam accompanied Selina to her departure gate, as his plane was scheduled to leave fifteen minutes later than hers. While they waited for her plane to start boarding, Adam tried his best to ignore his phone, which was indicating incoming messages with brisk regularity. He was also trying to avoid looking at the stalker still lingering around Selina; it had followed them from the Gideons' house and all the way to their departure terminal, with nothing more than a momentary power glitch in security scanners to indicate that anything was out of the ordinary.

"It's alright," Selina said. "You can take your messages. I know there are matters that you have to attend to."

"Mom, I hardly have a chance to see you," he said. "I feel like there are so many things we haven't discussed, that shouldn't wait until it's too late."

Selina took her son's hand between her cooler, smaller ones. "We've already talked quite a bit during this trip. There is such a thing as talking too much."

"I'm worried about Mina," he said quietly.

"Of course. What kind of brother would you be, if you didn't worry? Check your phone," she said, getting to her feet. "I want to wash my face, anyway." She pulled her silver hair comb from her hair to give her tightened scalp some relief and retrieved her cosmetic pouch out of her larger purse. As she tucked away her comb, avoiding its pointed tines, she fought the temptation to look whether the stalker was following, as she was sure it was.

Selina took her time washing her hands and face, waiting for a lull in foot traffic, as she kept an eye on her stalker in the mirror. She had had a difficult time keeping it in view, since it was always positioned behind her, but she saw it more clearly in the reflection, since the entity was drawn to her heat and energy and had no awareness of the mirror.

Selina passed her damp hands under the air hand-dryer and noticed that the stalker drew closer, attracted by the warmth and noise of the blower. It was distracted enough that Selina could take a step back without its notice, then another, before she pulled her hands away from the dryer.

When the stalker finally realized its distraction, it whirled around to try to get behind Selina again, but it was too late. She was looking at it, unblinkingly, and it was powerless to act while her eyes were on it.

Without averting her gaze, even as the restroom foot traffic began to pick up again around them, Selina felt around in her cosmetic bag for her silver hair comb. She hadn't lived centuries and traveled from the other side of the world to succumb to a base, crude creature like a shadow stalker.

As she let her eyes blink shut, it lunged at her, and she swiped the spiky silver tines against its body, scoring it with the silver tips. "Tell your masters that there are other powers and players that should not be discounted," she whispered, ignoring the alarmed sideways glances of the other women in the restroom.

Selina gave the stalker a couple of seconds to retreat, but when it lingered and seemed to be looking at the other, unwitting visitors as potential victims, she took a step forward and plunged the pointed silver teeth of her comb deep into its center, twisting her hand to embed the metal tines more deeply in its black core.

"On second thought," she said, as the stalker's dark spectral form dissolved into oblivion, unnoticed by all but Selina, "they'll figure it out on their own soon enough."

She tucked the comb back into her bag and returned to her gate, where some passengers were starting to collect their bags for early boarding. Adam stood when he saw her, looking past her, surprised that her stalker was gone.

"The less baggage, the better," Selina commented, returning her small makeup bag to her purse. "Let Mina know not to worry about me. I'll take care of anything troublesome on my end. Oh, before I forget, your father wants me to give this to you."

She slipped off a white gold chain over her head and over Adam's with ease, although his neck was more muscular than hers. The small, intricately-carved white jade pendant dangled just below his collar from the clasp-less chain.

Adam felt the relief pattern of the pendant, a piece of flawless, milk-white "mutton fat" nephrite jade, and he recognized its dimensions and shape. "This is Dad's jade. How didn't I notice that you were wearing it this whole time?"

Selina smiled patiently, patting Adam's smooth cheek. "Silly. Unless you look for it, why would you see it?"

"Why does Dad want me to have it?" Adam asked.

"Because it protects the wearer, and your father wants you to be safe," Selina said matter-of-factly.

"Maybe you should've given it to Mina, instead," he said. "Or keep it for yourself."

She shook her head. "We have our own means. This protection is meant for you."

"Okay," Adam said, skeptical but resigned. "Tell Dad 'thanks' for me." Adam gave Selina a hug. "I love you, Mom."

"How western of you, to state something so obvious," she teased, hugging her son back. "Call me, if you need anything."

Jonah found Connie in her favorite armchair, with her stockinged feet finally unshod and propped up on the chair's matching ottoman. She waved him over and motioned him to take a seat on the loveseat closest to her.

"Quite a week we're having, isn't it?" Connie remarked, brushing back a loose gray curl from her face. "And it's not even the weekend yet. How are you holding up?"

"Fine, Aunt Connie," Jonah said. "I'm more concerned about you and Uncle Teddy. If you need to talk, I'm always here to listen."

Connie reached over and patted Jonah's hand. "Sometimes, I wish Malcolm had followed your example more. Your uncle Teddy and I loved him more than anything, of course, but your uncle always said there was a darkness about him. Maybe now, your cousin's finally at peace."

"I'm sure he is." Jonah refrained from saying more, not wanting to explain to Connie how he knew how Malcolm's spirit was faring. Dropping his eyes, he noticed a small picture from Malcolm and Mina's wedding, on the end table next to Connie's chair. It was a spontaneous candid shot, of Mina beaming up at Malcolm during their first dance as husband and wife, with the lights illuminating the pearls on her dress and hair...

"It was nice of Mina to come," Connie said. "I don't think Malcolm was ever happier than when they were married. It's a shame that they couldn't make it work."

Jonah heard the regret in his aunt's voice. "Not all marriages are meant to last forever, and I'm sure there were reasons for their decision. It's not fair to make one partner stay in a relationship, just to keep the other one happy."

24

Connie looked at him askance. "Did Mina tell you something? I didn't realize you and she were so close."

"We reconnected when I was in New York last month, that's all," Jonah said. "Malcolm didn't like me talking to her when they were together." He realized after he spoke, that his words sounded more accusatory than he intended.

"He was very jealous about her, wasn't he? That just made a bad situation worse for them," Connie sighed. "Malcolm thought the world of you, though, and I think he would be very happy, if you took care of his widow for him."

"Excuse me?"

"The Book of Deuteronomy states that if a man dies without a son, his brother should marry his widow as part of his duties," Connie said. "Malcolm was an only child like you, but you were practically brothers to each other."

"You're quoting the Bible now, Aunt Connie?" Jonah laughed cynically. "As I recall, the passage after that one says that if I refuse, she should publicly shame me, hurl a sandal at me and spit in my face, for shirking my responsibilities."

"Then don't refuse," Connie joked. "Not *everything* needs to be taken literally, silly boy. All I'm saying is that we wouldn't be against it, if something happened between the two of you."

"That's a relief," Jonah said. "As I recall, Deuteronomy also has a few notes against marrying the same woman twice, cross-dressing and half the repass menu today, so our whole family would be in a load of trouble." Just to be safe, he decided not to mention Mina's actual work concerning divination and sorcery to Connie—that could be a bit too much for his aunt to handle.

"Here, while you're thinking it over," Connie said, holding out a small ring box.

Jonah took it from Connie but didn't look inside right away. "What is this?"

"It was your mother's ring, and your grandmother's before that," Connie said. "Your uncle Teddy said your grandmother gave it to your father when he was trying to save up for a diamond engagement ring. She told him not to wait, that if your mother was the right one, it would be good enough."

Jonah opened the box and saw the glimmering, brilliant-cut ruby set in a fine, yellow gold ring, with tiny diamonds on either side. It wasn't flashy or extravagant, but it was beautiful in its simplicity, just as how he recalled life with his parents. Briefly, he caught a flash of a memory of his mother, putting the ring on, as she dabbed on perfume and a touch of pink lip gloss. "My mom used to wear it on special occasions and holidays," he recalled.

"She left it to me, in her will," Connie said. "It still reminds me of her, and I could never bring myself to wear it, so I thought I'd hold onto it, until you were mature enough to know what you want to do with it. It's time you settled down—you're not getting any younger."

It was well past sunset and after rush hour by the time Jonah and Mina left Connie and Teddy's house. Mina slowed her step to let Jonah unlock the truck and open her door for her, although all she had were her small sling bag and a black canvas satchel that served as her overnight bag.

Jonah's truck was a powder-blue pickup that suited him: strong, dependable, and well-maintained. It wasn't new or shiny, but it was clean and comfortable inside. There were smudges of dried mud on the exterior, but no rust.

He eyed Mina's slim skirt and the height of the cab. "You need a step-stool or mounting block to get up in there?"

"I'm fine," Mina said, tossing her bag inside the cab and hitching her skirt up her thighs to climb up. Once inside, she noticed a small black pouch underneath her seat.

"Yeah, your mom left that for you," Jonah said, slipping into the driver's seat. "I know it's late, but did you need to stop at a pharmacy or someplace before we head back to Brookline?"

Maybe it was the long day finally taking its toll, but Mina didn't entirely comprehend what Jonah was asking. "Back to... I thought you were just going to drive me to a hotel?"

"No, I never said that," he said, pulling out of the parking space. "I promised your family that I would look out for you, and I can't do that, if you're in a hotel. You'll have to stay with me." He glanced at her briefly. "So, do you need to pick up anything, like a toothbrush?"

"No, thanks, I have that," she said. "My mom taught me to always keep a toothbrush, a hairbrush and flats in my carry-on bag, in case I get stuck at the airport. I didn't pack extra clothes, though. I thought I'd be home tonight."

"There are some stores on the way..."

"No, it's better that I stay out of sight, and away from crowds, in case Miranda tries to make a move against me." She leaned back against the headrest. "Are you sure I'm not imposing? This was all very last-minute."

"Imposing?" Jonah laughed. "After what you had to deal with, when I was in New York? Unless you change into an animal, I think we'll be okay."

"Not planning on it," Mina muttered, peeking into the zippered cosmetic bag that her mother had left for her. There were plastic snack bags filled with dried

27

herbs, whole spices and small desiccated animals, as well as a couple of filled glass jars, a lockpicking set, a pack of first-aid supplies… "Holy shit, Mom," she muttered. "How did you even get through airport security with this?"

Jonah kept his eyes on the road but asked, "What's in there?"

"Everything but a good weapon," she said.

He smiled knowingly. "You're suffering without your dagger, aren't you?"

"This is one of the reasons I don't travel: I like having my own supplies." At the sound of her phone chime, she glanced at it briefly. "Adam's back in New York, and our mom should be home by midnight." She let out a deep, relieved breath. "At least, they're both away from here."

"They wanted to stay."

"I didn't want them to," Mina said. "The less Miranda knows about my family, the better."

"Why?" Jonah asked. "You're worried that she'll try to use them against you, like she tried with Morgan?"

Mina recalled Morgan's hapless, guileless fall under the blood magical control of Miranda's sisterhood, and Adam's subsequently harsh technique to break him free of it. "No, my family's too knowledgeable and careful to let that happen," she said. "But the fact that they know to be careful, makes others curious enough to look at them more closely. My mom already had one stalker trailing her when she left for the airport."

"Is that why she didn't say good-bye to me?" Jonah scowled. "You should've said something earlier."

"What for? Connie was in greater danger from her stalker, and besides, my mom knows how to deal with them," she said, looking out the window. "She's the one who taught me."

"Does that make you a second-generation witch?"

"My mom's more than a witch," she smiled, thinking of the rare occasions when she caught a glimpse of her mother's true, original nature, those times when Selina Xing let down her guises and became *Jin Mudan* again. "She's descended from *huli jing*."

"Holy what?" he asked, unable to read Mina's lips with her face turned away.

"*Huli jing*," Mina repeated the Chinese, turning back to Jonah. "Fox spirits. Nature elementals, of a sort. They were revered once, and even had shrines built in their honor, but now they're hunted and scattered throughout the world."

"Your mother's a spirit?" Jonah asked.

"Not anymore, not entirely," Mina said. "When my mother was old enough to take a human form, she chose my father as her mate, but she never completely lost her identity. She was human when she had my brother and me, so we are genetically human," she said, wrinkling her nose uncertainly. "Or, at least doctors have never noticed anything atypical about us."

"Your family is just full of surprises," he muttered.

"Do you actually believe me, or are you just humoring me?"

"Baby, I've lived through and seen enough weird shit these past few weeks to believe just about anything you say," he said.

She simpered at being called "baby." Normally, she found it patronizing or chauvinistic, but coming from Jonah, it sounded like a genuine endearment. "And you're sticking with me, despite all the 'weird shit'?"

"Weird started feeling normal this week," he said. "When I got back, everything looked busier and more vivid, and it was a little stressful not to have someone around who could commiserate with me. Not anyone I could trust, anyway."

Mina hadn't really considered how isolated Jonah was, dealing with his recent changes without a support structure in place. "Are you noticing anyone hanging around you more? People taking a greater interest in you?"

Jonah raised his brow. "Besides my old girlfriend hitting on me again?"

"Yeah, besides Ellie," Mina grinned. "I'm thinking more like people who give you an odd vibe, who set off your 'Spidey senses.'"

"No one like that, just the general sense that I'm being watched."

"Miranda knows who you are, so it's in her interest to keep tabs on you," Mina said. "I don't expect that she'll try to capture you again, as long as she doesn't consider you a threat."

"I suppose I should be relieved that she thinks I'm 'mostly harmless,' but I can't help feeling a little insulted." He glanced at Mina. "What does she want with you, though? You were just visiting for the day. It's not like you were intending to single-handedly take over her turf or anything."

"I don't know. To humiliate me after the way I showed her up to her boss? To have me over for high tea? I don't know what that psycho wants," Mina said, as her phone chimed again. She didn't bother hiding her pained scowl of disgust.

"What is it?" Jonah asked.

"Miranda's summons: tomorrow noon, at the address on the business card. Come alone, no weapons… the usual conditions."

"You think it's going to be more complicated than a simple meeting," Jonah said.

"If it were a simple meeting, we could meet for coffee or chowder around Faneuil Hall, Harvard Square, or fifty other public places, not at an isolated warehouse."

"You can't go alone," he said.

"I have to," Mina said solemnly, texting back her confirmation.

"Why? Your safety—"

"Because of this," Mina said, showing him Miranda's text on her phone, as he slowed at a red light.

"I don't know what I'm looking at," he said, returning his attention to the road when the light changed to green. "I just caught a glimpse of a person, a man."

"The dark streaks on his face are his blood," Mina said, having more time to study the photo. "He's alive, but he's injured. There's a tattoo on his neck—a brand, really."

"What does any of that have to do with your going to meet Miranda alone?"

"Because he's her prisoner, and if I don't follow her instructions, she's going to kill him, or at least continue torturing him," Mina said. "And I know him. Or, at least, I know who he is."

"How's that?"

"Because Cindy rented some space from me, to shelter him and his family for a few weeks. He's an escaped indentured fae, and he's supposed to be living in my duplex."

Chapter 3

Morgan Crain nodded to Xani and his sister's boyfriend
and Mina's brother, Adam, as they passed Micah's
security check at the door of the Red Lotus. After
observing their jinn bouncer at his post for the past
couple of hours, Morgan was pretty sure that Micah
didn't have to look at the customer IDs at all to know
whether someone was allowed in—all Micah had to do
was give the customers a suspicious look to make
potential troublemakers and underaged drinkers rethink
coming in. If customers thought about causing trouble
once they were inside… well, Mina's wards were in
place to keep the peace.

Xani and Adam came to the booth where Morgan
was working and took a quick glance at the bar. "Cindy
stepped away?" Xani asked.

"Cindy said she has to take care of some personal
business and should be back in a couple of hours,"
Morgan said, shutting his laptop to take a quick break.
He had been working in the office before Cindy asked
him to watch the lounge while she was gone. Her team of
bartenders and waitstaff had everything well under
control, but it never hurt to have one of the co-owners
present, for questions or feedback. Personally, Morgan
found it less distracting to work in the office, not so
much because of the noise level, but because he often
found himself just gazing fixatedly and wistfully at

Cindy and forgetting all about work when he was in the main lounge.

Adam looked tired from his prolonged day. "Did you guys just get back from Boston?" Morgan asked.

Adam and Xani exchanged a meaningful look. "Just me. Mina stayed behind, hopefully not for too long."

Morgan frowned, focusing his clear green eyes intently on Adam. If Mina had just stayed behind to hang out with Jonah for a while, Adam wouldn't have looked so concerned. "Shit. Did something happen?"

"I don't know," Adam said, leaning against the booth. "But Garrison Brothers is based in Boston, so that's where Miranda's sisterhood is headquartered, too. We were hoping to pay our respects to Malcolm's family and get out before anyone noticed, but…"

"It's not your fault that Miranda's being an asshole," Xani said. "I'm sure Mina will be fine."

"I'm surprised you didn't stay in Boston with her," Morgan said.

"I would've," Adam said readily, "but Mina didn't want me there." He must have noticed Morgan's involuntary twitch, as he followed up, "It's not a Jonah thing, like she doesn't want me hovering. Mina didn't want either me or our mom around, in case Miranda tried to use us for leverage or control."

"Like she did with me?" Morgan asked quietly. He still bristled at the memory of when he had been under Miranda's control, thinking and acting in ways that he would've never otherwise considered, especially towards Mina.

"Yeah, something like that," Adam said. "In the meantime, Mina wanted me to check on a few things for her before she gets back." He took a quick look around the bar area. "No follow-up visits from the police?"

Morgan and Xani shook their heads. "Malcolm's death was an unfortunate traffic fatality, as far as they're concerned," Xani said. "And the medical examiner filed that Jack Mackay was an accidental overdose. The office had a hard time even tracking down his next of kin," she said sullenly.

"Either way, Mina had no motive or contact with either of them prior to their deaths, so the cases are closed," Morgan said, feeling relieved on Mina's behalf. She had been asked to come in for a police interview earlier in the week, as part of the routine investigation, but they had worked with Mina before on prior cases and saw no reason to trouble her further.

"It's been quiet this week," Xani said. "Even Lucifer's been scarce. He was in here earlier today to talk to Cindy, but it was a quick visit."

Morgan tried to manage his discomfort about Cindy being in regular contact with devils and demons, feeling in his gut that Lucifer was not to be trusted. It should've been obvious that devils were less than forthcoming or upstanding, but somehow Lucifer seemed to behave himself, as far as Morgan could tell, at least within the walls of the Red Lotus.

"I'm going to head over to Mina's building," Adam said.

"Want me to go with you?" Xani offered.

"No, I should be quick," Adam said, giving her a peck on the cheek and a quick nod to Morgan before he left the table.

Morgan watched his sister's adoring gaze after Adam until he disappeared out the door. "Wow, you really are smitten."

"Not that you get a say, but does it matter?" she answered smartly.

He shook his head, as he opened his laptop again. "Nah. I'm happy for you."

"What are you working on?" Xani asked, slipping into the booth next to him. "Looks fancy. And expensive."

Morgan ignored his big sister's affected air-headed tone. "Cindy asked me to see about installing high-intensity security lights around the duplex, just temporarily, until her friends move out."

"How high-intensity?" Xani asked, eyeing the specifications on Morgan's screen. "Mina's okay with you mucking around in there?"

"Yeah, Mina's cool with it, as long as I don't dislodge any old lead paint or asbestos insulation," Morgan said. "About three thousand lumens per bulb, one in each room," he said under his breath. "Some areas will get about thirty kilolux of illuminance, a little less than full daylight levels."

"Why does Cindy want that much light in there?" Xani asked. "That's enough to blind someone, if they're not careful."

Morgan shrugged. "Hey, if my girl wants the stars and the sun, I'm not going to ask her why, just where and how bright she wants them."

"You make it sound so romantic," Xani said. "So, is Cindy officially your girl, now?"

"I'm working on it," he said, looking at her askance. "You okay with that? She used to be your guy, when she *was* a guy."

"That was years ago," Xani said, bumping her brother's shoulder playfully. "As long as you're both happy, I'm good with it."

"Yeah," Morgan smiled. "I guess you could say I'm smitten."

Selina didn't like confined spaces, so she didn't particularly enjoy air travel, but she tolerated it for its speed, especially for transcontinental trips. To lessen her discomfort, she flew first class whenever it was possible, and requested aisle seats whenever it wasn't.

Thankfully, her plane from Boston to San Francisco had a first class cabin, so she was able to relax and catch up on some letter-writing on her way home. Despite the long day and the droning hum of the plane, she couldn't fall asleep. Something about hurtling through the air at forty thousand feet inside a tin can did not set her mind at ease.

Selina had also left her travel pouch bag of materials and supplies behind with Mina, so she felt more vulnerable than usual. She reassured herself with knowing that she only had a few hours until she was home, back within the safe boundaries of her adopted home.

She was drafting a note to old friends, when she sensed a figure coming down the aisle towards her, slowing to a stop next to her seat. She folded her note and looked up at the tall, handsome, dark-haired man smiling down at her.

"May I speak with you?" he asked quietly.

"Depends. Do we have business to discuss?" she asked coolly. She didn't recognize him as one of the passengers in the cabin, but he took the seat across the aisle from her without concern or even a look around.

"I believe we do," he said folding his well-manicured hands over his crossed legs. A golden pin shaped like a shofar glittered from his lapel. "Regarding your children."

"We have nothing to discuss regarding my children," she said. She glanced around the cabin and noticed that no one was listening or even glancing in their direction, not even the flight attendants. Even the air seemed to stop blowing through the vents. "Have you taken us out of time, in order for us to speak privately?"

The olive-skinned man smiled slightly, with barely a flash of his perfect white teeth. "You're still as wily and perceptive as ever, *Jin Mudan*," he said. "I didn't

36

think you would be as forthcoming, if we had an audience."

Selina noticed his subtle luminescence better when she didn't look at him directly, but the faint golden halo crowning his dark curls was apparent. "I haven't seen one of your kind in years. Which one are you?"

He set his fingers over his pin, as he bowed his head. "I am Gabriel. I believe you met my brother Michael previously."

Selina tucked her half-written letter into her notebook. "My husband deals more regularly with your master's agents than I do, so I'm perplexed about why you could possibly want to speak with me."

"You've undoubtedly noticed recent changes in your son," Gabriel said. "I wanted to clarify that I was partly responsible, in that I intervened to spare his life, but I didn't make any other alterations."

She nodded. "Thank you for confirming your involvement."

"You're very stoic about your son still being alive. Are you upset that he was saved?" Gabriel asked.

"Of course not," she replied. "I would've grieved losing him, but there are worse fates than death, aren't there?" She had lived long enough to understand that divinities and deities didn't interfere in mortal lives without ulterior motives. "What are your plans for him?"

"I cannot tell you," Gabriel said, almost apologetically. "I can only assure you that his decisions are his own, and he will never bring disgrace or dishonor to you. He may be tested—as most good humans are— but you've raised him well."

"What do you want from me, angel?" Selina asked.

"Your promise that you will not side against me or my Master," Gabriel said. "I wish to be forthright with you, as I'm aware that our human followers haven't always treated your kind with tolerance," he said, raising his hand at Selina's dismissive frown, "but I believe that you see us as the lesser evil, so to speak, at least compared to our diabolical counterparts."

"I don't take sides except to protect my family," Selina said, "but I don't respond kindly to threats against them either, so I'm leaning more towards your faction than the other, at the present." She had no intention of provoking divine wrath, nor would she allow herself or her children to be used for bargaining. "You have my word."

"The Master will be gratified to hear it," Gabriel smiled. "Thank you, Missus Xing."

Gabriel rose from the seat and bowed to Selina, and the activity in the cabin resumed with the clink of glasses and hum of the overhead air vents. He strolled towards the privacy curtains separating the cabins and slipped between them without anyone's notice.

I've given my word, Selina mused, closing her eyes. *But my dear husband hasn't.*

As soon as Adam stepped into the hallway on the bottom floor of Mina's building, the faint giggling he heard was quickly silenced and replaced by hushed semi-whispers, coming from behind the door of the duplex, which he had only seen vacant since returning to New York weeks before.

Earlier in the week, he had heard Mina and Cindy discussing some details about Cindy renting the space for a little while, until her guests were better situated for moving on, but Adam had heard little about the tenants themselves. After looking over Mina's apartment and checking in with Millie Krantz on the second floor, he was finishing his rounds and keeping his promise to Mina by looking in on the new occupants to make sure they were settling in comfortably.

To avoid startling the new dwellers, Adam walked with a heavier, shuffling step to signal his approach, and knocked on the half-open front door. "How's it going in there?"

As he listened more closely, he could distinguish two children's voices, or at least voices on the squeakier, higher-pitched end. Finally, he saw one of the figures peek at him from the edge of one of the doorways, and it was a small, dark-haired figure. As soon as the figure realized that Adam had noticed, it ducked behind the doorway again.

"It's okay, I'm a friend of Cindy's?" he called. "Mina asked me to check on things while she's gone."

Another figure peeked out from the other side of the same doorway, and Adam fought the temptation to enter the room uninvited. From his angle, the duplex was still mostly devoid of furniture and personal belongings or valuables that would tempt a burglar, but that didn't mean that his presence wouldn't be met with suspicion or hostility, anyway.

"Who's Mina?" the new figure asked quietly, in one of the high-pitched voices, and its form was taller and gently curved, definitely female, with short dark hair against her golden-tan complexion.

"Mina's my sister," Adam said. "She owns this building."

"The whole building?" marveled the first figure. "She must be a princess!"

"That would make me a prince, and I'm definitely not that," he replied. "My name is Adam. And you are…" he prompted.

"We're faeries!" the smaller one chirped, his wings buzzing like a bumblebee's, as he stepped out from his hiding place. Adam could only tell that it was a young fae boy because it wasn't wearing any clothing apart from a thin linen shirt that ended just below his waist, leaving his little boy parts unfettered and clearly visible.

The taller figure hissed at the boy to settle down. "You're going to get us in trouble with the humans!" she

39

cried, and Adam saw the edge of an iridescent wing tucked behind her back.

"It's okay, you're not in trouble!" Adam said in a rush. "Not with me, anyway."

The heavy front door of the apartment building opened, and Cindy's cheerful humming floated into the duplex. The boy zipped past Adam with wings beating excitedly, careening towards the apartment door to greet her but was stopped short, as Cindy shut the door behind herself, holding a large paper bag in her other hand.

"You're back!" Cindy smiled at Adam. "No Mina?" she asked.

"I'll tell you later," Adam said, more seriously.

"Oh," Cindy said, picking up on Adam's somberness. "You," she said gently, turning to the boy embracing her waist. "I've told you already, silly bean. No flying inside unless all the drapes and doors are closed. And where are your pants?"

"They're too warm," the boy complained, then pointed at the taller figure. "She doesn't have to wear pants!"

"My dress covers me enough," the other fae said, stepping through the doorway.

Adam reserved comment but shot Cindy a look, as the thin slip did cover her essential form, but just barely. There was little doubt in Adam's mind that he was looking at a teenage girl, and her pretty face and large wings allowed him to focus his eyes elsewhere besides her newly-mature body.

"I'll take a look in Mina's closet for some other clothes for you," Adam offered.

"Where is Fern?" Cindy asked, handing the bag to the boy.

"She's taking a nap," he said.

Adam recalled the giggling that had drawn him to the apartment and wondered if Fern was still asleep after the noise.

"If she's napping, then we'll let her sleep," Cindy said. "In the meantime, I brought you some extra food and toiletries."

The boy chortled. "'Toilet trees'?"

"Things to clean ourselves up, Fallon," the girl explained. "This is too generous, Miss Cindy. You've already done enough for us." Still, she peered into the brown bag that the boy was already digging through, curious about what was inside.

"We watch out for each other, remember?" Cindy said. "You kids have already been through enough to get here."

Fallon pulled out a pack of toddler training pants. "What's this?"

"That's for Fern," Cindy said patiently. "I don't want her to have any accidents, and she's nervous in this new place."

Adam looked at the pack of cartoon-decorated diapers. "How old is Fern?"

"Fern is two and a half, almost three," Cindy said.

Adam turned aside to speak to her privately. "They're all children here? Who brought them?"

"There had been others," Cindy said in a hush, "but two of the adults died in the voyage here, and the third is missing. Gia is the oldest of the remaining three, and she brought them the rest of the way to New York."

"Gia's the girl? She looks barely sixteen."

"She's actually fifteen, but she's been through a lot," Cindy said grimly. "This isn't what I had expected either, but they don't have anyone else."

A fussing, whining cry came from one of the bedrooms, and Gia's wings sprang open and propelled her towards the crying. Adam noticed small nicks and fraying along the corners of her lace-like damselfly wings, as she glided towards the back.

Fallon was busy unpacking the groceries and found a pack of juice boxes, and he took one out. "What happened to your wings?" he asked Adam. "Were they severed like Miss Cindy's?"

"Adam's not fae," Cindy said. At the boy's startled recoil, she said, "It's okay. He's human, but he's the good kind."

Fallon watched Adam suspiciously, as he stuck the juice box with its accompanying straw. Instead of drinking, he held the box and waited for Gia to return with a small toddler, whose dark hair and pale skin matched his own.

Fern was a small faerie child, with dark, nub-like protrusions growing from between her shoulder blades, fused to her pink skin, and Adam saw the growths clearly, as the child clutched a fleece blanket to her chest and belly. Gia was careful to avoid the nubs, as she held the toddler close, while Fallon held the juice box carefully to let Fern drink from it without having to release her hold on her blanket.

Adam pulled out his phone as it chimed in his pocket. It was a text from Mina, with a single question mark.

He texted back: *3 kids. I'm here with Cindy.*

"Mina?" Cindy asked, folding up the empty brown grocery bag.

"Yeah," Adam said, looking at his phone, at the ellipsis indicating a pending reply. "She had to stay behind in Boston."

Cindy stopped. "Is she okay?"

"So far," Adam said. "She's staying with Jonah, so at least she's not alone."

"Witches?" Cindy asked, careful not to say too much around the children.

"Who else?" Adam quipped, as Mina's reply came back.

"What does she say?" Cindy asked.

Adam held up the phone for Cindy to read for herself: *Tell Cindy I'll do what I can.*

It had been a while since Jonah had brought anyone back to his apartment, on a quiet residential street in Brookline, not too far from the birthplace of John F. Kennedy. Technically, it was Connie and Teddy's old house, where Jonah had lived with them years ago, before they decided to move to South Boston and convert the small house into up and downstairs apartment units. He lived upstairs rent-free, in return for maintaining the house and yard for his aunt and uncle. The young couple who had lived downstairs had moved out during Jonah's extended stay in New York, so he had the house to himself, essentially.

That is, he thought he lived by himself, until he returned from New York and discovered that he had the ghost of a child staying with him. It had taken a few minutes of patient coaxing for Jonah to learn that his roommate's name was Maggie, that she had died at age eight during a smallpox outbreak in 1721. The ghost was attired as she was when she died, in a plain muslin nightgown that fell to her bare feet.

Jonah unlocked his door but didn't bother interrupting Mina's phone conversations, first with Cindy, then with someone named Aciré, whom Mina trusted enough to speak openly about her family's whereabouts. The woman's voice was deep and resounding, and Jonah could hear her tones through Mina's phone.

"Okay, thanks," Mina said finally, as Jonah shut the door behind them. "I'll let you know if I need you. Good night, Aciré."

"Who's that?" Jonah asked, a little tersely, but he also taken aback by his ghostly border standing mere inches away from Mina, as Maggie openly stared at her in fascination. He presumed that Mina could see the

43

ghostly child with the light-colored hair clearly, but there was no reaction or acknowledgment.

"Aciré Hart, our family's counsel in Boston," Mina said, slipping her phone back into her pocket, as she left her heels by the door.

"How do you pronounce her name, again?" Jonah asked.

"Like 'Desiree,' but without the 'D,'" Mina said, poker-faced. "This is usually when she hears some snickers or lewd jokes at her expense."

Jonah wasn't a teenaged boy, but he was familiar enough with current crude slang to know the "D" reference. "I'll refrain, thanks."

"Anyway, her firm handles my parents' estate and manages their East Coast assets. Her partners, Bullfinch and Farrier, work more with my parents, but she and I go back a bit."

Jonah wondered about the Xing family's holdings, that they had ready access to their lawyer late on a Friday night. "Are you expecting legal trouble?"

"No, just letting her know that I was in Boston, in case I need to get into my mom's vault on Harrison Avenue, or anything else."

"Your mom has a vault here?"

"Just a small one," Mina said, dropping her bags on a chair in the living room and turned around, stooping to look at the child spirit in the eye. "Hello."

Maggie smiled shyly, shuffling her bare feet. *You can see me?*

"Yes, I can," Mina said, lowering herself to a crouch. "Do you live here?"

Sometimes. When Mister Jonah was gone, I visited downstairs, but I think those people were frightened of me. I like it better here, anyway; it's quieter and more peaceful. She leaned in closer to Mina, unaware that Jonah could still hear her. *And I think he is lonely.*

44

Mina smiled but didn't look at Jonah. "That's very observant of you. What is your name?"

My name is Margaret White, but everyone calls me 'Maggie,' the ghost introduced herself, just as she had to Jonah.

"It's nice to meet you, Maggie. Have you noticed anyone coming to visit Jonah's home recently?" Mina asked.

Jonah hadn't thought to interview Maggie when he had spoken to her, but in light of Miranda's hostile intentions, it was a prudent move on Mina's part. Thankfully, Mina was affable and gentle with the ghost child and gave her attention fully to her, so Maggie felt at ease to talk and seemed grateful for the chance to be heard.

No one comes inside, but sometimes there are people who look around outside, by the windows and doors.

"This week?" Jonah asked, then noticed Maggie's confusion about the measures of time. "Since I came home a few nights ago," he clarified.

Yes, Maggie said, seeing his agitation. *Is that bad? Did I do something wrong?*

"No, Maggie, you haven't done anything wrong," Mina said tenderly. "I'd like to hear a little more…"

As Jonah excused himself to change out of the suit that he had been wearing since that morning, he listened to Mina's gentle questioning of Maggie for details of who had been around, how the spirit spent her days, and even helping her figure out why she hadn't yet left the material world to join her family.

When Jonah returned to the living room, he found Mina alone, sitting on the floor, with her head against her drawn-up knees.

"What happened?" he asked, looking around the space for Maggie. "Are you okay?"

"Yeah," Mina said breathily, wiping at her eyes.

"Where's Maggie?" he asked.

"Gone to wherever she goes, to rest. She'll be back tomorrow," she said. "She's afraid to move on. She thinks her family blames her for her baby brother's death from the pox, and that she'll go to hell for killing him. I was trying to help her get 'unstuck.'"

Jonah held out his hand to help Mina to her feet, and he noticed that her hand and her eyes were damp with tears. Instinctively, he tugged her hand to draw her into an embrace, but she pulled back, just as instinctually.

"I'm fine, but thank you," she said, wiping at her eyes as she rushed past him, to her small bags. "So, should I just sleep out here on the couch?"

"No, I have a guest bedroom," he said. "Second door on the left. Bathroom is the door on the right, and there's a washer and dryer in the hall, if you need it." He hadn't expected to give Mina such a rushed overview of his apartment, but she was already heading down the corridor to get settled. "Please ignore my laundry basket. It's all clean, I just haven't had a chance to put anything away."

Mina paused in the doorway of the guest room and eyed the stacked washer and dryer. "Actually, would you mind terribly, if I did a quick rinse of my stuff and borrowed some of your things for tonight? I'll even fold your clothes for you."

The thought of seeing Mina in his clothes was immediately compelling. "That sounds very reasonable. Help yourself."

Chapter 4

While her clothes were sloshing around inside the efficiency washer, getting cleaned of other guests' wine and sauce stains from the repass earlier in the day, Mina picked through Jonah's clean laundry and found a black t-shirt, a front-zip heather gray sweatshirt, a pair of boxers and clean crew socks. She was disappointed in herself, that she hadn't thought to pack an extra set of underwear, but she was more relieved not to find another woman's undergarments mixed in with Jonah's clothes.

She had to think for a moment about why that mattered. Despite Jonah's consideration and her mother's observation that he liked her, she and Jonah had yet to talk about their friendship. It seemed unnecessary to have a discussion over it, and raising the topic risked complicating what appeared to be a straightforward relationship.

She didn't want complications or distractions. Everywhere she went, there were people and creatures who needed her help and undivided focus, if possible, whether it was a fae fleeing servitude, a demon looking for their wayward spawn, or a centuries-old ghost seeking peace and absolution. She didn't expect or want Jonah's involvement in any of it—he had his own life, with his own obligations and duties.

Mina followed the upbeat tempo and guitar riffs of an old Aerosmith album—*Toys in the Attic*, maybe?—to the kitchen, where Jonah was drumming along, as he watched the simmering pots of pasta and sauce, with an assortment of cutting boards strewn across his countertop.

She watched him silently for a moment, impressed by his ability to multi-task in the kitchen. She waited for the song to start fading out before she cleared her throat gently. "Need a hand with anything?"

She didn't seem to catch him off-guard, as he didn't even flinch, as he piled his used cutting boards in the sink. "I'm good, thanks. I don't know about you, but I didn't get to eat very much today, and now I'm famished."

He did do a double-take, though, at what she was wearing.

"I hope you don't mind me borrowing your hoodie," she said sheepishly. "The shirt's a little thin. I matched your socks and folded your other shirts, though."

He shook his head. "I don't mind at all. They look better on you than on me."

He motioned her towards the dining table, with two place settings already arranged on the side that was not covered with file boxes and books. He started to straighten the table, as he caught her glance at his clutter.

"It's okay. You can leave it," she said.

"I don't want it toppling over while we eat," he joked, shoving the piles just a little further over before he returned to the kitchen for the plates. "Uncle Teddy was talking this week about selling this place finally, so I started cleaning out my stuff. There's nothing like a month away to provide some perspective about what's actually important to keep."

Amid the clutter was a glass mug filled with pencils and pens, and a stiletto-like letter opener. She pulled it out of the cup and noticed its shine and resonance.

"Silver?" she asked.

He looked over. "Yeah, the blade is, but the handle's steel. One of my cousins brought it back as a souvenir from Spain."

Mina recognized the handle's ornate black and gold damascened design as typical of metalwork from Toledo. "Do you mind if I borrow this?"

"Um, okay. Do I want to know why?"

"In case I feel a little stabby," she said. "Away from home, I have to improvise."

She took the seat across from him as he set down their fluted bowls, each containing a generous tangle of *al dente* linguine noodles bathed in cream, egg, cheese and pancetta, dusted with freshly-ground black pepper and chopped flat parsley from Jonah's window box of new herbs.

"Bacon, gluten, dairy and fat: all my favorite comfort food groups, in one bowl," she said, admiring the expert plating. "This looks incredible."

He smiled. "It'd feel gluttonous to make it just for myself, but since you're here I figured: why not?" He shrugged, "I wish I had some wine or beer to offer, but…you know."

"Don't worry about it," she said, twirling some of the pasta on her fork for a small bite. She closed her eyes at the first taste. "Oh, my God," she sighed. "That's the most delicious—" She snapped her eyes open. "Don't tell the elves at the Lotus I said that. They'd be devastated."

He laughed, and the sound of his spontaneous laughter made her smile, in turn. He had been so serious all day, and probably all week, given all the preparations and support needed for Malcolm's funeral, and hopefully, he could now breathe and relax a little. She had confirmed with Maggie White's spirit that Miranda's agents were keeping Jonah under surveillance, but at least they hadn't moved on him.

The conversation over dinner was light, as Mina caught Jonah up on what their friends were doing back home in New York, and he seemed to welcome the brief diversion from his own personal life. Jonah moved to take her empty dish, but she waved him away and cleared the table for both of them.

As Mina set all the dishes and empty pans to soak in the sink, Jonah packed away the leftovers. She paused for a moment to savor the domesticity of the moment. She missed those days from the months when she and Malcolm were married, when it was just a quiet evening with the two of them in their tiny apartment.

"You can leave the dishes, really," he said.

"It's no bother," she said, pouring some dish soap on the sponge. "You cleaned up glass shards for me while you were barefoot. This is nothing," she said casually, then remembered his permanent condition. "How does it feel, having to cut out alcohol and the rest?"

He reached past her to slip a couple of sauce-coated utensils into the sink. "Some days are harder than others," he admitted, "especially this week. But it's worth it, and I wouldn't change a thing."

She was reminded of something that Malcolm had told her before his spirit left. "Did you really tell Malcolm the night before our wedding that you'd swear off drinking if you were married, because you'd want to remember every moment you spent with your wife?"

Jonah was still for a moment. "Malcolm told you about that?"

"He told me after he was dead, but yes, he told me," Mina said, focusing on the dishes to avoid looking at Jonah. It was most likely a private comment, and she was already sorry for bringing it up so randomly.

"As I recall, I told him that I would quit drinking, if I were in his shoes," he said solemnly, "so that I'd remember every single moment with *you*, specifically."

"Oh," she said, now feeling even more chagrinned, as she turned her attention to vigorously scrubbing the pans. "I'm sorry, I shouldn't have mentioned it."

"I'm sorry he told you," Jonah said quietly. "He shouldn't have burdened you with something from years ago."

"He just didn't want to leave any lingering secrets," Mina said, noticing Jonah's discomfort. It was a remark made in confidence, possibly even on impulse. "It's not a big deal—it's ancient history." She finished rinsing and looked over her shoulder at him. "Right?"

"Malcolm could be a thoughtless shit, sometimes, but he had me pegged pretty well." He shook his head dismissively. "In any case, that's my baggage, not yours."

"Wait, what are you saying?" she said. So, Malcolm was right about Jonah feeling something for her?

She dried her hands hastily and followed him to the living room, where he had the changed the playlist to something mellower, not necessarily quieter. Miles Davis's *Kind of Blue*, if she wasn't mistaken.

"Maybe we should call it a night," he deflected, stepping around her. "We don't know what Miranda has planned for you, so you should get some rest, and then we can figure out how to get you home. It's not safe for you to stay here."

"Given what Maggie's said, it doesn't seem like you're completely safe here, either."

"I mean it's not safe for *me*, to have *you* here," he rephrased pointedly. "I might do something that I shouldn't."

She shook her head, not quite understanding. "You wouldn't hurt me."

"That's not what I'm saying," he said sharply. "Let's just drop this. The less said, the better."

Xani Crain noticed Adam and Cindy laughing together as they slipped past Micah on their way into the Red Lotus. Cindy was wearing Adam's jacket to stave off the evening chill, and she hurried to take it off before she circled back behind the bar.

"Everything go okay?" Xani asked, sensing a connection between the two of them.

"As well as can be hoped," Cindy said, more seriously, mixing up a gin and tonic with an extra twist of lime, which she set in front of Adam. "The three of them are healthy and resilient, but of course, there's a great deal of work ahead." She looked over the Friday night crowd—they were in that brief lull between the departure of the business crowd heading home and the arrival of the post-theatre revelers.

"Morgan went home," Xani said. "He was going to finish up the plans tonight and get the supplies and light fixtures early in the morning." *For you*, she stopped short of saying.

Everything Morgan was doing was for Cindy, and as Xani watched her friend and former lover's casual flirtation with Adam, she couldn't help wondering if Cindy was as invested in the relationship as Morgan was. Unlike Morgan, Cindy was irrepressibly outgoing and social, able to command anyone's attention with a flash of her smile or a wink of her glittering lashes. She did it for the business, but she also basked in the adoration.

Thankfully, Adam was more worldly and experienced in the art of innocent banter with Cindy than an initial acquaintance would be, and Xani didn't worry about him falling under Cindy's spell during their verbal wordplay. Xani did notice that Cindy liked to touch him, though, as she often noticed faint glimmers of fae dust left in Adam's hair or on his hands.

Adam turned his dark eyes to Xani and flashed a smile. "Long day?"

"I guess so." Xani hadn't realized that she had been scowling until Adam's glance got her to relax her brow. "Not as long as yours," she said, recalling his 3AM text that morning that he was heading to the airport.

Adam took her hand and kissed it, and Cindy mimed a swoon behind the counter, out of his line of sight. "Let's call it a night and get out of here, then," he said.

Xani shook her head. "Not my place. Morgan's probably going to keep me up with work tonight. He usually keeps all the lights on and likes to barge into my room at weird hours to pick my brain."

Adam held onto her hand. "You can crash at my place, if you want."

That sounded tempting, but Xani knew she wouldn't actually sleep much if she went back to Adam's apartment with him, if past experience had taught her anything. "You should go home and get some rest. I think I'll go lie down in the office," she said, getting to her feet.

"Hey," Adam said, turning around on the stool to face her, as Cindy moved down the bar. "Is something bothering you?"

"No," Xani said peevishly. "I'm just tired."

"You're very quiet tonight," he observed.

"I'm sorry if I don't have Cindy's boundless energy and wit," she said smartly, regretting the slip of her tongue. "Forget it. I'm just going to say more stupid things, if I stay out here," she said, tugging her hand free.

Adam set his hands on her hips to keep her in place, between his knees. "It's not stupid. I want to hear what's on your mind. I know Cindy and I were gone for a while, but things took longer than we expected…"

"It's not that," Xani said, rolling her eyes at how silly she felt. "I know we haven't even been together for a week, so I may sound a little clingy, but the way you

53

talk to other girls just feels—I don't know—like you're already looking for your next girlfriend."

"Next girlfriend?" he asked, tugging her closer. "Does that make you my current one, officially?"

"I don't know that we've formalized that," she said. "And if you're still shopping—"

He interrupted her with a kiss. "I'm not. You don't have to be jealous."

"I'm not," she said quickly.

"Good, there's no reason to be. Even with Cindy; she's gorgeous and brilliant, but…"

"But what?" Xani frowned, wondering if Adam had something against non-humans, or transitioned individuals like Cindy.

"But she's not you," Adam grinned, pulling her against him.

"Good answer, honey," Cindy remarked, returning to them.

"It's an honest answer," Adam said, keeping his eyes on Xani.

"Ooh, even better," Cindy cooed. "There's nothing Xani hates more than a lying, indecisive piece of shit. I should know," she murmured, pulling beers to take to the other end of the bar.

"Cindy!" Xani shouted after her.

"What does she mean?" Adam asked.

If we're going to be honest… "It doesn't matter," Xani said quietly. "Cindy cheated on me a couple of times, when we were together. It was before she decided to transition, and I think she was still trying to find out what she wanted. When I found out, that's what I called her. I never really hated her, but in that moment, I wanted to hurt her like she had hurt me." She took a deep breath. "It was a long time ago, and like I said, it doesn't matter."

Adam brushed back her red curls. "It sounds like it still matters, to both of you," he said. "I'll never cheat on you, Xani."

"You don't have to promise me anything," she said. They hadn't even agreed on whether they were exclusively dating.

"It's not just about you," he said. "Honestly, *I* don't want to be with anyone else. Would you mind terribly, if we just cut the crap, and I started calling you my girlfriend?"

"Not at all." Xani couldn't help grinning. "I kind of like how that sounds."

As Jonah got ready for bed, he heard Mina in the hallway moving her clothes between the washer and dryer. She had looked very cute in his clothes, especially his boxers, which ended at the very top of her thighs and showed off her long, lean legs, and he had tried very hard all evening not to stare. He was a gentleman and wouldn't do or say anything untoward, but he was undeniably affected by her—"besotted" was probably the better word—and he was less distracted when she wore her own severe, dark suit. Her mourning clothes.

Shit, we just buried Malcolm this morning, he reminded himself. While they hadn't been married for years, Mina was still treated like Malcolm's de facto widow, as he had never spoken unkindly about her, and neither of them had ever remarried. In a way, Jonah still harbored some jealousy towards his cousin, as Mina had once been Malcolm's, emotionally and physically, on a level that was beyond Jonah's own reach.

Why? Because Jonah was too cowardly to tell her how he felt? If he did, the worst she could do was reject him, which he had already accepted was the most likely outcome. She had seemed embarrassed earlier, after mentioning that Malcolm had shared with her Jonah's warning about the drinking interfering with their relationship. Jonah had avoided discussing it further with Mina, but maybe they needed to talk about it, and clear up any uncertainties between them.

At least then, he could move on from it, move on from her, and focus on getting on with his life. In the meantime, he would do his best to ignore her presence in his thoughts...his life, really, even when she was hundreds of miles away. Every time a trace of his altered, canine nature resurfaced, he remembered how he had come to be that way, and how comfortable and content he had felt to be hers.

An urgent knock shook the door, and Mina entered without an invitation.

"Did you need something?" he asked.

"Yes," she said breathlessly. "You haven't cut yourself or anything today, have you?"

"Ah, no," he said tentatively. "What is this about? Hey!"

Mina braced her hands on his shoulders and kissed him deeply. Her tongue pried between his lips and touched his, but she withdrew almost before he realized what had happened. It felt as passionless as a cheek swab, but he still needed a moment to catch his breath.

"Oh, fuck," she murmured, stepping back and dropping her hands. "I'm sorry, but I needed to taste you."

"No, I'm...totally good with that," he said, a little flustered.

"Thanks," she said. "Now, I need you to get into the closet."

"The what, now?"

"Closet, now!" she said urgently, pushing him toward the slatted door. "This shouldn't take long."

From her poker-faced expression, he guessed that she had a serious reason for her peculiar demand, and he ducked inside without argument. Once inside, he heard another knock on his bedroom door, which Mina answered. He peeked through the slats on the closet door to see what was happening.

Mina had come to his room, again. Except that this was a different Mina, because the one who had kissed him had somehow taken on his appearance and still wore his t-shirt and boxers, while the new arrival wasn't wearing anything at all.

The second Mina kissed the first—the one who looked like him—without preface or greeting, and Jonah raptly watched his own fantasy play out, as the two fell back onto his bed. The two figures slowed their pace to a more sensuous rhythm, with the second Mina moaning his name. Even knowing that the second figure was not the real Mina, Jonah felt himself responding to her voice.

Suddenly, the real Mina—still looking like Jonah—took his silver letter opener from the back of the boxer waistband and plunged it into the chest of the pretender, who shrieked in pain and outrage but was too weak to throw off Mina's weight, even as it reverted back to a demonic form, charred-skinned and misshapen. Despite the direct strike, it didn't bleed and just howled furiously.

Mina's illusion gradually faded, and she changed back into herself, and the demon screeched even louder at being deceived. Mina stayed unmoving and expressionless, keeping the stiletto-like silver spike in the wounded demon's chest, as she kept it pinned underneath her, between her knees.

"Stop struggling," Mina said. "You failed. It's over."

"It's not over," it croaked. "She will call forth others."

"I'll be ready," Mina said quietly, then began whispering under her breath rapidly.

"You won't always be here," the demon chuckled, stopping its struggle, as it began to recognize Mina's incantation.

Mina climbed off the bed, taking the letter opener with her, as a swirling red vortex of brimstone smoke and fire formed next to it. She pointed the silver spike at the portal with a stern, disappointed glower, as though sending a misbehaving child to her room.

The demon got to its feet with an effort, still glaring at the make-shift weapon in Mina's hand. "You will not kill me, witch?"

"You wouldn't have killed me, even if I was your intended target," Mina said. "Go, before I change my mind."

The demon staggered through the vortex, which vanished in its wake, and Jonah emerged from the closet.

"Are you okay?" he asked.

"Yeah." Mina didn't look hurt, just vaguely disgusted. "Do I really look like that when I kiss?"

"It didn't look so bad from where I was standing," Jonah said, checking the bed for bloodstains, but aside from some flakes of char, it was clean. "Do you mind telling me what just happened?"

Mina took a deep breath. "I don't have my supplies, so your house isn't protected like my hangouts in New York. I thought I could just keep an eye on things, since it was just for the night, but I guess your location is already compromised, and Miranda is testing what defenses are in place. When I went to get my clothes out of the wash, I felt a sharp tug, like I had caught my hair on a nail or something, but there wasn't anything by my head. From what Maggie had described to me earlier, I suspected that someone had snuck into your house."

"That's when you rushed in here," Jonah said. "Why did you ask me if I had cut myself?"

Mina hesitated. "Kissing you was sort of my second choice. I would've preferred to take a drop of blood to assume your guise."

"Ouch," he said in mock insult.

"I had to keep my focus," she said. "Sorry."

"You didn't want to pluck a hair from my head, like the demon did to you?"

"That's more of a demonic practice. Besides, I don't like eating hair," she said, wrinkling her nose. "As it was, it didn't try very hard to look or taste like me."

He briefly contemplated how Mina would know her own taste, then moved on. "It probably thought that I wouldn't be able to tell the difference," he said, hastily adding, "I would've noticed, I'm sure."

Mina shot him a doubtful glance. "If you didn't realize by the time you were fucking it, you would have guessed it, when it started chewing off your balls." At his incredulous stare, she said, "That's why it was here. Not just the last part, but to fuck you and harvest your seed, first. The castration just ensures that no one else gets to harvest you," she said, "but I think the demon actually considers it a dessert treat. Now that I think of it..."

Mina grabbed a tissue from a box on his dresser and spit into it, even wiping her tongue. "If you'll excuse me, I have to use your mouthwash. If I had to guess, I'd say that you weren't its first visit tonight."

"Oh! Yeah, sure, help yourself," he said, realizing what she meant. Listening to Mina rinsing, spitting and even gagging a little, he sympathized with how repellant it would be to taste another guy's junk, in addition to knowing how the whole process ends... *She's certainly dedicated to her work. Wow.*

Mina emerged from the bathroom looking more composed, wiping down the bloodied letter opener with a wad of toilet paper. "So, that must have felt strange," she said casually, "watching us rolling around on your bed, while not actually participating. Is it like watching your own porno tape?"

Jonah wasn't sure how to answer. "First of all, I don't know it feels to watch my own performance, live or recorded. Secondly, I'm not sure whom I was more jealous of: you, for being able to feel yourself up, or the demon, for being with the *actual* you."

"For what it's worth," she said, tossing out the soiled tissue, "the imitation of me was pretty shoddy, so you didn't miss much."

"You got my impression down pretty good," he said.

"Sure, because I pay attention to details," she said, "and I've had more time to study you."

Study me? "If you didn't just come to my rescue, I'd be feeling very unsettled right now, especially with you carrying that sharp, pointy thing," he said, leaning against the doorframe. As she laughed and turned towards the spare bedroom, he called after her: "In case this happens again, how can I tell if it's a demon pretending to be you?"

"If I show up in your room again?" she asked, pausing at her door. "I'm not going to go in there uninvited, I promise. Just give a shout, if you're not sure. Better safe than neutered."

Chapter 5

Mina jumped at Jonah's sudden appearance in the kitchen, as he had yelled her name in his surprise. She straightened and hid her hands behind her back.

"Oh, you're still awake," she said blandly, but from the look on his face, it was clear that he was not convinced by her feigned nonchalance.

"I can smell your blood in the air," he said, glaring at her. "What the hell are you doing out here, cutting yourself?"

"I'm trying to protect you," she said. "And I didn't cut myself, I used a needle to draw blood into a vial." She showed him the fine brush and small flask of blood that she had in her hands, and even the tiny bandage that she had taped over her needle mark. "I have to finish marking your doorways and windows before my blood starts coagulating, so just give me five minutes, okay?"

"No, not okay!" he returned. "You haven't told me why you're doing this. Where did all this stuff even come from?"

"It was stuff in my mom's emergency kit. My blood will act as a protection ward against anything else trying to come into your home, as long as I don't miss any of the openings. I was hoping not to resort to this, but after this last visit, I didn't want to take any more chances."

She swirled the vial to keep her blood from clotting. "I was just about to finish in here, then it's just your room left. I already did the front door, the bathroom and the guest room." She dipped her brush into the vial and painted a thin crimson line across the window ledge. It didn't have to be a lot, but enough so that losing a fleck or drop wouldn't compromise the ward. She made sure to paint a line under his kitchen vent, as well.

"It's a quick, temporary fix," she said, "but it's effective for keeping most creatures away, human or otherwise, for at least a day or two."

"I guess I should be relieved that you didn't paint your blood around your own apartment, too," Jonah said, keeping his breath shallow, as he left the kitchen.

"I did, when I first moved in, but I replaced the protection wards with stronger spells over time," she called to him in the hallway. "I'd do the same, here, but I don't have my kit." Looking around the kitchen to make sure that she hadn't missed anything, she turned the lights off and easily navigated the darkened hallway by the light from Jonah's room.

"The smell was potent enough to wake me up," he said. "I thought something had happened to you."

Mina recalled what she had said to him about going into his room uninvited, and she gestured to him for permission to enter, which he granted with a flourish.

"Thank you. Anyway, if something had happened," she said, crossing the room to mark the window frame, "I'd sound an alarm to warn you to get to someplace safe." With her measures in place, she breathed a sigh of relief and grimaced. "Oh, that's a stronger odor than I thought."

"That's what I'm saying," Jonah confirmed testily. "And since I still scent like a dog, that smell is going straight to my head."

"I'm sorry it's keeping you awake," she said, turning towards the door. "It's just for tonight, and then I'm gone tomorrow."

"It's actually that part about you leaving, that's keeping me awake."

She stopped in the doorway to face him. "I'll be fine once I'm back in New York," she said. "And before I leave, I'll make sure Miranda and her followers know to leave you and your family alone."

"That's not it, either," he said softly, meeting her at the door. "Stay."

"You know I can't do that," she said. "I have obligations and people who need me at home. I have to get back."

"Then stay for tonight," he said, cupping her face in his hands. "With me."

Mina felt rooted in place, as though her body had already decided for her, before he even kissed her. She had convinced herself that it had been a mistake to kiss him earlier, even if it had been for his own safety, but now she couldn't imagine anything more perfect than the taste of him.

The hard glass vial and bamboo brush digging into her clenched fists reminded Mina of why she was even in Jonah's room, and why it was unwise to stay. Her body's instincts begged her to reconsider, fighting to move towards him instead of retreating. Then, Mina felt the chain against her skin, the thin gold rope that held her rings, and her cool-headed sanity reasserted itself.

"I can't do this," she said, savoring his kiss and the tickle of his new beard for a last few seconds. "I can't let myself be distracted."

Jonah was slow to release her. "You can't, but you want to?" he whispered against her lips.

Fuck, yes! she wanted to scream. She stroked his face with her free hand, knowing that if she ventured lower, she wouldn't want to stop. "Don't do this to me now, Jonah."

He kissed her a final time, slow and sweet, before he let her go. "Later, then?"

"Not later tonight," she clarified, backing away.

"I got it." He chuckled, his laughter low and teasing, as he leaned against his bedroom doorway. *"Later* later, when things calm down."

Back in the guest room, Mina shut the door and leaned heavily against it. *Shit, I have to keep my head straight.* The more involved she got with Jonah, the harder it was going to be to leave, to get back to her responsibilities in New York.

Or worse, if she really lost her focus, there was a chance that she'd get herself killed in Boston, and then she could *really* forget about getting home, ever.

Cindy let herself into Mina's building quietly, careful not to disturb Mrs Krantz upstairs. It was long past midnight, and Cindy had let Xani take care of closing up for the night, as she took some kitchen leftovers for the children, for them to have for breakfast in the morning.

Letting herself into the duplex, she noticed the glow of a dim incandescent bulb from one of the living room end table lamps and heard a chorus of quiet, peaceful snores.

Setting down the bag of food, Cindy crept to the living room to see who hadn't made it to their beds, and found instead an idyllic scene: Gia bundled up in a blanket on the floor on a pile of pillows, and Fallon and Fern curled up on an oversized armchair, on either side of Mrs Krantz, snoring the loudest, with a storybook open on her blanketed lap—all deep asleep.

Millie, you have a visitor, whispered Arthur Krantz's voice, even though he was nowhere in sight. Mrs Krantz stirred awake, but moved carefully to straighten her reading glasses without waking the children.

Cindy smiled and waved soundlessly to Mrs Krantz. "Thank you," she mouthed.

Millie Krantz waved Cindy's thanks aside. "It's nothing," she mouthed back, gingerly extracting herself from the armchair without displacing Fallon and Fern too much.

"It *is* something, Missus Krantz," Cindy said, helping Millie steady her feet. "That was very kind of you to visit with them. The children miss having an adult present. They weren't difficult with you, I hope."

"They have no parents here, so of course, they were unruly, at first. They calmed down in time. They are very special children, though, aren't they?" Millie smiled affectionately. "All my life, I've believed in faeries, and now I've seen them with my own eyes! And they're as delightful as I always imagined."

Cindy gave Millie a hug on impulse. Over the past few days, after Millie was discharged from the hospital, Mina had looked in on her elderly tenant more often than she had in the past, and Millie seemed to appreciate the extra visits. On a couple of occasions, Cindy had accompanied Mina on her check-ins with Millie and had cautioned Mrs Krantz not to be concerned if there were noises coming from the downstairs unit, but to let her know immediately if the new residents were too boisterous.

Now, knowing that Millie had taken it upon herself to see to the children's well-being, Cindy adored the sweet old woman even more. Hugging her, she felt the fragility of her limbs and was careful not to squeeze too hard, but she felt Millie's fingers rest on the old scars on her shoulder blades.

"Good heavens," Millie whispered. "Are you one of them, too?"

Cindy pressed her fingers to her lips in a gesture for secrecy. "Can I trust you to keep my secret, Missus Krantz?"

"Whom would I tell?" Millie giggled. "And who would believe a silly old lady like me, anyway?"

"Thank you," Cindy said with a bow of her head. "It's late. Why don't you get some sleep, and I'll get the children to their beds?"

"I'll leave you to it," Millie said. "Let the children know that they can come up and visit me anytime. If we're going to live by ourselves, we may as well be alone, together."

"Do you need help getting upstairs?" Cindy asked, noticing Millie's slow, shuffling pace.

"No, dear," Millie said, scuffling to the door. "This is the only exercise I get nowadays. Good night."

After Millie left, Cindy unpacked the food onto the counter and put the perishables into the refrigerator. She took pains to be quiet, but Gia trundled to the kitchen, still enveloped in her blanket.

"Miss Cindy, you didn't have to bring us more food," Gia said, staring at the assortment of sweets and pastries that Cindy had brought.

"It's no trouble; the kitchen had plenty left over." Since much of the prepared food would not keep long enough to be served a second day, Cindy always let the kitchen staff take leftovers home, and the elves were always appreciative of her generosity. "You're all still growing and regaining your strength, so you should eat as much as you want."

Gia looked around. "Did Missus Krantz leave? We didn't have a chance to say good-night to her, or thank her for the bedtime story. She taught us how to make hot chocolate, too."

She sounded disappointed, and Cindy studied the girl for a moment. Gia had been born into servitude, but her parents had not, so they had raised and taught her and her siblings how to live among humans. The children had manners and language to blend in, but from their initial reaction to Adam, clearly they had been taught to avoid and fear people, yet they hadn't shown that same fear towards Millie Krantz.

Cindy realized that, despite whatever horrors they had seen and experienced during their captivity, Gia and the others were still children, who sought and craved comfort and genuine love, regardless of the source.

Cindy passed Gia a plastic take-out bowl of cut fruit. "Are you hungry now? If not, you can put these in the fridge for breakfast."

Gia looked through the clear plastic and frowned skeptically at the colorful, uniform bite-sized balls and cubes.

"Open the lid, honey," Cindy said, taking a last look at the counter to make sure all the perishables were away.

Gia's eyes crinkled with delighted recognition at the smell of melons and pineapple. "Oh, it's fruit! I've never seen such small pieces," she said, marveling at the product of the kitchen elves' knife skills. "We usually are just given the rinds and trimmings left over from the master's meals."

"You and your siblings are free from that life," Cindy said, passing Gia a fork. "We're never sending you back to your captors."

"What about our parents?" Gia asked. "Have you heard from them?"

"Not yet." Cindy remembered her last exchange with Mina in Boston, and the image that Mina had forwarded of Gia's beaten father was seared into her memory. "Whatever happens, honey, remember your parents' sacrifice. They risked everything to make sure your lives will be better than theirs."

"What happens to us, if something happened to them?"

"We fae stick together, always," Cindy said solemnly. "I promised your parents that I would take care of you, so anything that tries to hurt you again will have to go through me."

67

✧✧✧

Jonah awoke early Saturday morning, despite having a restless night, thinking of Mina on the other side of the plasterboard wall. He had been more alarmed than he had let on when he scented her blood, and he was far more nervous about propositioning Mina than he had sounded.

Jonah liked to think of himself as an experienced guy, with no lack of attention from women, and certainly no trouble talking to women he liked, but something about Mina threw him off his game. Maybe it was because of her innate suspicion or her ability to see through his bullshit, but talking to Mina required a little more effort on his part.

Her response to him had been encouraging, though. Although she didn't accept his invitation to spend the night with him, she seemed tempted by the idea and by him, so there was a chance. He could work with that.

Jonah threw on a pair of jeans and a t-shirt before he opened his bedroom door, tucking his mother's ring into the snug coin pocket of his jeans, for luck. His gray hooded sweatshirt hung off his doorknob, so he pulled that on, too, with Mina's scent still lingering on it.

He realized as soon as he stepped out of the room that Mina was gone. There was a coldness and emptiness in his apartment from her absence, masked by her scent still lingering throughout the apartment, in his clothes that she had borrowed, left folded on the bed in the open guestroom, and her bag neatly packed on the living room couch, with her smaller sling inside the satchel: ready to grab on the run.

Crazy witch. Jonah had assumed that Mina would let him drive her to the rendezvous with Miranda, or at least wait for him to wake up so that they could plan whatever came next. Of course, that was Jonah's assumption, but Mina wasn't wired the same way, and he should've known that. He had observed her enough over the past month to know that Mina didn't like extra thoughts and fancies cluttering her mind, sidetracking her before she tackled a task that required her full focus.

So, he was surprised to get a call on his phone from her, and he picked it up readily. "Where are you?"

"Good morning, Jonah," she said brightly.

"Mina," he said entreatingly.

"I'm near...the Riverway? It's only a couple of miles from your place to the meeting place, and I didn't want to wake you, so I decided to walk it," she said.

"That's bullshit!" he snapped. "Stop treating me like I'm your dog again! I don't appreciate being left behind without explanation, with the expectation that I sit here and wait for you to come back."

"That's not my intent," she said calmly. "But I don't want you exposed, and we don't need Miranda pissed off that I'm not arriving alone like she wanted. I still don't know what she's planning for her hostage."

"Uh-huh," he said skeptically, noticing Mina's black high heels peeking out the top of her mostly-zipped satchel. At least she had had enough sense to wear her more comfortable flats to the meeting. "You want to text me the address of the warehouse? Peterborough and Jersey, right?"

"There's coffee in the kitchen," she deflected. "I'll text you when I'm done..."

"Wait a second—"

"And maybe we can continue our exchange from last night?" she said coyly, then disconnected.

"Fuck!" Jonah yelled, hearing the hang-up beep, then dead air. He calmed himself when he caught a pale flicker out of the corner of his eye. His resident ghost, Maggie, was cowering behind the couch, peering at him over the edge of the cushion.

"How long have you been listening, kid?" Jonah asked, heading towards the smell of fresh-brewed coffee from the kitchen.

I watched Miss Mina prepare to leave, Maggie said. *Are you angry with her?*

Jonah shook his head, as he poured himself a cup and switched off the coffee maker. "No, Maggie, I'm not, but I'm worried that Mina is in over her head." At Maggie's blank expression, he clarified: "Getting into more trouble than she can handle."

When my brother tried to do things that he couldn't, I would follow him to make sure he didn't hurt himself, Maggie said, trying to be helpful.

"I'd like to, but Mina won't tell me where she went." He had half a mind to drive to the area where he thought she had gone and just cruise the streets until he saw her or came across the likely building. It was barely 9AM, so there was plenty of time.

Jonah's conundrum was solved by a text from Adam: *Mina not answering?*

He texted back: *She's meeting Miranda this morning.*

A pause, then: *Alone?* followed by a frown emoji.

Jonah tapped back: *Not my choice.* Angry emoji.

Recalling his interactions with Adam the day before, he typed: *Address from business card?*

Promptly, Adam replied with the address from the card that Mina had shared with him, and Jonah breathed a grateful sigh for Adam's ready recall.

Jonah? Maggie's voice quavered.

"What is it, kid?" he replied automatically, typing his thanks back to Adam.

There's someone outside the window.

It took Jonah a moment to register Maggie's alarm as a legitimate warning, as it didn't make sense that anyone should be outside any of the windows of his upstairs unit. As he looked to the window, he backed up into his kitchen, away from the window's vantage.

It was a shock to hear and see the cinderblock crash through his window, but it struck the frame and tumbled to the floor by the sill, doing minimum damage. Jonah's relief was short-lived, however, as he then saw a bottle fly in after the cinderblock, with a burning rag hanging from its neck, reminding him of a Molotov cocktail. He dove behind the counter and covered his ears. *Motherfuckers!*

Jonah felt the room shake around him with the blast, but the counter structure held and shielded him from any direct damage. The explosion was loud enough to leave his ears ringing and, instinctively, before he remembered that she would be unaffected by physical forces, he shouted: "Maggie!"

Don't shout! They can hear you, and they're coming up, she replied urgently.

The fear in Maggie's tiny voice impelled Jonah to move quickly and stealthily, and he scrambled on his hands and bare feet over the splinters and debris to look where his window had been blown apart. Sure enough, shadowy forms crept through the opening, no longer protected by Mina's ward, their gnashing jaws and spiderlike appendages moving jerkily towards him, as though they sensed him clearly.

Shit. He reached over the back of the couch and snatched Mina's bag, before he even thought to grab his keys or his shoes. He heard a cacophony of hisses and howls, almost like cruel laughter, as he bolted from his crouch. "Get somewhere safe, kid," he whispered to Maggie. "I'll come back when I can."

Be careful, she said and vanished.

As the invaders swept through his living room towards him, Jonah grabbed his essentials: his phone, his wallet, the keys to his truck, and his sneakers on his way out the door. He flew down the stairs and out the front door, and discovered that he didn't need his car keys after all.

His blue pickup was consumed in flames, with pieces falling off and littering his driveway. He would've gawked at the wreckage longer, had he not been aware of the chittering and screeching demons in the stairwell, closing on him, as well as the ones emerging from behind the fiery ruins of his truck.

Motherfucking demons! He made sure Mina's bags were tightly secured, as well as his running shoes, as he mentally plotted out his course. He lowered himself to all fours and let his canine instincts take over. *Let's see you try to keep up, you cocksuckers.*

Sinking more deeply into the hand-me-down armchair in the living room of the duplex, Adam scowled at his phone, waiting for an answer that never came. He was aware of Xani playing with the two younger fae children on the floor by his feet, and Morgan crisscrossing the floor with tools for mounting the extra light fixtures, with Gia helping him run the cables and wires, but Adam stayed riveted on his phone.

He resisted the temptation to fiddle with the white jade pendant and its accompanying white gold chain around his neck. He had fond, gentle recollections of playing with it, when it had hung from his father's neck, as Adam was being carried or tucked into bed, at various times during his childhood.

Although the pendant was clearly visible to him, peeking out from under the open collar of his shirt, no one had commented on it or even seemed to notice that he was wearing jewelry. It was as his mother had said: unless one knew to look for it, one wouldn't see it.

"What's the matter?" Xani asked, looking up from the building block playset. She and Morgan had arrived some time ago, while Adam was in the middle of his text exchange with Jonah, but he was still waiting for a reply.

"I asked Jonah how long it would take to get to the address, and he hasn't answered. I also asked him to keep me posted when he met up with Mina, and he hasn't acknowledged that text either. I tried calling him—nothing."

"Maybe he got busy, or his phone died," Xani shrugged, pretending to voraciously nibble on a plastic cupcake that Fern had handed her, to make the toddler squeal with laughter. "There's nothing you can do about it from here."

Adam slipped his phone back into his pocket. "You're right. We just have to trust that they can take care of themselves."

"We'll try them again later." Xani reached up to the armchair and intertwined her fingers with Adam's, in part to keep him from reaching back into his pocket.

Adam gave Xani's hand a kiss, and he noticed Gia's casual glance in their direction. She seemed fascinated by human interactions, particularly between Xani and him, and he wondered about the extent of socialization that Gia and her siblings had received prior to arriving in New York.

"Hey, is anyone hungry, yet?" Xani asked, as enthusiastically as a kids' party hostess. Since their waking that morning, the children had been so busy playing and running around that breakfast was the furthest thing from their minds, despite Adam's regular reminders, but Xani's simple suggestion was enough to persuade at least the two younger ones.

Fern and Fallon's hands shot up, as they both raced to the kitchen, with Xani jogging after them. Even Morgan had joined them, to top off his coffee, but Gia lingered in the living room and picked up a few errant blocks that had tumbled off the edge of the rug.

"Not hungry?" Adam asked, glancing at Gia to make sure that Mina's halter-style tank top and jogging pants fit her comfortably. It had been a challenge to find something in Mina's closet that Gia could wear that wouldn't impede her wings while covering her sufficiently. He was glad that Cindy had assumed the task of purchasing undergarments for the children, as that was more than he felt comfortable doing for kids that were not his own.

Gia shook her head. "I had some fruit this morning, before you arrived."

She stepped to his side, and the alarms sounded in Adam's head, spurred by her warm, enticing smile. He stayed calm and seated, but he did sit forward a little more, to subtly dissuade her from coming any closer.

"You're not as aggressive as other men," Gia noted. She didn't advance, but she didn't back away, either. "But you seem to like women, like Xani and Cindy."

"I like Xani very much," he said pointedly, "and Cindy is a good friend. I don't need to be aggressive to let someone know that I like them."

Gia swayed and flitted her wings lightly. "Do you like *me*, Adam?"

Shit. She's precocious for fifteen. Adam no longer felt safe in the chair, where he could easily be trapped, so he jumped to his feet, but she misinterpreted his maneuver as an invitation, and she leapt nimbly in front of him and kissed him before he could back away.

Fuck! Her kiss was like a flood of warm, intoxicating honey flowing into him, and he locked his arms at his sides, digging his nails into his palms, to free himself from her hold by focusing on the pain. He did manage to sidestep her and put a few feet between them before he could trust himself to look at her.

"You can't do that!" he chastised, regretting the pained confusion on her young face. "Most men will

74

absolutely take advantage of you, and you're too young for that."

"I've already witnessed the 'advantage' that humans and demons would take," she said quietly. "I'd like to give myself to someone willingly, instead of having the decision made for me."

The rips and holes on Gia's wings reminded Adam that she had already lived a difficult life. "I'm sorry, and I'm very flattered," he said gently, "but I love Xani."

"What does even mean?" Gia scoffed. "If you don't want me, just say so."

He smiled sympathetically, seeing her disconnect. "For me, love means that I want Xani more than I want anyone else, and I never want to do anything that would hurt her. That includes kissing other people, even the very pretty ones."

"So, if you didn't love Xani, would you like me more?" Gia asked.

"You're lovely and clever, and clearly very determined," Adam said, "but you're also less than half my age. It wouldn't matter how much I liked you, because you still have some maturing to do. Anyone who tells you that you're already an adult is either lying, unstable, or immature themselves," he said bluntly, "and doesn't have your best interests in mind."

His words seem to resonate with her, and her demeanor became more serious. "My father said something like that to me, before we started on our way here."

"He must be an astute man," Adam said. "Especially to raise such a capable daughter."

Fallon and Fern were calling their sister from the kitchen, asking if she wanted her hot chocolate with marshmallows or gummi bears. With a laugh, Gia pivoted on her heel and glided with her open wings towards their voices, skimming past Xani in the doorway.

"You said you loved me," Xani said with a sly simper. "Did you mean it?"

"I don't lie to kids," he said with an affronted scowl. "How much did you hear?"

"I heard enough," she said, stepping closer to him, carefully avoiding the minefield of building blocks. "What happened? Did she try to kiss you?"

He hesitated in answering, caught by the "try" part. "She stole a kiss, but it was quick, and it won't happen again."

Xani nodded. "That's actually pretty impressive. A lot of guys would fall under a fae's spell after a kiss like that." Adam scowled at her feigned ignorance. "Yes, I admit it: I saw it happen. But even if I hadn't," she said, running her finger across his lips, brushing off a trace of glittery dust, "her fae dust would have given it away."

"You're not mad?" he asked.

"That someone else thinks you're handsome and approachable?" Xani laughed, giving him an affectionate hug. "No, I'm not mad, silly. As long as you don't make the first move, it's just something I'll have to live with."

"Xani!" Fallon screeched. "Are gummies and marshmallows made from pigs?"

Adam laughed. "I'm pretty sure Cindy gets them the vegetarian kind."

"Oh, good," Xani said, as she followed the sound of the children's disgusted uproar towards the kitchen. "I wasn't looking forward to explaining the sourcing of gelatin to them."

As he watched Xani disappear into the kitchen, he touched the white jade at his neck. If his mother was right about the pendant's power, then it had helped to shield him from the full effects of Gia's kiss. It could've been luck, too, but that didn't mean that Selina wasn't also right.

Somehow, he marveled, *Mom always knows.*

Chapter 6

Mina walked a little around the building perimeter before approaching the front door of the two-story warehouse where the business card had directed her. Not trusting that she would be allowed to keep anything of her own, she had left most of her belongings behind in Jonah's apartment, and had brought only her phone, and a twenty-dollar bill for incidentals, and her pissed-off mood.

She knew that Jonah would be annoyed about being left behind, but there was no way she was dragging him into this situation. Hopefully, she could come to an agreement with Miranda quickly, and be allowed to go on her way, but that would've been less likely with Jonah at her side, acting as her backup. The less Jonah was associated with Mina, the better and safer for him. It was possible that Miranda had her own plans for Jonah, too, but that was also a topic Mina preferred to discuss with Miranda without Jonah present.

Mina rapped on the steel door and flipped her middle finger at the faceless figure who appeared in the tiny window to confirm her identity. The door opened after a noticeable pause, but Mina stayed outside, waiting until she saw an actual person in the doorway.

"You are welcome," greeted Miranda's voice from inside. Despite the large glass-block windows all around the building, it seemed inordinately dark beyond the door. "You are still protected, so you will not be harmed."

From the disdain in Miranda's voice, Mina believed it to be so, but she forewarned: "My friends in New York expect me to contact them this evening, so if I am late to the conference call, there will be repercussions."

A slender blonde appeared in the doorway, wearing the white robes of Miranda's sisterhood. She no longer wore the caterers' monochrome uniform from the day before, but Mina recognized her as Miranda's intermediary at Malcolm's repass. "We've invited you here for a simple conversation, that is all."

In Mina's experience, employing shadow stalkers and keeping tortured captives to ensure compliance didn't generally precede simple conversations, but if Miranda felt threatened by Mina's presence, then her measures were understandable. Cowardly and morally reprehensible, but understandable.

"I want to see the fae," Mina said, venturing into the doorway.

"All in due time," Miranda's voice replied through an intercom speaker. "He is alive and alert, rest assured. And the stalkers have been recalled, as you've arrived alone, per our request." There was an edge to her voice, as though she wasn't sharing the whole story.

"You'll excuse me, if I don't take you at your word, especially if we can't even speak face-to-face," Mina said acridly.

"Kelsey will bring you to me," Miranda directed, and the blonde nodded. "I trust that you came unarmed?"

"I'm not here to cause trouble," Mina said, holding out her arms. "Even my phone is turned off.

Kelsey shut the heavy door behind them and with a silent gesture, invited Mina to walk ahead of her.

Mina didn't bother engaging the girl in conversation, instead taking the uninterrupted silence to study the building interior. There was no second floor, just some loft areas and very high ceilings that reached to the rafters, while the free-standing brick walls stood a few feet taller than Mina. The building looked and felt like a derelict warehouse, and sections of the exposed walls still supported the remnants of cross-beams, suggesting that there had been an upper floor at some point, but the building interior had been gutted and never restored.

The glass block windows that Mina had seen from outside were painted dark on the inside, limiting the amount of natural light that entered the building. There was also a fair amount of foam insulation on the exposed walls, which kept out cold drafts out but also muffled any ambient sounds.

Kelsey knocked on a steel door at the end of the last corridor, and another of Miranda's white-robed acolytes opened the door from the other side.

Miranda would meet Mina in person, but not alone. She stood at the center of the vast closed chamber, one of the few rooms that actually had four walls and a ceiling, but no windows. She still resembled a comely young woman with long brown hair and heavy goth-style makeup, as Mina had seen her in New York the weekend before.

Standing near her were six of her followers, their heads and faces covered by their white cowls. There was a single light bulb hanging overhead directly over Miranda, like a dim spotlight.

An eighth figure awaited in the chamber, trussed and dangling from chains suspended from the ceiling. While Mina couldn't see the man's face in the dim chamber, she recognized him from his limp, dark hair and his bound, chitinous fae wings, as the injured man in the photo. She smelled his syrupy sweet blood and stale sweat in the air, but the occasional clink of the chains and labored breath signaled that he was still alive.

"You recognize it, don't you?" Miranda asked.

"He's fae," Mina answered, not giving anything away, as she looked up at him. "Why is he here?"

"It disobeyed its master," Miranda said. "It tried to escape with its young, but we recaptured it. Do you recognize this fae, in particular?"

Mina shook her head, realizing that Miranda suspected some familiarity and was trying to find out more. "I've never seen him before."

The fae laughed weakly, its chuckle sounding pained and sickly. "You're reaching, witch. It doesn't matter now what happens to me, as long as the children are safe."

"They'll be found," Miranda said. "They're naïve little whelps, and without their adults to guide them, their fate is better if we find them first, rather than the regular humans." She looked up at the bound fae suspended above them. "The other adults have already perished. You can escape their sentence, if you tell us where you sent your young."

"Fuck you," he spat.

"Torture won't work," Mina said. "He'll die before he gives them up."

"That's why you're here," said Miranda, sweetly. She motioned to one of her followers, who wheeled out a tray cart from one of the shadowed corners. "We don't want it to die prematurely and in pain, and most likely, neither do you. You've dealt with these creatures before and consider them like people, I hear?"

Mina narrowed her eyes. "Did you call me here just to help him or did you have other business with me?"

"Two for one, Mina," Miranda said. "You and I still need to discuss your unauthorized incursion into my territory, but while you're in town," she said, gesturing to the injured man, "you may as well make yourself useful. I also wanted to be certain that you would come, as agreed."

"I always keep my word." Mina looked at the tray cart. "Leave the supplies, and I'll treat him. Then, we can talk."

"You're very compassionate, to risk coming here for a stranger," Miranda said dubiously. "Perhaps you can persuade it not to sacrifice itself needlessly. Its master has invested a great deal in the family and would prefer not to lose his outlay. You can understand its master's concern, can't you?"

I don't give a fuck about a slaver's feelings, Mina wanted to say, but she didn't want to chance that any punishment for her lip would be dealt to the fae. "You're wasting precious time. I can't work with an audience hovering."

"Very well," Miranda said, waving to her entourage. "In case you're thinking of escape, there are guards posted outside the door, and unlike me and my followers, they're not forbidden from hurting you."

As Miranda and her minions filed out, Mina switched on a dim clip-on reading light that illuminated the tray of assorted metal implements. They were used typically for medical or dental procedures, but with the wrong intentions, they could be utilized for malicious torture, too. There was a basket of gauze and assorted bottles underneath the tray, too, but she didn't touch anything until the door was shut, and she and her patient were alone.

"I won't tell you anything, either," the fae growled. "I won't betray my family."

"Uh-huh," Mina said absently, following the chain to where it was fastened against the wall, and letting him down to the floor so that she could get a better look at him. "Have you been cut or maimed?"

He allowed himself to sink onto the floor, to give his long limbs some relief, but he remained wary and sat upright. "I was cut and stabbed, but nothing that hasn't healed. I don't want your help!" He tried to push himself away from her, but was constrained by the chains and his own exhaustion.

Mina found an unopened water bottle, which she uncapped and held out to him. "I will help, whether you want me to or not." As he stared at her, she had a moment to study him, too, more clearly than what she could see from the picture that Miranda had sent her. He was olive-skinned, with dark, wavy hair that drooped around his scruffy face. He was young: no wrinkles or grays, and almost gaunt, but that could have been from his recent trials.

"You don't think I can tell when someone's used fae dust?" he said. "Do you harvest us for it, like your friends out there do?"

"They're not my friends," she corrected. "Do you want water, or not?" She tilted the bottle slightly, threatening to waste the precious life-saving fluid.

"I'll take it!" he said. "But you have to free my hands, if I'm to drink from it."

Mina shook her head. "I can't trust you not to kill or ditch me, so sit up a little. Please."

Carefully, she drizzled a small amount into his open mouth, waiting for him to swallow before she gave him a little more. "I am a witch, and I've had fae dust used on me, but I've never taken anything that wasn't freely given."

"Why the fuck should I care? You'll probably cremate me and harvest my dust as soon as I stop breathing, maybe even before."

"You should care because I'm the best chance you have at getting out of here, alive. You want to see your children again, don't you?" She held up a finger, as she recapped and set down the half-empty water bottle. "It was a rhetorical question; don't bother answering."

She reached into the basket under the tray and pulled out a bottle of witch hazel tincture and a wad of gauze. "Some of your old injuries need to be cleaned."

He balked and backed away from her. "I told you. I'm already healed."

"The cuts are gone, yes, but there are poisons being absorbed into your skin through the new flesh," she said. "They prevent you from healing completely, and they'll continue to build up in your body unless I clean them off."

Mina knelt in front of him and cleaned off a tar-like stain by his elbow, revealing the reddened skin underneath. She was familiar with the substance, a mix of nightshade, milkweed and mushroom extracts, with other toxins. She found a few other similar patches on his shoulder and his thigh, near tears in his clothes that indicated recent cuts.

"How do I know I can trust you?" he asked.

"You don't," Mina said, tossing the soiled gauze aside. "I don't trust you, either. You could be a test that Miranda is using to find out how much I know and how she can try to use me, but your injuries were real and needed care."

At the sound of the door opening again, Mina returned to her feet, as did the fae. He stood only an inch or two higher than her, but his long, slender frame made him seem taller. Miranda motioned to her assistants to hoist the man back into the air, and Mina blocked them.

"His limbs aren't made to withstand that kind of stress!" she said. "You don't have to do that; he's too weak to fly or run away."

"Did it tell you that?" Miranda smirked.

"Look, he can barely stand," Mina said, as the fae balanced unsteadily near her. "If you want to keep him alive, don't suspend him like that."

"Fine, we'll let it rest on the floor, for a little while," Miranda said. "But we still have this hook and chain already set up, and it would be a shame to let it hang there idly. I have an idea," she smiled, and signaled to her acolytes, who held Mina in place.

Off the tray, Miranda lifted a syringe that with filled with the tar-like substance that Mina had cleaned off the fae, and Mina stiffened momentarily, worried that Miranda would use it on her. Such a high dosage of the mixture would kill a fae, for certain, but it would certain incapacitate her, too. She lunged but was held back, when she saw Miranda step over to the fae. To ensure his compliance, Miranda drove her knee up into his groin, and he curled over in agony.

"This isn't for him, not yet," Miranda assured her, standing over him. "But I'm curious how much you would endure for the sake of another's comfort, especially someone that you claim to not even know."

One of the assistants dragged out another length of chain, as Miranda pulled the fae's head back by his hair with one hand and held the syringe to his throat with the other. "One sudden move, and I start pushing the plunger."

"How do I know that you won't hurt him anyway, once you have me chained?"

"If I'd simply wanted to have you restrained, I could've ordered it sooner, before we even brought you in here," Miranda said. "No, it's your behavior that I wish to study."

Mina remained unmoving, as the chains were pulled taut around her, binding her arms against her body. She watched Miranda for any break in her concentration, any window to allow her an escape attempt, but Miranda seemed intent on watching her put into shackles. Once Mina was chained, the cold hook latched onto the links behind her, tightening the chain to bite into her skin, as it hoisted her at an angle—not far, not even a foot, but too far for her feet to reach the floor, as her body pitched forward.

Miranda smiled bemusedly and switched another syringe for the first one, this one smaller, with a maroon-hued liquid. She came closer and looked into Mina's face. "Interesting. I don't know that I would've subjected myself to the same." Not hearing any rejoinder from Mina, Miranda grabbed her chin and kissed her on the mouth. The unexpected move distracted Mina for a moment, but not enough to keep her from jerking back from the syringe that Miranda had at her arm. Some of the dark red liquid still seeped under her skin, but it didn't burn as much as the tar serum would have.

"No, Mina, I don't want to poison you," Miranda said, looking at the needle to see how much had been administered. "This serum is for extracting information from stubborn creatures, like yourself, and to keep you docile. When the burning starts in the blood, you'd be amazed at what you find yourself confessing."

One of Miranda's followers rushed into the chamber and whispered something to his mistress that darkened Miranda's expression and mood.

"I'm surrounded by incompetence," she muttered, then glanced back at Mina. "Let's give you a moment, while I tend to some matters, and let the serum work its magic."

Mina felt her vision blur and dim, and she focused hard on the fae still chained on the floor, now shackled to a tether on the floor. It was easier to give her attention to him, than to think about her own discomforts.

"I'm sorry," he said. "You shouldn't have intervened. Now we are both prisoners."

"But we're both alive," Mina said, feeling her head weigh as heavy as her limbs. "That's what counts."

"You don't even know me," he said.

Mina's thoughts drifted to people, spirits, demons and other creatures she had helped over the years, when she had provided aid and mercy without knowing why or anything about their histories. "I don't have to. Sometimes, it's easier not to know."

As Mina's mind began to slow, her thoughts drifted further afield, to her friends, to Adam, to their parents...

"My name is Galen," the fae said.

"It's nice to meet you," she said, trying to keep herself from rotating on the chain. "I'm Mina."

"Thank you," Galen said. "Did you have a plan for escaping here?"

"I *had* a plan," she said, flexing her arms to test the chains. "This complicates things a little." Her head was too muddled to strategize, and she was tempted to close her eyes and sleep, in hopes of waking up more refreshed, but she didn't want to risk waking up to an even worse predicament.

It was better to try to stay awake and fight the effects of the substances in her system, as well as she could, but that carried its own risks. Already, she could feel her inhibitions lessening, and the desire growing to talk about everything that came to her mind, as though she would break down or break apart if she didn't let the words spill out. *Shit, if I tell Miranda that Galen's family hiding out in my duplex, before Cindy's done securing it...*

Mina looked down at Galen and saw his look of concern. *Better talking to him than talking to Miranda, I suppose.*

"Are you any good at keeping secrets, Galen?"

"Only as good as the next fae," he said warily. "Why?"

"Because I think I'm going to say a lot of things that I probably shouldn't," she said. "So in case I tell you something that you'd rather not hear, I'd like to apologize preemptively."

Galen smiled tiredly and tried to get into a more comfortable position on the floor. "I have a willful and outspoken teenage daughter, Mina. There's not much you can say that will shock or offend me."

Jonah was getting better at sneaking around and dispatching the warehouse's demon guards, but he tried not to be cocky about it. He had promised Adam before they parted ways that he would protect Mina, and he couldn't do that if he was caught or killed.

The demons that patrolled the warehouse were tougher than the ones that had guarded the brownstone in New York. They were certainly bigger, filling the more spacious dimensions of the corridors, and of the building, overall, but they were slower and more lumbering. Their presence assured Jonah that he was in the right place, and Miranda's white-robed followers confirmed his supposition further.

Thankfully, he was still stealthier than the guards, so he was able to avoid most of them, once he caught their odors in the air or heard their stomping footsteps. Only once did he have to engage someone in a fight and it was one of Miranda's human followers. It was easy to put him in a sleeper hold and shove him into an electrical closet—well, easier than trying the same maneuver on a demon. Jonah stole the man's white robe and slipped it on, just for extra cover.

Jonah followed Mina's scent and voice to a guarded room, and he recognized her tones and speech patterns more than her actual words, but she seemed to be talking a lot, and not quietly.

Once he knocked out the two guards and unlocked the door using keys he found on one of them, he took one of their clubs and entered the vast, dimly-lit space cautiously. There were only two people that he could detect: a slender, dark figure on the floor, bearing a set of black, diaphanous wings, and Mina, wrapped and dangling by a chain, speaking in one of her Chinese dialects.

Noticing Jonah's silent approach, the fae man on the floor staggered to his feet to take a defensive posture, with his wings pinned back, but he didn't look strong enough to put up much of a fight against him.

"It's okay, I'm here for her," Jonah said, tossing back his cowl. He then noticed that the man was chained, too. Venturing a longer glance, he saw the fae's resemblance to the beaten one in the photo that Mina had been sent. "Hey, Mina?" he called.

She stopped her soliloquy and beamed at Jonah, as he went to the winch on the side to lower her to the floor. "You found me!"

"Of course, I found you," he said, catching her as she sagged, and unhooked the chain that held her. "Are you drugged?" She seemed in excellent spirits for someone imprisoned by her nemesis.

"Yeah... You're so pretty," she murmured, stroking his whiskered face. "Even as a human."

"She's been talking non-stop for almost ten minutes," the fae said. "You must be Jonah. She's mentioned you, a lot."

"That's Galen," Mina said, as Jonah found a way to untangle the chains for him. "He's fae like Cindy, and he's a really good listener, too."

"Cindy?" the fae said, his wings twitching with agitation, as he stepped back from Mina and Jonah. "How do you now Cindy?"

Mina giggled. "Everyone knows Cindy! She used to be such a cute boy. She's renting out my duplex for a couple of weeks—" She covered her mouth belatedly and looked around to see who had heard. "Oops, I think that was supposed to be a secret."

Jonah looked at the table tray and basket underneath for anything else he could use as a weapon, or to neutralize whatever was affecting Mina. He noticed with some irritation that Galen seemed in no rush to help him look.

"He's on our side," Mina said. "Or, at least he's not against us. Right?"

"I need to find my children first," Galen said.

"Let's get out of here *first*," Jonah said, "then we can talk about what's next. What did they give her?" he asked, checking Mina's eyes and pulse when she finally stayed still. Her pupils were a little dilated, but her pulse was normal.

"Is there a vial with a thin blue liquid?" Galen suggested. "That should be a diluting draught, in case of an accidental overdose."

Jonah found a small flask, filled with something that resembled and smelled like glass cleaner, but Galen nodded. Jonah hesitated in giving it to Mina, wondering how reliable Galen's knowledge was.

"Come on!" Galen urged. "I don't want her to slow us down, either."

Mina held out her hand, looking the steadiest and most clear-eyed since Jonah's arrival. "Listen to him, Jonah. Galen served masters who used potions all the time, so he knows his stuff."

Jonah passed the vial to Mina with reservation. "Drink it slow, in case it's the wrong thing." He tossed a half-empty water to Galen to test the fae's reflexes and was relieved that Galen caught it easily. "Can you walk?"

Galen nodded, but Mina started keeling to the side, slowly enough that Jonah caught her easily. Feeling her weight settle against him, he looked at her eyes and saw them still dilated and half-closed.

"She risked herself for me, so I will help you get out," Galen said, picking up the fallen club from the floor. "But once we are out, we will separate. Deal?"

Jonah lifted Mina easily in his arms, but his speed and mobility were hindered, so they needed Galen's help, if they were to escape cleanly. "Deal. Lead the way."

They left the room just in time, as they heard voices and footsteps approaching from around the corner.

Guided by Jonah's silent gestures, Galen led a brisk but cautious pace through the building the way Jonah had entered, avoiding the guards and Miranda's followers that had been alerted to their escape by the blaring alarms. Jonah's hearing was more sensitive to the jarring cacophony, but he tightened his hold on Mina, covering her ears as well as he could, and pressed on, focusing on remembering the twists and turns he had taken.

At last, they were by the door, and Jonah could smell the fresh air and see the glow of daylight through the doorway seams. As Galen slid open the heavy steel door, Jonah heard an explosive pop, and felt a sharp pain pierce his lower back. Galen immediately looked back to see if Jonah was still standing.

"Go!" Jonah said, ignoring the pain as much as he could, to reach the safety of the outside. Galen waited at the door and began sliding it closed, timing it to shut as Jonah slipped through with Mina. "Use that to jam the door," Jonah gestured to a length of lead piping that he had found and left by the doorway on his way in.

Galen darted over and grabbed the pipe, wedging the sliding door tightly closed on its track, just in time, as banging and other sharp pops reverberated through the door.

"Other doors," Mina said weakly.

"She's right," Galen said. "We need to get clear, before they come out the other entrances." Jonah's lower back was starting to feel numb now, and he set Mina down rather than risk dropping her. Jonah touched the cold, wet patch on his side, and his hand came away bloody. "Fuck!" Galen exclaimed.

"Just need to get to the car," Jonah said with an effort, pointing towards the street where he had parked. "Behind the wall."

Mina was unsteady, but she was alert. "How much can you carry?" she asked Galen.

"More than you," he replied, swinging around with his wings unfurled, scooping Jonah under the arms from behind. "By the gods, you humans are heavier than you look," he muttered, but he managed to alleviate some of Jonah's pressure and pain.

Jonah's vision was blurring, and he expected that he was hit with something more than a small-caliber slug, despite how localized the pain felt. He ran as quickly as his legs would carry him, with Galen's support buoying him and occasionally lifting him off the ground, especially in the last few hundred yards to the car.

"Black Charger," he said, gesturing to Malcolm's car when he noticed Mina looking around for his truck. He sank against the hood, barely feeling the sunbaked surface against his legs and held out the keys to Mina with a shaky hand. "You're going to have to drive."

Chapter 7

Mina had always hated Malcolm's car. It wasn't so much the color or the model, but what it represented during their relationship. It was his vehicle to get away from her, when he didn't want to deal with her or face the aftermath of lashing out at her. Sometimes, when she rode with him, it had felt like a prison, when she was secured in the passenger seat and unable to escape his rants or interrogations. Increasingly over time, Malcolm was drunk when he drove it, but he somehow always managed to come back safely.

Shit, I never thought I'd be in this thing again. In the all-black interior, the red dashboard lights were menacing and glaring, and Mina avoided looking at the crimson displays and concentrated on driving. At least, she was in the driver's seat this time; Malcolm had never let her drive *his* car.

She had hoped that Jonah was joking when he had pointed to the car, but it wasn't the right time to balk about transportation. In fact, none of them—Jonah, Galen or herself—said a word until they were across the Charles River, on a quiet street not too far from Briggs Field, in Cambridge. Mina hadn't received any direction from Jonah, so she just picked turns at random, until she had gotten them far enough away to feel safe.

Mina pulled over and turned off the engine, looking in the mirrors and windows to make sure they were alone. She wasn't quite up to turning her phone back on, in case Miranda had decided to bombard her with excoriating text messages for their audacious getaway. Mina unbuckled her seat belt and peered in the back seat, where Jonah and Galen had been eerily quiet.

Jonah had taken off the white acolyte robe and had it folded into a makeshift cushion that supported his wounded side. Galen had closed his eyes, finally allowing himself to rest in relative safety, with Jonah's gray sweatshirt balled up as his pillow, but he stirred quickly when he noticed that the car had stopped.

"Relax, Galen. We'll get you on your way to reunite with your family, as soon as we can assure your safety, and theirs," Mina said. "First off, I need to take a look at Jonah's bullet wound."

"Already done," Jonah said, lifting the cushion to show her the bandaged wound that peeked through the stained hole in his t-shirt. "Galen pulled out the slug and dressed the wound."

"I treated it for the usual contaminants and poisons," Galen said, "but the hole didn't go very deep, given the distance."

"Treated it with what?" She looked in the back seat for the first time and saw her plaster-dusted satchel on the floor, with the contents of a first-aid kit and some of her mother's herbal salves scattered across the seat. "Why are my things here..." In the bright daylight, she finally noticed slight scratches on Jonah's face, and what looked paint chips and splinters strewn in his gray-peppered black hair. "What happened?"

"Too much to get into now," Jonah said tiredly. "I'd say Galen's more than honored his end of the bargain, so let's get him away from Boston and back with his family."

Mina turned on her phone, expecting a slew of missed messages and calls, but she had only missed two: one from Adam and one from Cindy. She texted Adam a smile and a thumbs-up emoji, then called Cindy.

93

"*Dime*," greeted Cindy in Spanish upon pickup.

Mina heard the din of the Red Lotus's kitchen in the background. "Got a minute?"

"For you, honey? As many as you need," Cindy said.

"Hold on, let me put you on speaker," Mina said. "Jonah and Galen are here."

"Galen!" Cindy exclaimed. "How are you, darling?"

Galen smiled at Cindy's familiar, teasing tone. "Better than I was this morning, better now than I've been for days." He hesitated about asking, but he needed to know. "Are the children with you?"

"Yes," Cindy said solemnly. "Fern saw them all here safely."

Galen scowled. "Are you testing me, Cindy? Fern can barely speak. You mean Gia, of course."

"Of course," Cindy said easily. "Forgive the caution, but I hear that there's a considerable bounty on your heads, especially for the children, so one must be careful. We have security systems in place at the safe house, and someone watching them at all hours."

Mina could only imagine what Cindy and Morgan had decided to rig up at her duplex. "Do you have a contact who can get Galen out?" Mina asked. "He doesn't have any travel documents, and his wings are too conspicuous for him to travel publicly."

"I have someone that I trust, who can transport him tonight. What about you, honey?" Cindy asked. "When are *you* coming home?"

Mina glanced at Jonah. "Not until business is finished."

"I see," Cindy answered. "You're awfully quiet, Jonah. Do you agree with Mina?"

"No," he said readily. "I think she should leave at the first chance, but if she wants to stay, I'll keep her company until her work is done."

"I think you're both crazy to stay there, but what do I know?" Cindy sighed. "Okay, I have to run, but I'll text you the details later."

Lucifer swirled the icy vodka around in his glass, but he didn't drink. He was too busy trying to hear the tail end of Cindy's conversation, which she cut short as soon as she saw him waiting at the bar.

"Something you didn't want me to hear?" he asked, finally taking a sip of his drink.

"Mundane mortal concerns," Cindy smiled prettily. "Too boring to hold your interest for long."

"Try me," Lucifer invited. "If you're right, I'll tell you to stop."

"Mina's in Boston," Cindy started. "Your witches feel that Mina trespassed, I suppose, so they wish to keep her from leaving until they've had a conversation."

"Really?" Lucifer asked. "That sounds very reasonable. She's in their territory, after all."

"She was there to bury Malcolm and pay her respects to his family," Cindy reminded coolly. "Miranda knew that she was only planning to be there for a few hours, but she even resorted to using shadow stalkers and hostages to secure Mina's cooperation. Those are extreme measures for simply ensuring a conversation, wouldn't you agree?"

"Would it ease your mind, sweet Cin, if I told you that they're not working under my direction?" Lucifer offered. "Miranda is still in my service, but she acts on the order of one of my underlings."

Cindy wiped down the counter with a sideways glance at him. "Actually, that doesn't ease my mind at all, Luci," she said. "Because that means that you're out of the loop now, and any horrible outcomes that may result from Miranda's spite towards Mina will only reach you after the fact, too late for you to prevent."

"Prevention is overrated," Lucifer said. "Anything can be fixed or remedied, and in some cases, remade to be even better."

To demonstrate, he picked up his empty glass and let it fall directly against a tile, shattering it. Ignoring the stares he drew, he leaned over, and with a grasping motion, he collected the shards. By the time he straightened on his stool and faced Cindy, he had reconstructed the glass, and he set down a faceted, cut crystal glass on the counter to replace the plain glass highball he had destroyed.

"Better than new," he smiled.

"You can try to justify your delegation of Miranda's oversight however you wish," Cindy said. "But I've heard about the demon that she now serves. He lacks your perspective and your restraint, and if Miranda picks up any of her new master's bad habits, she may be more of a burden than an asset."

"Whatever restraint I show in your presence is forced, I assure you," Lucifer said, almost as a growl, irritated by Cindy's warning. "If not for Miss Xing's wards and your patrons' regular blessings, I could have you easily, in whatever way I wanted. Warlords and prophets have fallen at my feet to do my bidding and speak my words, at a snap of my fingers or a careless slip of my tongue, so I assure you: however mild-mannered I appear in this space, I am still very much in control, outside of it."

Cindy smiled at Lucifer's bluster. "Yet, you keep returning to our little watering hole, when there are so many places that are more accommodating and suitable for expressing your desires and whims."

"I visit those, too," Lucifer said. "But I also enjoy a break, now and then, as a respite from exploiting the darker nature of lesser beings."

"Just to be clear," she said, humorlessly, "I am Mina's friend, and not yours, so I will choose her over

96

you, every time. If you ever cause her pain, either through your action or inaction, I reserve the right to banish you from the Lotus. Is that clear?"

"Perfectly, Cin," he replied. "Why the condition? If you don't trust me to keep my word, if you think that I could ever harm Miss Xing, you could eject me now."

"You haven't done anything to warrant that, yet. Until then," Cindy said, placing another vodka on the counter in front of him, "you're welcome to enjoy your respite here, anytime."

Adam started when he heard his phone chime, as the duplex had been quiet for the past hour, ever since the two younger fae children went to bed, and Gia went upstairs to help Millie Krantz with chores and cleaning. Gia liked to listen to Millie's exploits of her years spent as an army nurse—she had met her sweetheart Arthur when they were stationed overseas together—and Millie enjoyed Gia's company and appreciated her energy and nimble hands.

Adam found his phone on the coffee table in front of him and answered promptly without looking and was relieved to hear Jonah's voice.

"We just saw Galen off, about half an hour ago," Jonah said. "Cindy's contact was waiting at Rowe's Wharf, as planned, and there was some cosplay festival going on, so no one even looked twice at Galen's wings. Text me when he gets there, okay?"

"Will do," Adam said, hearing a profound exhaustion in his friend's voice. "You sound tired. You must be ready to head back to the house and crash."

"Yeah, that's not happening anytime…ever again," Jonah said wearily. He was quiet enough that an elevator chime in the background sounded clear and sharp.

Adam settled in the armchair. "What happened? Are you and Mina okay?"

"Mina and I are fine. My place, however… The reason I left you hanging this morning was because a bunch of demons decided to firebomb and invade the house and torch my truck. The building's a total loss."

"Holy shit!" Adam exclaimed, surprised at Jonah's calm. "You sound surprisingly chill about it."

"Well, I've had the past few hours to process it," Jonah said. "Connie and Teddy are a little in shock about losing their old house, but their insurance will cover the loss, and then some. Most of my stuff can be replaced. I went back to pick through the rubble and found some clothes, my passport and documents."

Adam then recalled the brief video chat he had had with Mina, to make sure she looked okay, and the dark interior of the car she was in. "Oh, that's why you have Malcolm's Charger."

"Yeah, it turns out I can outrun most demons when I'm really motivated and my beast mode kicks in," Jonah said blithely. "But I was still carrying Mina's stuff, and I still had to find her, so I jogged to Connie and Teddy's, and they were more than happy to let me borrow the car. They want to get rid of it, anyway—it reminds them too much of Malcolm."

Adam nodded. "Mina always hated that car."

"I sensed that, when I asked her to drive," Jonah said. "I would've borrowed Connie's Beetle, if I'd known beforehand."

The image of Jonah's long frame crammed inside Connie's mint-green VW Beetle made Adam chuckle, and he heard Mina's light laughter from Jonah's end. "Don't coddle my sister. She needs to toughen up a little," Adam joked. "Where are you staying, if your house is trashed?"

There was a muffled exchange between Jonah and Mina before he answered, "Mina called Aciré Hart earlier, and she apparently keeps a magically-secured hotel room as a safehouse for her firm's clients? We're getting up to the suite now."

Adam knew the penthouse suite in question. It had a great view overlooking the Charles River, from what he recalled. "Aciré's an old family friend, so she'll take good care of you and make sure no one gets near you."

"That's assuring. We learned our lesson: no more staying with known associates."

Adam fought the temptation to ask whether Mina and Jonah were sharing a bedroom, reasoning that it really wasn't any of his business. "I still think you guys should just come back to New York, where you at least have some support."

"I told Mina she should go, but she says she doesn't want to leave me and our family unprotected," Jonah said, sounding resigned. "It's a big suite, so we're in different rooms, by the way, in case you're wondering. We even have separate phone chargers."

"Of course, he's wondering," Mina remarked in the background. "I'm going to take a shower now, *ge-ge*," she announced, "in my *own* room."

"Thanks for staying with her, Jonah," Adam said. "I'm not happy that she's still there, but I'm glad you're with her."

"About that," Jonah said, tentatively. "I feel like I should talk to you first, before I consider talking to your parents."

Adam was intrigued. The last time he heard such words, he was getting rebuked by his high school principal for smoking in the boys' bathroom. "Okay?"

"It's about Mina."

"Yep, I figured as much."

Jonah took a slow breath. "I want to ask her to marry me."

Adam was astonished by the suddenness, more than by Jonah's sincerity, which sounded heartfelt. "Are you asking me how to go about it, or..."

"No, I guess I'm asking for permission?" Jonah asked, sounding chagrinned. "I wasn't sure how traditional your family was about this sort of thing."

Adam laughed. "Why? Would you really show up at our parent's house with red envelopes, a whole roasted pig and red baskets of pastries and cakes?"

There was a pause on Jonah's end. "Is that something that you actually do, or are you just picking on the *wàirén*?" he asked, poking fun at himself as the "outsider."

"We're not *that* traditional," Adam grinned. "But you'd probably do it, if we told you to, wouldn't you?"

"For Mina, I'd do and give anything, in case that wasn't clear."

Adam thought of everything Jonah had endured for his sister, and everyone else in their close-knit circle, not even counting the loss of his worldly possessions just hours before. "No, I think you've demonstrated your commitment enough."

"Good." Jonah paused, then added, "I'm also a little scared of your mom."

"Who isn't?" Adam commented. "She likes you, though. Better than she liked Malcolm. That's not to say that she *disliked* him—she just found you more mature."

"I've got at least three years on you," Jonah reminded. "I should hope I came across as more mature."

"It's not about age," Adam said, "but more about attitude. My parents gave their blessing to Malcolm, in part because they liked you and your family; they saw that there was love and respect in how you treated one another, and they wanted to be sure that Mina would be happy and accepted by her new in-laws. My mom finds you to be good and trustworthy, so I don't think she has a problem with you."

"But?" Jonah spurred, sensing Adam's hesitation.

"What's the rush?" Adam asked. "You know how Mina hates having her attention pulled in different directions, so you could just wait till everything settles down."

"That's just it," Jonah said. "Going after Mina today, I realized: if anything had happened to her, or to me, and I never had the chance to ask her, I'd always regret it. I want to be there to support her, especially if things get messy."

"Okay," Adam said, as he spied the baby monitor light turn on next to him. "Do what you feel you must, with my blessings, and as our parents' proxy, too. Good luck."

Adam cut short the call and pocketed his phone to give his attention to Fallon, who flitted out from the bedroom, rubbing his eyes tiredly. "What's the matter, buddy?"

Fallon landed lightly in front of Adam. "Fern woke me up with her fussing."

Adam heard a quiet, complaining kind of wail though the monitor. "Alright, let's go see if she needs changing or something." He followed Fallon's aerial zigzag to the children's rooms, and turned on the dimmer switch in Fern's room to partial brightness.

Fern sat up in bed, on her knees, whimpering quietly. "It hurts."

"What hurts, sweetheart?" Adam asked, sitting on the edge of the toddler's bed. "Your head? Your tummy?" She shook her head and pointed her finger over her shoulder. "Your back." She nodded and showed her back to Adam.

He noticed a warmth emanating from her back and thought he noticed that her nightgown stuck to her skin, as though it was soaked in sweat. "Fallon, can you turn up the light for me, just a little, please?"

As the room lights brightened, the source of Fern's fretting became painfully obvious, as Adam saw the reddened, oozing, open welt-like sores on Fern's tender skin through the cotton knit of her night gown.

Oh, fuck. "Okay, Fern, hold still for a moment. We have to get your gown off." He loosened the ties of her nightgown and helped her slip it off over her head, taking care not to touch her back more than absolutely necessary. While the gown was stained, Fern hugged it to her chest for comfort, as she liked the soft flannel and the unicorn and princess print.

The dark edges of her small wings were visible through her thin, fragile skin, as they struggled to erupt from her back, almost as if they had a life of their own, like a butterfly writhing free of a chrysalis.

The pterostigma of one of Fern's wings tore out through her back, and she shrieked in pain. Fallon jumped back, shutting his eyes and holding his ears at the sound of his sister's screams.

"Fallon, get me the tray of ice from the freezer, and then fly upstairs and get your sister." Adam was just blindly grasping for ideas on how to help Fern, but Fallon didn't need to see or hear his panic. This was far more dramatic and sudden than a human baby's teething, but maybe he could try similar methods to soothe the pain.

He texted Cindy, the only adult fae he knew, and prayed that she was near her phone: *Wings. Need help ASAP.*

With her hair still damp, and her oversized towel wrapped around herself, Mina frowned at the sparse contents of her bags. Without question, she was thankful that Jonah had rescued her satchel, her mom's pouch and everything else that was hers, before his apartment was destroyed, so she was more annoyed with herself for not having the foresight to bring more clothes. She had spot-cleaned her suit of the worst stains and left her clothes drip-drying in the bathroom, but it still seemed that she would go to sleep in a towel, or naked.

Humbly, she knocked on Jonah's bedroom door. He looked surprised to see her, especially clad in just a towel, but she was glad that he managed to keep his eyes on her face. He had showered, too, and had on a clean t-shirt and a different pair of jeans.

"I don't suppose you packed any other extra clothes?" she asked covetously. "I'm out of options."

He stepped away from the door, grinning. "I may have a few things I can share. I'm all out of bras and panties, though."

Mina looked around the bedroom and noticed that Jonah's bed was larger than the one in her room, a king instead of a queen. She had the better view, though, a more direct north-west vantage of the Charles River and the park-like campuses and river walks that lined its banks.

"I have no idea how this will fit you," he prefaced, handing her a weathered black sleeveless concert t-shirt with red and white printing.

"Early U2," she noted, shaking it out. She laughed. "There's no way this is yours! You would've been a toddler or preschooler at that time, if you were around at all."

It was an original shirt from U2's War Tour in the early 80's, which Mina only recognized because lead singer Bono had immortalized it by wearing it during the recording of their concert video at the Red Rocks Amphitheatre in 1983. She was too young when their early albums first came out, but she watched the video on repeat until she had memorized every lyric to every song. She had coveted Bono's shirt for years, and now, she was wearing it.

"It was my dad's," Jonah said fondly. "I kept a lot of his concert shirts after he died, but *that* was my favorite. I couldn't leave it behind in the rubble."

"This is a very cool shirt," Mina said, slipping it over her head and pulling it down over her hips before she tugged her damp towel free. "Thank you for letting me have it. I'll take very good care of it."

"I'll want it back," Jonah said. "It looks good on you, but it's still mine."

"We'll see." Mina cackled and raced back towards her room, with Jonah at her heels. She hurled her towel at him, but he was still able to catch up, wrapping his arm around her waist and tickling her until she conceded: "Okay, fine, I'll give it back!"

She darted away, as soon as he released her, as her phone chimed with an incoming text.

As she reached for it, Jonah said: "You could leave it for a moment. I need to talk to you," he said.

"I have to check, in case it's important," Mina said, picking up the phone.

It was a message from Miranda: *You took something that doesn't belong to you.*

It took Mina a second to refocus her attention and realize that Miranda meant Galen, and she typed her response: *Fae are not things.*

"There's always going to be something important that needs your attention, and I don't want to put this off," he said. "Please turn around."

Mina tossed her phone face-down on the bed and turned around to give Jonah her full attention. "What is it?" She wasn't expecting him to stand so close to her, and she took an unconscious step back before she noticed the ruby ring he held between his fingers. "What is *that*?"

"It's my mother's ring," he said, holding it out to her. "Would you..." His voice caught, and she waited a beat.

Was he giving it to her for safekeeping, or was he planning to give it to someone else? The idea of him being with another girl saddened her, but it was unfair of her to think of him as hers. He didn't need to get entangled in her shit, risking his life for matters that didn't involve him.

Mina reached for his hand and froze when he started to aim the ring towards her finger. She had a flashback of Malcolm's grand proposal gesture, on one knee in the middle of Boston Common, offering her a three-carat diamond in full view of their friends and total strangers, and she yanked her hand back reflexively. "Jonah! What are you doing?"

"Mina," he said with an effort, "I'm trying to ask you, not very successfully, it seems: would you do me the honor of being my wife?"

Of course, yes! She fought her instinct to accept and considered the consequences. She wanted him and thought of him more often than she should have, but it had been that way at the start with Malcolm, too. *He's not Malcolm.* That was true; Jonah was brave, selfless and sweet…and he deserved a better, more peaceful life than any that he could have with her.

"Jonah, I…" She wanted to say "no" but couldn't work up the courage for that, either, so she was stuck in her indecision.

"Okay," he said gently, but she could see that he was wounded by her hesitation. "It's not a flat-out rejection, so at least I know you don't think of me as a complete asshole." He slipped the ring back into his jeans pocket. "Let's forget the last five minutes ever happened."

"Jonah, if I were anyone else, I'd consider myself the luckiest girl in the world, and I'd say 'yes' without a second thought," she said, reaching for his hand, but he walked away, beyond her reach.

"Maybe, but I didn't ask anyone else," he said, his voice cool.

The phone chimed again, and Mina was torn between answering the new text, or continuing the agonizing exchange with Jonah. She knew it was

105

cowardly, but she reached for her phone. As soon as she picked it up, she heard her bedroom door shut quietly, and she knew Jonah had left.

Fuck! She took a deep breath and looked at Miranda's new message: *Its master wants it returned.*

She fired back: *Fuck him. Too bad. He's left.*

As she waited for Miranda's reply, Mina realized that this was their first exchange since her escape from the warehouse and since her learning of what had happened to Jonah's place and truck. She typed a follow-up: *Consider it part of compensation for unrequested Brookline demolition.*

Miranda's reply: *Greater losses to follow, unless meeting tomorrow.*

Mina sighed heavily. Until Miranda was dealt with, there would always be a threat, either latent or immediate. Perhaps they could come to some sort of agreement or truce, but nothing would happen unless they met again.

Miranda texted an address, which thankfully did not point to the warehouse again. *9AM. Come alone, no weapons.*

Fine, Mina replied, wary of the regular pedestrian traffic around the address that Miranda had indicated. *No more threats or hostages, either.* Whether Miranda would uphold her end…well, that remained to be seen.

Chapter 8

Cindy asked Xani to cover, as soon as she received Adam's urgent text, and sprinted to Mina's building. If she still had her wings, she would have flown the entire way, witnesses and amateur videographers be damned, but she had to settle for weaving through the throngs of tourists and ridiculous street traffic on foot.

Inside the front door, she listened momentarily for sounds of crying or screaming, but there was only silence. She went directly to the duplex and let herself in. "Hello?"

"Back here," Adam called from the living room, sounding more relaxed than she expected.

Adam was nestled in the armchair with Fern curled against him on his lap. She was sucking furiously on an ice pop that was dripping purple syrup on Adam's white shirt, as she clutched Mina's fleece Star Wars blanket to her chest. Slowly and rhythmically, like a breath, Fern's new wings flapped, still filling with her blood until they would extend fully.

"Hey, honey, how are you feeling?" Cindy asked gently, peering at Fern's half-covered face.

Fern nodded and tucked her free hand tighter against Adam.

"And how are *you* feeling, honey?" Cindy asked Adam. "Sorry it had to happen on your shift. I was hoping Galen would arrive in time to see his daughter's wing-sprout."

"I'm just glad that Gia was here," Adam said. "She knew exactly what to do: how to treat her skin around the wounds and what to give Fern for the pain. She and Fallon are changing the bedding, so that Fern can get back to bed. It's been a busy night, huh?" he asked Fern, giving her a gentle kiss on the forehead, as he rocked her in his arms.

"You're really good with them," Cindy smiled.

"It's easy when they're good kids," Adam said simply. As Gia appeared in the doorway, cueing that Fern's bed was made, he tried to get up from his seat, but Fern held fast.

"Come on, Fern," Gia said. "Let's give Adam a break. I'll let you pick out a bedtime story."

As she jumped off Adam's lap, her ice pop still in hand, Fern flitted her wings, but they weren't yet strong enough to support her weight. She continued to hug Mina's fleece blanket, gazing up at Adam with her dark eyes wide and inquiring.

"Yes, you can take it to bed with you," he said. "But you have to brush your teeth before you fall asleep, otherwise that popsicle might turn your whole mouth purple *forever*."

Gia and Cindy chuckled, as Fern ran to the bathroom to see her purple lips and teeth. "Do you need anything?" Cindy asked the older fae girl.

"I don't think so, Miss Cindy," Gia replied. "Thanks for coming to check on us."

"I hear you handled everything like an expert," Cindy said. "Well done."

Gia nodded with a proud smile and went to help Fern with getting ready for bed.

"You haven't told them that their father is on his way?" Adam asked under his breath, as he finally got to his feet.

Cindy shook her head. "There's time for that. If I tell them now, they'll be too excited to sleep. Speaking of sleep," she said, glancing at him, "you look like you're ready to pass out."

"I wanted to wait up for Xani," Adam said, blinking to clear his tired eyes. "I've barely had any time alone with her since I got back."

"Let me get back to the lounge and relieve her, then," Cindy said. "We wouldn't want you falling asleep in the middle of sex. Maybe you can find a clean shirt, in the meantime." At Adam's blank look, she laughed and pointed at the drying ice pop stains down the front.

"It's alright," he smiled, looking down at the purple blotches. "If I were worried about stains, I wouldn't wear it around kids."

"They're not even your kids," Cindy said, marveling at his lenience.

"They don't have to be," he said. "They still give me a hug and say good-night before they go to bed. After what they've suffered, they deserve a chance to just be children."

"You're unreal," Cindy said. "I could kiss you. On the cheek, of course."

Adam took a cautious step back, and Cindy noticed his sudden, serious alertness. "What's the matter?"

"I'm not sure," he murmured. "I thought I heard a noise from the alley." Just as they turned towards the window, a shrill chirp sounded from the alarm system, and a floodlight switched on outside. Adam ran to take a look, but he shook his head. "Nothing there now."

"False alarm?" Cindy asked hopefully.

"Maybe, but it was enough to trigger the motion sensors," he said. "Maybe Morgan or Xani can check the sensitivity on it tomorrow. We don't want the alarm going off every time a stray or a rat passes by."

Jonah listened to his Aunt Connie's concerned rant without interrupting. She and Teddy had gotten worried when they didn't hear from him, especially in the hours after they found out what had happened to the house. Did he get hurt at all? Was it a gas leak, like the fire department was saying? Why did the truck get burnt up, then? If someone did it on purpose, who could have done such a terrible thing? He could use the car for however long he wished, and where was he staying, in the meantime? They had a spare room, so he could stay with them indefinitely, until he found a new place. Even his old friend Ellie had come by to offer him a place to stay, if he needed it.

As Connie continued her questioning, Jonah stood in front of the full-length closet mirror to check the bandage over his gunshot. Thanks to Galen's skills, Jonah's wound wasn't bleeding anymore, but he was still sore. Even Adam had to keep a bandage on when he was hurt, and he healed at an unnaturally fast rate.

He caught Connie's question: did he have enough clothes?

"Yes," he answered shortly, but Connie didn't seem to hear him, as she began to list off the clothes they had unused, especially Malcolm's, that she was thinking of donating, but if he needed anything...

The door creaked open, and Jonah had to think whether he had heard a knock before he had said "yes" to his aunt, as he pulled his shirt back down.

"I'm fine, Aunt Connie. Tell Uncle Teddy not to worry, and I'll stay in touch."

Jonah disconnected and set his phone on the nightstand before he faced Mina.

They had stayed in their respective rooms after his failed proposal, and Jonah had used the break to reconsider his rashness. After their brief horseplay, Mina's unguarded laughter and vulnerability had stirred him, reminding him how much he wanted her to be his. He hadn't planned to be so spontaneous about his proposal, and her shock and subsequent fumbling made him realize how thoughtlessly he had gone about it. At least she was nice enough to turn him down without making him feel like a total idiot.

Mina looked a little uneasy, too. She seemed more unsettled and less self-assured now than when she was in his room before, when she was wearing nothing but a towel, but there was something appealing about her shyness. In his hand-me-down concert t-shirt, which looked oversized on her, she was much more covered but looked so much sexier.

"I'm meeting Miranda in the morning, at nine," she said. "But before I do, there are some things I need to say."

"If it's about before, I'd rather forget about that," he said.

"I'll be brief," she said. "I was caught off-guard before, but I owe you an explanation."

He shook his head. "You don't owe me anything, really."

"I *do* like you, which was why I hesitated," she continued. "I care about what happens to you, and I hate endangering you or seeing you get hurt, because of me."

"I'm not stupid!" he shot back. "I realized within the first couple of days of being your dog, how chaotic and dangerous your life is, but I want to stay in it. I didn't forget what we've been through, when I asked you to marry me."

"I'm not willing to risk your life," Mina said. "I've already let myself become distracted and careless, and you're paying the price for it. If anything else happens to you…"

"Hey," he interrupted, taking her hands in his, "there are never guarantees. We just buried Malcolm, who shouldn't have died before me, or his own parents. All that these past few weeks have proven is that being with you or knowing you means absolutely shit when it comes to determining who lives or dies."

111

Jonah lifted her hands and kissed them. "I love you, and all I'm asking for is a chance to spend the rest of my life with you, whether that's five days or fifty years."

He was secretly pleased with himself for leaving Mina speechless. Now that she was there, he was determined to get through to her, to strip away all her excuses and barriers. If, at the end, she still didn't want to be with him, then it would at least be an honest answer.

"You..." she started hesitantly. "You love me?"

"I thought that was a given," he chuckled incredulously. "Baby, I wouldn't have offered you my mother's ring, if I didn't love you."

"You barely know me," she said, shaking her head, trying to pull her hands free.

"I know more than you think," he said, refusing to let go. "I know you play Billie Holiday when you feel sad and Metallica when you're angry. You use one Chinese dialect to speak to your parents, but curse in another..."

Mina narrowed her eyes. "That's not fair. You learned all that when you were living as my dog."

"Okay," he conceded. "You're also secretly afraid that you've inherited more from your mother than from your father, and you don't want anyone to get close, in case it's true." He didn't know exactly how Selina Xing's spiritual nature affected her children, but he knew that Mina was holding something back.

"Fine!" she cried, jerking her hands free. "You've made your point. Yes, I'm scared of sharing too much of myself. It's too painful, and I have enough to focus on, for tomorrow and afterwards, so I'm not exposing myself like that anymore. To you, or anyone else."

Jonah seized on something that he hadn't realized earlier. "Malcolm knew, didn't he? He knew about you, and about your family."

112

Mina nodded stiffly. "I was in love with him, and we were thinking of starting a family, at some point, so yes, I told him everything. He said he accepted it and that it didn't matter, but it did," she said bitterly. "I won't go through that again, for anyone."

"You wouldn't have to," Jonah insisted. "I'm not him, and I would never treat you like he did. I would never resent you for keeping secrets or use them against you. If that's your main reason for turning me down, it's a pretty shitty one. What else you got?"

"I can't stay," she said quietly. "This isn't my home anymore."

"There's not much left for me here, either. Next?" he asked, as he sensed her resolve flagging through the uncertainty in her eyes. "If you want to speed up the process," he said, with difficulty, "you can just tell me honestly, if you don't feel anything for me, and we'll call it a night."

She looked pained. "I don't think I can do that." She took a step towards him, reluctantly. "I can't bring myself to say 'no' outright, because I *want* this. I want this feeling to stay, I want you in my life. It's shitty and selfish, and I really should let you go, but I can't!"

Her words were labored and agonized, as her tears started.

He hated seeing any woman he cared about in tears, but Mina's crying wrecked him. He gathered her in his arms and let her sob into his chest. He had been ready to argue with her, point for point, but forget about that, now. "I'm sorry, baby," he said gently, kissing away her tears. "Fuck what I said. You don't have to give me an answer. Whatever and whenever you decide, I just want you to be happy."

Even through her tears, she looked beautiful to him. Mina looked up at him and touched his cheek and jaw, as if memorizing the contours of his face. An enigmatic mix of wonder and despair showed in her unsmiling

113

expression, as she kissed him. Slow and sensual, her lips and tongue touched his, as her hands began a torturous descent.

Fuck. If he had let Mina return home without letting her know how he felt, he would've never forgiven himself, but now that he had her in his arms, he couldn't fathom how he could possibly let her go. He pulled back from her kiss when he felt her fingers unbuttoning the top of his jeans. "We don't have to do this, unless you want to," he whispered, stroking his fingers along her lips, along her jaw and down her neck.

"I know," she said, leading him to his bed. "I want to."

Mina lay back on his bed and pulled him closer, and once their bodies touched, their primal instincts took over. She was clawing into him and panting for breath, desperate for release, before they were even undressed. She reached for the light switch at one point, but he pushed her hand away. "I want to see you," he whispered against her ear. "I don't want to miss anything about you."

He refused to be rushed by her pace and savored every moment, exploring every inch of her, until she was literally cursing and pleading, crying out for him. So that when Jonah was finally inside her, hearing and feeling her come, as Mina screamed his name, he knew that she had completely, unconditionally, finally given herself to him.

Adam eased his eyes open to find himself lying on the sofa in the living room of the duplex. From the stillness in the room and darkness outside the windows, plus Xani's red curls spread across his chest as she slumbered on top of him, he guessed that it was sometime in the middle of the night.

He caught a silvery, glowing swirl, like the tail of a cirrus cloud, out of the corner of his eye, and followed it to the silent, mid-air pacing of Mina's *ruishi* around the back of the sofa. Technically, Dawa didn't belong to Mina, but the Tibetan spirit lion-dog had spent the past few years watching over her in New York—most likely at their mother's request—and sometimes assumed the role of her nanny dog.

Selina had befriended the *ruishi* during one of her solitary trips back to mainland China and regions further north, when Mina and Adam were both children. What had started out for Dawa as a curiosity-seeking visit to the United States extended into a semi-permanent residence. The *ruishi* came and went as he chose, and as children, Adam and Mina had learned not to talk about him to their friends, who could not see him as the family did.

As Adam and Mina grew up and left home, Dawa had paid them occasional visits on their mother's behalf, and for his own peace of mind and desire to explore. When Mina moved to New York, he visited her more often, but Adam guessed that Dawa also liked the higher vantages and thinner air of the burgeoning number of skyscrapers throughout Manhattan and the boroughs.

Dawa was fretfully panting, open-mouthed, as he flowed back and forth through the living room, and seemed to yowl soundlessly to Adam.

"I don't know when Mina's coming back," Adam whispered, careful not to wake Xani. "You want to go check on the kids and see how they're doing? Don't wake them!"

Dawa bounded off eagerly, with a flourish of his white tail and mane, as Xani stirred, raising her head. "Did you say something?"

"It's the middle of the night," he said. "You can go back to sleep." Adam eased himself upright, as Xani started getting up from the sofa. "You can crash at Mina's upstairs, too, if you want."

"What time is it?" she asked, looking for her phone with her eyes half-opened. "I wonder if Cindy wants help closing up. The crowd was rowdy tonight, even for a Saturday."

"I didn't hear either of our phones go off, and I'm sure she would've texted if she needed anything." He stood and stretched his arms overhead to alleviate his muscle aches from falling asleep half-curled on the sofa, and felt Xani's arms wrap around him from behind, and her head resting between his shoulder blades.

"I love you," she said, almost like a sigh.

"I love you, too," he replied, pleased but surprised to hear her say it. "But…?"

"No buts, that's it," she said, giving him a little squeeze around his waist. "I've just never said it to you before, and I thought I should start. I'm still a little rusty with this relationship thing."

Adam laughed and covered her hands with his own, the golden color of his skin contrasting with the pale, translucent white of hers. "It doesn't need saying. I can hear in your voice, see it in your smile." He turned around in her arms and cupped her face, as he kissed her. "I can feel it in that," he whispered against her lips.

Xani groaned with annoyance, as the front door opened with the familiar, deliberate jingle of Cindy's keychain.

"Ten…nine…eight," Cindy began her whispered countdown, ending at "one" with her arrival in the living room, bearing a neatly-creased brown paper bag with leftovers. "Already dressed? Damn."

"We weren't going to start anything with children in the other rooms," Adam said.

"My parents felt that way. I think that's why I was an only child," Cindy smiled, returning to the kitchen, with Adam and Xani in tow. She unpacked the food and stowed them in the refrigerator with minimal noise, except a couple of bowls of what looked like cubed, dark red yellowfin tuna and seasoned octopus over rice. "Leftover ahi and tako poke from the kitchen, if you guys are hungry. The kids don't eat fish, either."

Xani's green eyes glimmered with interest. "I could eat."

"What time is it?" Adam asked, then checked his phone. "I can't eat anything at three in the morning."

"Suit yourself," Cindy laughed softly, passing one of the bowls and a pair of disposable chopsticks to Xani. "But if the girl's hungry, she's hungry," she shrugged, then turned at the sound of her phone in her jacket pocket.

"Who calls you at this hour? That's not Morgan checking up on you, is it?" Xani remarked, inhaling the aromatic blend of soy, ginger, sesame and chilis in the poke marinade.

"No, he would text," Cindy said, taking out her phone and going into the living room for privacy. "There's only person who ever calls me to talk at these ungodly hours," she said, holding the phone to her ear. "*Dime.*"

Mina awoke in Jonah's bed, with Jonah still asleep next to her, his hand resting loosely on her hip, guarding her even in his sleep. She was reminded for a second of when he used to do something similar when he was in his husky form, planting his paw on her hand or knee when she tried to get up from her sofa. As a dog, he would usually also stare with his black-lined, ice-blue eyes to entreat her to stay a little longer.

God, I have to stop remembering him as a dog, or this will never work.

She gingerly eased back a wisp of his silver-shot black hair out of his closed eyes, and contemplated the possibility that she had made a huge mistake in sleeping with Jonah. Not that she hadn't enjoyed herself—shit, she felt her pulse quicken in anticipation of an encore, just thinking about it—but it was more difficult to leave him now. She didn't even want to think about going home to New York and waking up in her bed without him there.

She wasn't used to letting her guard down like that. She rarely let herself fall deeply asleep when anyone else was in the room with her, even with people that she trusted. She recalled once passing out in the office of the Red Lotus after an all-nighter job and waking up to Cindy's startled shout, just as Mina's small, clawed, black-furred paws changed back into hairless hands, and a luxuriant auburn tail curled out of sight and vanished.

To this day, Mina couldn't determine whether she had actually changed in her sleep, or whether she had just dreamed it, but Cindy refused to speak about what she had seen, one way or the other. Mina also wondered how much Jonah had noticed and learned about her during their time together, as he seemed to accept her words unquestioningly, regardless of how outlandish or cryptic she sometimes sounded. He accepted her, and wanted her, exactly as she was.

Jonah had been generous, kind and passionate when it came to her happiness, as well as her pleasure, in a way that Malcolm never was. Perhaps it was due to Malcolm's comparative immaturity, but there was also Jonah's patience: the care and time he took for her seduction, until all her doubts and defenses were stripped away, and she surrendered completely to him… Mina felt a little guilty about comparing men with whom she had sex, but it was hard not to, when there were only two, who happened to be first cousins.

Shit, why does that feel so wrong, like I've seriously fucked something up?

Mina slid Jonah's hand off her hip and slipped from the bed silently, careful not to disturb the bed. She took the discarded t-shirt from the floor and slipped back into it, as she tiptoed back to her room, where she went to find her phone.

No messages. That was a relief. Mina's first instinct was to call Adam to ask for his sage advice but reconsidered. *He won't want to hear about my sex life… But I know who would.*

Cindy picked up on the third ring. "*Dime.*"

"Is this a good time?" Mina asked.

"If it wasn't, I wouldn't have picked up," Cindy said tartly. "What is it?"

"I think I'm going to hell," Mina said. She was being overdramatic, but she was feeling so torn and frazzled, that it was the first thing that came to mind.

"Honey," Cindy said, with a steady, soothing voice of reason, "if you mean the Christian one, you and I both know the managers that run that place, and it's pretty clear there's no vacancy for you there, unless you've done something catastrophic and unforgivable." She paused. "You haven't, have you?"

Mina took a breath. "Jonah and I had sex."

From Cindy's muffled squeak of surprise, Mina knew that Cindy was somewhere where she didn't want to be overheard. "I'm sorry, but why do you think you're going to hell for that?"

"Maybe not literal hell," Mina amended, "but is it wrong that we slept together?"

"Did it feel wrong?"

"Fuck, no, it was mind-blowing," Mina blurted. "It was probably the best sex I ever had. I think I even blacked out, at one point."

"Okay," Cindy laughed. "So, are you guilt-ridden about being with Jonah? There's no reason to be: it's been more than four years since you and Malcolm split, and your dead ex literally gave you his blessing from the

119

afterlife. You and Jonah clearly care about each other, so have some fun."

Mina considered Cindy's comment, while Cindy was speaking to someone in the background. "You think I may be feeling guilty for enjoying myself?"

"Or enjoying *him*, as it were," Cindy rejoined. "I don't know everything that's going on inside that pretty head of yours, but I know you deny yourself the same happiness you wish for everyone else. You have to allow yourself to be vulnerable."

"I do," Mina insisted. "I lean on you guys all the time."

"For some things," Cindy said. "Where's your chain, with your rings?"

"In my bag, side pocket," she said easily.

"That's my point, honey. You don't need those reminders of your pain, because you've moved on. Or, you should've by now, anyway," she said. "Let them go, and get yourself something better. *Someone* better."

"Thanks, Cin," Mina said. "I'd give you a hug, if you were here."

"Me, too. Go give Jonah a hug, instead, and see where that leads you," she teased. "If you're only having sex every four or five years, you'd better make the most of it, while you can. Quick, hang up before Adam grabs the phone from me!"

Jonah became fully awake when he noticed Mina's absence from his bed, although the space she had vacated was still warm. The reading lamp over the bed was on, the only light source at that late hour. It was still hours from dawn, judging from the darkness of the room, even with the drapes open.

He craned his head around to see where Mina was. She had left his bedroom door ajar and was emerging from the other bedroom with her phone in hand, laughing quietly, as she said good-bye to her brother. The air was slightly chilly, so she had wrapped herself in a blanket. She had the shirt on, too, of course.

The call disconnected with an electronic chirp, and Jonah closed his eyes, pretending to be asleep. Mina returned to Jonah's bedroom, setting her phone down on his dresser before she tossed aside her blanket and crawled back into his bed, into the cozy hollow waiting for her. She slid her hand across his chest and lay her head over his heart, lying still for a moment.

"You faker," she murmured. "You're awake."

"I never said I wasn't," he returned. "What did Adam want? Is everything alright?"

"Everything's fine. I called Cindy, and he and Xani happened to be in the duplex with her, so we just talked briefly."

Jonah raised his head to look at her. "You had to talk to Cindy in the middle of the night?"

"It wasn't the first time, and it won't be the last," Mina said, curling more snugly against him. "We're sounding boards for each other, whenever we need a sympathetic ear."

"You could always talk to me," he offered, wondering how long it would take for her to trust him to the same extent that she confided in others.

"Not when it's about you," she said drowsily. "Don't worry; I didn't share any intimate details with her. I just needed a sanity check."

He pulled the bedcovers over her chilled shoulders. "Do you regret last night?"

"No, but it just makes it harder for me to leave." She kissed him, but it was a lingering, melancholy kiss. "It doesn't change what I need to do."

"I'll go with you, then," he said. "It's just New York, not half a world away." He had no right to dictate or interfere in her decisions, but he could at least make it clear that her choices and her fate mattered to him, and he still wanted to be with her.

"Let's see how my meeting goes," Mina said evasively. "It's still a few hours away, and I'd rather not think about it now. I don't want to think about anything, really."

With her eyes drifting closed, she stroked the edge of his jaw and curve of his neck in that slow, deliberate way, like she was studying his face. He watched her delicate features soften and slacken, as she fell back to sleep, and he imagined that if he lived to be a thousand, he would never tire of watching that.

He brushed back her sleek, night-black hair; it was straight, smooth and strong, sliding against his fingers like woven silk or a raven's feathers. Over the years, he had imagined its texture, and the feel of her skin and the taste of her lips... "I love you, Mina."

Even as her breath changed to signal that she was already asleep, she whispered with a smile, "I love you, too."

Chapter 9

Cindy awoke in the spare bedroom in the duplex's upper floor, to the aromas of eggs and butter, and something herbal and savory, like oregano. There was also the sound of pans and a whisk against the inside of a metal bowl, coming from the kitchen.

Cindy descended from the loft and peeked into the kitchen, where Adam was scrambling eggs and sautéing mushrooms, while Xani watched raptly from the other side of the counter. It was strange to see the kitchen in actual use, not just used for microwaving leftovers or storing prepared foods.

"I didn't even know there were pans and cooking utensils," she said, joining Adam and Xani in the kitchen.

"I brought them down from Mina's," Adam said. "She barely uses them, anyway."

"The children apparently told Adam at some point that they've never tasted certain foods, so he's on a mission to expand their palates," Xani said with amusement.

"From their past experiences, fresh foods are a privilege for their masters and human guests," Cindy said. "The proper care and feeding of fae slaves are not generally priorities for their masters."

"That's not their life anymore," Adam said, retrieving a pan of blueberry muffins from the oven. "Don't look at me like that," he said, catching Cindy's stunned expression. "Mina's fridge hasn't been touched in three days, and it seemed a waste to toss berries and mushrooms. No meats, right?"

"That's right," Cindy said. "Nothing taken from the flesh or bone of an animal. Dairy and eggs are fine."

"Good, because Adam uses a *lot* of both in his cooking," Xani commented.

"Not in everything. There's some fruit in the muffins," Adam grinned, pouring some of the eggs into a pan glistening with melted butter and stirring the well-browned mushrooms in the other pan. "Have you had breakfast yet? I can make something for you," he offered Cindy.

Cindy shook her head, but the smell of butter and eggs was making her mouth water. "Maybe after the kids have eaten. I'll take a muffin for now."

Xani passed her one, as she piled the rest onto a plate.

"You're spoiling them," Cindy said, savoring the smell of vanilla, lemon zest and nutmeg in the crisp berry-studded muffin top.

"I don't have nephews and nieces, and probably won't for a while," Adam said, turning out the fluffy, creamy eggs onto a plate for Xani. "This is my chance to be the 'fun uncle.' Besides, I'm not buying them video games or designer sneakers; I'm just feeding them a proper Sunday morning breakfast."

The sound of adults conversing and the savory aromas were enough to rouse the children, who swept into the kitchen with beating wings, even Fern, who lagged behind the others but managed to stay hovering about a foot off the ground.

The toddler stomped her padded bare feet, clearly indignant about coming in last.

"Fern's the littlest, and she just got her wings, so she deserves the first pick of what she wants for breakfast," Xani suggested, and Gia and Fallon nodded, albeit reluctantly.

Beaming, Fern climbed onto Xani's lap for a better view of the offerings and pointed to Xani's plate of fluffy soft-scrambled eggs. "That."

Adam laughed and turned back to the stove to start the next batch of eggs, and Xani groaned melodramatically about losing her food, as she passed a small dessert fork to Fern to let her dig in. Gia and Fallon chuckled, content to start with the warm muffins.

A knock sounded at the back door, and Adam and Xani were immediately on alert, but Cindy gestured to them to stay put, as she went to answer it. Bad guys wouldn't knock before barging in, she reasoned. Still, she approached the back door cautiously, only relaxing when she saw the winged silhouette through the small window, next to the taller, more familiar wingless shape.

Cindy opened the door with a broad smile. "Welcome to New York, Galen," she greeted the fae, then gave the older, taller man a big bearhug. "Hi, Daddy."

Mina was lost in her thoughts during the whole taxi ride from the hotel to the North End, staying alert enough to watch her driver's turns and heading, but otherwise letting herself drift back into her memories of the morning, from waking at dawn to Jonah's kisses and caresses, to when she finally dressed and left the suite, promising Jonah that she would keep him up to date, in return for him agreeing not to try to follow.

Exiting the cab, Mina breathed in the aroma of morning pastries wafting from the Italian bakeries and cafes from all areas of the neighborhood, as she watched the early bird tourist crowds filing back and forth across Unity Street between the Old North Church and the Paul

Revere Mall to for views and selfies at that eponymous statue.

As she often did when she had lived in Boston, Mina visited the gardens of the Old North Church and stopped to stroll through the Old North Memorial Garden, in the company of ghosts of soldiers and their loved ones, who came to see the blank dog tags hung in remembrance of the fallen, one for each servicemember killed during recent conflicts. She noticed, to her dismay, that there were hundreds more now than when she had last visited. As the wind blew between the metal tags, or as the visitors—both alive and deceased—gingerly touched them, they harmonized together as a solemn, serene chime.

As the doors of the old Episcopalian church opened in preparation for the weekly 9AM Sunday services, the regular congregation filed into the Old North Church from all corners, but a young woman with long, coffee-brown hair, in an ankle-length, cream-colored woolen coat walked at her own leisurely pace, lagging behind the worshippers and watching them with a condescending simper.

"Off they go, to wipe their slates clean and start their debauchery anew tomorrow," Miranda smiled, approaching from the Charter Street end of Unity Street. "You're early, Mina."

"I don't like wasting time," she said.

"Good," Miranda said, stepping closer to the buildings with Mina, to avoid the pedestrian traffic. "We can get to the point then."

I wish you would.

"I suggest a truce, a ceasing of hostilities. We agree not to interfere in each other's affairs when we cross into each other's jurisdictions. As part of the terms, we both agree not take any lives or prisoners, when we pay our visits."

Mina found the conditions curious. "It's not my norm to kill, maim or kidnap anyone, so I wouldn't have any issues. How do I know you'll honor your end of the bargain, and not harm anyone when you come to New York?"

"I have responsibilities to my sisterhood," Miranda said. "And to my masters, as well. It wouldn't sit well with my colleagues, if I renege on any agreement like this, especially if we expose ourselves to your retribution."

Mina didn't trust that there wasn't a catch. "What do you want from me?"

"From you? Nothing," Miranda smiled. "As a show of good faith, I will even release Jonah Gideon and his family from our jurisdiction. They will no longer be visited by stalkers or demons, or any of the other creatures that you seem to find some odious."

Mina didn't bother correcting her, that her feelings towards such beings were entirely neutral: as long as they didn't trouble her or her loved ones, she didn't trouble them. "And I'm free to come and go from Boston, without having to look over my shoulder, or anyone else's?"

"That is correct. As long as you don't direct your attacks towards me or attempt to remove me from my seat of power, we will allow you to keep yours." She extended her slender hand. "Do we have a deal?"

Mina looked at the hand offered to her. "If this is all you had wanted, you could've saved us both a great deal of time and effort, and come to me two days ago, after the funeral, in person."

Miranda smiled with a conciliatory nod. "Perhaps, but this is not an offer I make lightly, or often. To warrant this gesture," she said, turning up her hand, "you had to demonstrate a certain level of acumen and talent, to be worthy of regard as an equal. Jonah Gideon will be compensated for his losses and his time, once you've left Boston."

The hair on Mina's neck prickled at how Miranda said his name. "Is he also free to come and go from Boston, as he chooses?"

"Of course," Miranda said amicably. "He'll no longer be under our watch, as we'll no longer have a need to monitor him, once you leave."

"You also firebombed and demolished Connie and Teddy's house—" Mina started.

Miranda waved it aside. "Yes, yes, they'll be reimbursed, too."

"—and caused the death of their only child," she finished. "There's a dollar amount for that, too?"

"Older generations are more pragmatic about loss," Miranda said dispassionately. "You should follow the example of your elders, and not cling to grievances that are beyond your power to resolve. You have our word: the Gideons will be recompensed to their satisfaction."

The safety and security of Jonah and the rest of the Gideon family was paramount to Mina, so she took Miranda's hand, still with reluctance, but confident that Miranda was sincere. It was true, that without Mina around, their lives were less fraught and complicated, so she and Jonah would have to discuss where she fit, if anywhere.

As their hands unclasped, Miranda bowed her head slightly. "I'd say that I look forward to seeing you again soon, but I don't think you'd take my meaning the right way, so I'll simply say: 'Safe travels.'"

Jonah heard the door open without a prefacing knock, which signaled Mina's return. He jumped to his feet, feeling a familiar excitement and relief about seeing her again, as he had been waiting anxiously ever since her earlier text indicating that her meeting with Miranda was over, and that she was on her way back to him.

He met her in the alcove, refraining from sweeping her into his embrace when he saw the packages in her hands: a colorful shopping bag in one, and a blue-lettered, white pastry box in the other. She handed him the pastry box. "Sfogliatelle and cannolis from Mike's."

He gave her a deep, appreciative kiss. "Could you be more perfect?"

She laughed and turned towards her room, her mood and expression lighter and more playful than when she left that morning.

"Adam texted that Galen arrived this morning with Cindy's dad," Jonah said, stopping at her open door, "so that's one less thing to worry about. I take it that the meeting with Miranda went well, then? Or, at least well enough that you decided to go shopping?"

"As well as could be expected," Mina said, shedding her black jacket before reaching into her shopping bag and pulling out more black garments to add to her monochromatic wardrobe. "And the shopping was a necessary evil. I can only wear certain clothes for so many days." Noticing that Jonah was watching, she motioned for him to turn around.

"I've already seen you naked, so there's no need to be shy," he grinned, peeling back the tape holding the pastry box closed. "So, what did you discuss?"

Mina turned her back to Jonah anyway, as she slipped her dress up over her head. "A truce. Miranda will stay away from you and your family, as long as I don't threaten her position. I have my doubts about her honesty, but she's bound to her word, so if she tries anything, she'll have to answer to other powers, not just me."

Jonah paid close attention to every word and took a bite from one of the lobster tail pastries, if only to keep from drooling with his mouth agape like an idiot, as he watched Mina change into her new black lace undergarments. She was magnificent unclothed, but the little scraps of embroidery served to accent all her beautiful curves.

"You're free to leave, then," he said, trying not to sound disappointed.

"Yes, finally," she said, ripping off the tag and slipping into a pair of curve-hugging pants. "Ah, shit," she muttered.

"What?"

"I forgot to pick up a shirt while I was out," she said, not too convincingly.

Jonah laughed. "You, of all people, forgot? Come here, you liar."

She stepped over to him, batting her straight black lashes up at him. She took a bite of the flaky, half-eaten lobster tail he held out for her and smiled coyly. "I don't suppose I borrow one of your shirts?"

He knew exactly which shirt she meant, as the black sleeveless concert t-shirt was still neatly folded and sitting on his bed where she had left it in the morning. It was hard not to say "yes" to her, when she was standing in front of him wearing just a black lace bra and skin-tight leggings, but he resisted. "Uh-huh. And when are you getting it back to me?"

"I don't know," she said, more seriously. "I haven't planned that far ahead."

"Okay, you can have it, on one condition," he said, putting the pastry back into the box and reaching into the coin pocket of his jeans with his free hand. With his heart pounding furiously and a bead of nervous sweat forming at his nape, he showed her his mother's ruby ring again. "This has to go with it."

"Jonah, I..." She still hesitated in her answer, but it was different this time. "I love you, but I don't know if I'm ready to do this again."

She loves me. "Just take it with you, and think about it," he said, kissing her forehead. "If it's not meant to be, you can give it back to me when you've reached your decision." He smiled. "Along with the shirt."

She flashed her eyes at him defiantly, but without heat in her gaze. "That may not happen for a while."

"I'm not in a rush," he said, looking at her expectantly. "Don't leave me hanging; I've only got one free hand here."

Mina laughed, taking the box from him and setting it on her dresser near the door. As she turned away from him briefly, he grasped her hand and touched the ring to her fingertips, just to see her reaction. She flinched instinctively, her fingers stiffened and her brows knitted with consternation.

"Don't freak out, baby," he said soothingly. "It's not a promise, or an obligation; it's just a piece of jewelry. And not a very expensive one, at that." As her hand relaxed in his, he pried her ring finger loose and slipped his mother's ruby onto her hand. It was a perfect fit. "Thank you," he said with a relieved breath.

She didn't smile or have the beaming, euphoric glow of someone in love; in fact, she had the slightly panicked, wild-eyed look of an animal caught in a snare. But Jonah knew her tells, mainly that she didn't curse him out or tear the ring off and fling it back in his face. Mina was willing to consider it, and that was enough for him, for the time being.

"Let's get your shirt," he said lightly, leading her out by the hand. Her fingers felt different against his now, with the gold band pressed snugly between them. He liked the new sensation, but it was too early to tell whether she would get used to it.

Mina paused in the alcove, as she noticed a large white envelope on the back of the sofa in the living area. "What's that?"

131

Jonah turned around. "That came for you, while you were out."

"Something came addressed to me, *here*?" Mina frowned.

He nodded. "It was hand-delivered from Bullfinch, Farrier and Hart. That's Aciré's firm, isn't it?"

"Yeah, but they don't typically use couriers for their clients' materials," she said, picking up the envelope. "Not for Sunday deliveries, especially."

"She didn't look like a courier. Hourglass figure, expensive suit, and short, curly burgundy hair?"

"That would be Aciré Hart, herself," Mina said. "I'm sorry I missed her."

"She didn't introduce herself, but she said you would know who she was. She said that the envelope arrived for you at the State Street office and to text or call her, if you need anything."

Mina scowled at the return address on the white envelope, as she opened the envelope. "The only party that would send anything to their attention for me, would be Malcolm's lawyers. Do you know what this is?"

"A copy of Malcolm's will," Jonah said. He hadn't opened the envelope, respecting Mina's privacy, but he had recognized the name of Malcolm's advisor from the return labeling and guessed from the heft of the packet what it was.

"What the fuck, Malcolm?" Mina muttered, pausing before she pulled out the sheaf of papers. "Killing a tree for a document that tells me what, exactly?" She looked evenly at Jonah. "Before I sift through this whole thing, do you know?"

"Sure. I was in the lawyer's office with him when he finalized it, but I think you should read it for yourself, anyway," Jonah said, returning to his room to give Mina a moment of privacy.

Jonah recalled all the details of Malcolm's will, but his perspective had evolved and changed since it was written. He had a better understanding now of why Malcolm had included certain clauses and statements, particularly those that had pertained to Mina. He picked up his shirt from the bed and returned to the living area, where Mina was sitting on the sofa, with her eyes closed in a pained scowl.

"He didn't have to give me anything," she said. "I would've preferred it, if he hadn't."

"He wanted to make sure that everyone he loved was taken care of." Anticipating the possibility that his parents would outlive him, Malcolm had left them his real assets and investment holdings to ensure their comfort for the remainder of their lives. After whatever few debts were settled, a portion of the residual cash was bequeathed to Mina, as well as the remaining patents he still held in his name.

"Your name's not in here as a beneficiary," she said. "Just as his executor."

"I told him to leave me out of it," Jonah said, taking a seat next to her. "Anything he wanted me or our cousins to have, he already signed over or gave us in person. It made for less drama and fewer arguments."

He looked over her shoulder at the page she had left on top, which detailed a clause indicating that she no longer needed to keep the Gideon surname until remarriage, which had been a condition of the original divorce settlement. "He wanted to ensure that you had your life and name back."

"Only *after* he was gone, when he couldn't keep me, anyway," Mina said. "I've only kept my married name this long because I couldn't be bothered with filing all the paperwork for the name changes on my legal and financial documents, not out of any obligation."

"It's your choice, either way," Jonah shrugged, and handed her the t-shirt. "Here. A deal's a deal."

Mina set aside the papers and pulled on the shirt. "Thank you. I really do love this shirt."

"Enough to be bribed with it, to wear my mother's ring," he said.

She turned around and leaned against him. "I love and cherish them both, because they're your links to your parents, and whenever I wear them, I will think of you." She stroked his bristled cheek and kissed him. "And I like how you look at me when I wear them."

"I can't imagine anyone else in them," he said sincerely, kissing her hand, with the glistening ruby brushing against his skin. "I know they're not as impressive as a three-carat diamond or a portfolio—"

She kissed him soundly and pressed herself against him, to ensure that she had his full attention. "None of that was enough to make me stay with Malcolm, but your gifts are meaningful and priceless; they're pieces of you."

"Hmm," he grunted shrewdly. "'Gifts' imply that you're not giving them back."

She played with his hair and the front of his shirt, distractedly, but her dark eyes were distant and thoughtful. "Did you mean what you said?"

Jonah chuckled. "Yeah, probably, but you'd have to be more specific. I've said a lot of shit these last couple of days."

"That you wanted to spend your life with me," she reminded. "That you want to marry me, even knowing the crazy and dangerous shit that goes on?"

"I definitely meant every word of that," he said, pulling her closer. He felt her softening in his arms, surrendering in a sense: not in fear or resignation, but in placing her trust and faith in him. "I also meant it when I told you that I would never hurt you, and I just want you to be happy, whatever happens."

Mina lay her head against his shoulder. "I believe you, but I still need time to think about it."

"I know," he said, kissing her forehead. It still wasn't a "yes" but it was incrementally closer. "Take all the time you need. I'm not going anywhere."

Galen took the cup of tea from Cindy's hand with a grateful nod. "I still can't believe I'm here, and that the children are finally safe." He breathed in the warm, fragrant steam from the lemon-zested cup of black tea, savoring its fresh tartness before he took a sip. "I don't know how I can ever repay you."

Dan McManus patted Cindy's knee, as his daughter perched on the arm of the sofa next to him. While his hair was finally thinning and already silver-white, Dan knew he still looked imposing, as he was as sturdy and solid as most of his crew members, but he was starting to feel his age in his weathered, arthritic hands and knees. Soon, he probably would have to slow down and cut back on the number of these transport jobs, but as long as his mind was working and his crew was loyal, he would lend his services and his resources whenever his child needed him.

Cindy handed her father a glass of his favorite Irish whiskey and passed a woolen blanket to Galen to help him warm up. This was their first opportunity to speak in private since Galen's arrival, as the children had been so excited at being reunited with their father that it took Xani and Adam a bribe of hot chocolate to coax the children into allowing their father a few minutes of rest after his grueling journey.

"Your freedom is payment enough, Galen," Cindy said. "I'm very sorry about the loss of your wife and your sister."

Dan recalled the two fae women, flying away from the weeping children, charging back to meet their pursuers, fighting valiantly to buy the transport more time. He had watched them in the mirrors of the truck as long as he could, but they eventually vanished into the dust and darkness. "They wanted to make sure the children were safe, whatever happened. As we were separated from you, we didn't know if you had been captured or killed."

Galen took a slow sip of the tea. "We made a pact that, no matter what befell us, the children had to reach New York. When the three of us were captured as youths, we were branded when we were enslaved," he said, gesturing to the tattoo on his neck, "but our children were still pristine and had a chance to live as free fae."

Dan remembered something that the eldest child, Gia, had told him. "Gia said that you were running short on time. She had heard that the demon was going to brand her upon her next birthday?"

"Yes," Galen scowled. "That was as much as we could allow ourselves to tell her, but my sister and my wife also remembered, when they were captured, that along with the branding came their physical initiations, when the master tested their tolerance and suitability for his…entertainment," he said with a grimace.

Dan squeezed Cindy's hand, as he felt simpatico with Galen's protective instincts. "I understand your determination. I would do anything to spare my daughter from that kind of abuse."

"We were concerned for Fallon, too," Galen said. "Most boys have an easier time in servitude, as most are trained for aide or household duties, but some of them catch the eye of one of the master's associates or allies," he said grimly. "The boys reassigned to the harem often live short lives, mercifully so."

"Papa!" squeaked Fern, flitting into the living room with madly beating wings, trying to maintain her hover. "Look!"

"I see you!" Galen beamed. He set his teacup on the corner end table and caught Fern, as she bounced onto his lap. "I'm so proud of you, little bean."

He was so overwhelmed by his adoration for his daughter that his throat seized briefly, and his eyes blurred with a sheen of tears, as he hugged his daughter. "I wish I could've been here for your wing-sprout."

"Okay, Papa," Fern said gently, squeezing his whiskered face between her little dimpled hands. "Here now."

Dan got misty-eyed for a moment, remembering when Cindy was little, with the same boundless energy to climb over him for hours. Dan gave Cindy's hand a final squeeze and got to his feet with a habitual grunt. "Let me get back to the crew, and maybe we can head out while there's still light."

"I'll walk you out," Cindy said, taking his empty glass for him. "Dad's leaving," she called towards the kitchen, where everyone had gathered. Xani and Adam came out together, with his arm around her waist, and Dan grinned.

"I always liked that girl," Dan said quietly to Cindy. "I'm glad she found someone who makes her happy, if it couldn't work between the two of you."

"Me, too, Dad." Cindy smiled encouragingly at Morgan, who came forward and offered his hand to Dan, who still stood a couple of inches taller than him.

Dan shook Morgan's hand vigorously and slapped him on the back, just a little harder than he needed to, to make sure Morgan knew he meant business. "Take care of my little girl."

"Yes, Sir," Morgan said earnestly. "You don't have to worry."

Dan frowned at him with a suspicious glance, his hand still clamped on Morgan's. "What do you mean by that?"

Morgan reddened and froze. "Ah…"

Cindy slapped Dan's hard, sinewy arm. "Dad!"

Dan's frown vanished. "I'm just kidding, Morgan. I know you'll do right by my Cindy." He leaned closer, as he released Morgan's hand. "But in case you don't, remember that my work involves smuggling people and goods across state lines, so I can make you disappear so fast—"

"Not helping, Dad," Cindy rebuked, dragging her father to the door.

"Alright," Dan acquiesced. "I won't say another word."

"That's unlikely," she rejoined, but she gave Dan a final hug. "But I love that you're still looking out for me."

"Always," Dan said, kissing her forehead. "Whatever changes you go through, and whatever makes you happy, I'm still your father."

Chapter 10

Jonah stirred from his reverie at hearing Aciré Hart calling his name. He looked around the spacious black seat of the black town car limousine, which seemed too empty now that Mina had gone. He also felt a little chilled since she stole his gray hooded sweatshirt, too. He peeked out the window and noticed that they were still in the Logan Airport terminal areas, so they hadn't dropped Mina only a few minutes ago for her late afternoon flight home, but it felt like longer.

"Are you alright, Mister Gideon?" Aciré asked through the open privacy screen separating the front and back seats. She sounded more amused than concerned.

Jonah had been thinking of his last few minutes with Mina, when the privacy screen was still closed, as they gave each other a bittersweet good-bye kiss. She promised to call him when she got home, and he promised that he would finish up his business in Boston and join her in New York soon. There was no mention of how long he would stay in New York this time, nor how long they expected their relationship to last. It seemed like too much to discuss for a twenty-minute ride from the hotel to the airport, especially when all he wanted was to hold and kiss her, for however much time they had left.

"Do you mind if I sit with you back there?" Aciré asked. "I'm going to strain my neck talking to you like this."

Jonah gestured to the ample seating next to him. "Go right ahead."

At the next red light, Aciré got out of the front passenger seat and slipped into the back, tucking her briefcase between herself and Jonah, on top of Mina's satchel that she promised to ship overnight to New York, to spare Mina the trouble of taking non-essential luggage. "Thank you. I figured a face-to-face would be easier, and more private. Not that I don't trust Iago," she said, glancing at the back of the driver's head before she closed the privacy screen, "but client matters require discretion."

She brushed back a sleek burgundy curl and straightened her tailored gray suit jacket, outfitted more for a day in the courtroom than a lazy Sunday afternoon. Except for the bright plum lipstick on her bee-stung lips, which was more festive than corporate. "I don't dress down often, Mister Gideon," she said, noting his passing curiosity. "The Xing family has used our firm since its inception, and we value their loyalty, as much as they value ours. How I dress reflects my respect for my clients, whether or not I'm officially acting on their behalf."

"About that," Jonah said. "Earlier, you mentioned that you wanted to discuss the insurance settlement and compensation regarding my aunt and uncle's house, and I'm not sure if there's been some misunderstanding, but I don't believe we're using your firm's services." He gestured at the pristine limousine interior. "To be honest, I don't know that we could afford to."

"Oh, I see," Aciré said, with an enlightened smile. "I apologize for any confusion. No, I'm not acting as an agent on the Gideon family's behalf, but rather as an intermediary for Garrison Brothers."

Jonah stiffened at the name of Miranda's parent company, under which her sisterhood operated.

"Please let me explain," Aciré said mildly. "Garrison is a shell company, among other things. Part of the enterprise is managed through the sisterhood, but Garrison Brothers also deals in more conventional businesses, such as global trade, real estate and insurance."

"My aunt and uncle's house was insured under Garrison?" he asked.

"One of its wholly-owned subsidiaries, yes," Aciré said. "Anyway, I'm authorized by Garrison to approve whatever disbursements are necessary to compensate you and your family for your troubles and time, as it pertains to the Brookline property," she clarified. "There is a limit to my scope, I'm afraid, in that I can only negotiate on this event, and only in monetary terms."

"So, you can write us a check to cover the house and what we owned, but what happened to Malcolm is an entirely separate matter," Jonah said. "I suppose that's fair; it's difficult to put a price tag on the emotional toll of losing a family member."

"For what it's worth, Mister Gideon, I've buried my parents, and my child, also," Aciré said evenly. "No amount of money will ever erase the pain or undo the damage entirely, but money can become a tool and a resource. You can either use it to weaponize your grief, or build a legacy to honor the lost."

"I'm curious, Miss Hart," Jonah started, trying to read her. "Why would someone with your intellect, ethics and compassion work for Garrison, given what you seem to know about their business?"

"Why would I agree to represent such a soulless, monolithic conglomerate, you mean?" she paraphrased, with the trace of a smile. "To be clear, Garrison is partnered with Bullfinch, Farrier and Hart, as a firm, not with me, as an individual, so my loyalties remain with my colleagues and my clients. However, to serve my clients' best interests, I sometimes have to insert myself into the process, to see how the sausage is made, as it were."

"To get an insider's view of the organization," Jonah said.

"And to exploit what I can, for the benefit of my clients," Aciré said. "When Garrison hands me their blank checkbook, they don't look too closely at how many zeroes are in the sum they're paying, as long as I make sure that they don't have to worry about paying again, later."

"I can't even think of a number right now," Jonah said. "Like you said, it's hard to quantify or price out certain kinds of loss."

"I can empathize with that," Aciré said, pulling out a notepad from her briefcase, "and you shouldn't think of this as selling out or abandoning your principles. I can tell you from experience that Garrison ultimately won't care whether the settlement is six figures or eight, nor will they care whether you burn their check or blow it on drugs and hookers, but you'll gain nothing at all by ignoring them."

Aciré wrote a number on the notepad and passed it to Jonah for his consideration, and he almost had to count the digits to confirm what she was offering.

"Stay with your friends and fight, or leave all this behind and start anew," she said. "It's ultimately your choice, but I think you'll find your future easier to plan, if you don't have to worry about how to fund it."

Adam could tell the hour by the children's routine of picking up their toys before washing up for dinnertime, more than he could by looking out at the darkening sky. The late autumn storm clouds didn't help, as their rain-heavy slate hue blotted out the setting sun, making the Manhattan sky look more like night than dusk.

He started at the piercing sound of the perimeter alarms, and the sharp screeching drove the children to their father's side. Galen's wings spread protectively around his brood, as he shot Adam an inquiring look.

Adam knew it wasn't a false alarm, as Morgan and Xani had meticulously recalibrated the sensors to only trigger after a certain threshold of movement or energy. Plus, the hair on the back on his neck prickled, as he felt instinctively that something was wrong. He looked to see that Mina's sheathed *kaiken* dagger was still on corner table, next to the armchair.

"There's a false wall in Fallon and Fern's room, inside the closet," Adam said to Galen. "Get inside with the children, and we'll let you know when it's safe."

Galen nodded stiffly and rushed the children from the room, as Morgan darted to his laptop to check the activity.

Xani went to her bag and pulled out a compact .23-caliber gun, which Adam recognized. He'd never forget the silver and gray finish as long as he lived. "Is that the gun that shot me?"

"The gun didn't shoot you, in the literal sense," Xani said. "But yes, this was the weapon used. Mina didn't want it, so she gave it to me for safekeeping. It's okay; I'm trained and licensed for it."

Adam heard a crashing garbage can outside the window. "Galen will make sure no one gets near his children, as long as we ensure that no one gets near him."

"The sensors are only picking up movement from the side alley and back," Morgan said. "If they're sensitive to light, like Cindy said, it would make sense they're on the move now, and avoiding the side with the streetlights."

"How does Cindy know them?" Adam asked, approaching the window from the side to steal a peek outside.

"She's familiar with the demon who enslaved Galen and his family," Morgan said, typing away at his keyboard while maintaining eye contact with Adam. "Her contacts passed on some intelligence when they were planning his family's escape; most of his minions are subterranean demons."

"That's why Cindy wanted all the ultra-bright lights installed," Xani said, checking her gun and pocketing some extra ammunition.

Adam noticed some jerky movements in the shadows outside, but it was difficult to tell whether they were they were made by wind-blown debris, or actual potential intruders.

"This is my fight, more than anyone else's," Galen said, returning to the living room. "The children know to stay silent and still."

Adam nodded, admiring Galen's resolve and commitment to his family. "We could use your insight. Aside from the light-sensitive demons, what kind of creatures are we facing?"

Galen peered through the window over Adam's shoulder. "Our master's minions were mostly lesser demons, not particularly strong or big, but they're fast, and they swarm," he said. "There are a great number of them; it appears that Ashu'ral has spared no effort to repossess us."

"Yeah, that's not happening, if I can help it," Adam muttered, gesturing to Mina's dagger, sitting on the end table. "You know how to use that?"

Galen shook his head, pulling out a pair of black gloves while carefully avoiding their palms and finger pads. "I have my own defenses." At Adam's dubious look, he said, "I was trained to use poisons and potions in my master's service, so I know what works on contact against his lackeys," he said, wriggling his gloved hands to ensure their proper fit. "Cindy said I could borrow these, as well as some ingredients, from your sister's supplies upstairs. I hope she won't mind."

"I don't think she'd mind at all," Adam said. "You, two," he called to Morgan and Xani. "I'd still feel better if you were watching the kids."

"Cindy texts that she's on her way," Morgan said, ignoring him. "Galen, how did your master even know to find you here?"

"For better or worse, Cindy's reputation hasn't gone unnoticed by those in the fae community," Galen said, "and unfortunately, not all fae are strong enough to endure interrogations. I'm sorry that our troubles have led our enemies here to you," he said to Adam. "You and your sister have been most kind."

A window shattered in one of the back rooms, and a chorus of unearthly howls erupted, as the bedroom was filled with blinding white light, some of which spilled out into the hallway. An avalanche of glowing white flooded out further, as the agonized howling dwindled, and the *ruishi* galloped from the bedroom into the living room, its toothy maw opened wide in a jovial grin.

"What is that?" Galen asked, aghast.

"That is our family spirit dog, of a sort," Adam said. "Dawa, go watch the kids and Missus Krantz! Atta boy!"

The sparkling white lion-dog gave a silent yap of acknowledgment and bounded away, vanishing into the wall, as quickly as it had arrived.

Before anyone was lulled into complacency by Dawa's antics, the sound of another shattering window came from the children's room, where the younger fae were hiding in the closet. There was another flood of dazzlingly bright light, and another outcry of hisses and shrieks.

"They're not stupid," Galen said. "Most of them will keep their distance while the lights stay on, but the ones that can get closer will look for your electrical box to shut off your power and lights, to let the others in."

"The previous owners of the building had a backup generator installed in the basement years ago," Xani said. "As long as these things don't get close enough to sabotage it, it'll be enough to last until morning."

"I'd like them to be gone long before then," Adam said, then turned at the sound of droning voices, like chanting, approaching from the back room. "What is that?"

"No, no, no," Galen muttered, despondently, shaking his head. "This is really bad. They're opening a portal, probably trying to bring Ashu'ral through." He leapt into the air and barreled towards the back room, with Xani close on his heels. "Go for the chanters first, I'll take out the swarmers."

"Morgan, watch the doors and windows," Adam said, backing from the window reluctantly. "Holler, as soon as you see or hear something," he said, snatching and unsheathing the *kaiken*, as he ran towards the echoing gunshots from the back room.

By the time Adam arrived in the room, the furniture for what was Gia's room was broken and in disarray, with several demonic forms littering the floor. In the center of the chamber stood a large black oval, and as Adam looked into its growing center, almost unable to look away, he noticed shadows moving within it. Next to him, Xani was carefully aiming her shots, each one hitting one of demonic chanters in the head or the throat to silence them. Galen was skirting the room to stay out of Xani's range, felling the swarming creatures with a swipe or slap of his gloved hands.

There were three chanters left, and Adam tackled the closest one to the floor, muting it with a dagger slash across its throat, but its bones were harder than his, and he felt a jarring pain shoot up his arm. Behind him, Galen had taken down the second to last, covering the mouth and nose until it was forced to breathe from his glove. Xani was trying to get a clear shot at the last chanter, which had ducked behind the yawning portal.

She managed to kill it, but too late, as a crimson-skinned hulk stepped through the open portal on black, knife-like claws. The demon also had a snaking, black-spiked tail, that trailed behind it out of the portal. Unlike the swarmers, this demon seemed irritated by the brightness of the room but was unhindered by it. Xani immediately turned the gun on the new arrival, but the bullets ricocheted off its broad, bare chest, with one of the shots grazing Adam's leg. *His* bare chest, Adam guessed from what he saw of its naked form. *Ashu'ral. Galen's former master.*

Galen took advantage of the giant demon's focus on Xani to finish off the last swarmers, and Adam saw the bitter loathing in the fae's dark features at the sight of the hulking red demon. As Ashu'ral approached Xani at a leisurely rhythm, almost stalking her, Adam lunged forward and felt the stinging pain in his thigh as he landed, and he gasped involuntarily.

Ashu'ral looked aside at Adam with its black, pupil-less eyes, and Xani shot once more, aiming at the groin, but that bullet was deflected, too. "Spirited, fragile mortals," the demon seemed to laugh, slapping its tail onto the hardwood floor to create a barrier between Adam and Xani. Adam read his lips, and while what the demon uttered didn't match his words, Adam understood him.

The demon turned his head a little more and spotted Galen stepping forward. "Using humans to save you from your duties, little fae?" he mocked. "Come home, Galen, and all will be forgiven."

"Stay away from him!" Xani spat. She didn't know exactly what Ashu'ral had said, but she got the gist. She was feisty and furious, but she had the wherewithal to not betray the presence of the children.

"You know nothing, little girl," Ashu'ral said, leveling his eyes at her. "Fae are willful beasts, who need a firm hand to become useful." He grinned, flashing pointed teeth, jet-black and gleaming like his claws. "Not unlike yourself."

Undaunted by Ashu'ral's looming form and threatening tone, Xani squeezed off her last shot, and it struck the demon's black, pupil-less right eye squarely but dropped to the floor uselessly. Before the shell had landed on the hardwood, Ashu'ral had grasped for Xani, but his claw was deflected by Galen's desperate charge, as the fae threw his full weight against his former master's shoulder with a defiant shout. Even with Galen's gloves firmly wrapped around Ashu'ral's arm, the demon was unaffected by any toxins or physical agents.

Adam held out his free hand to Xani, who darted towards him. Ashu'ral swatted Galen into the wall, and the fae struggled to regain his footing with one wing drooping. With Galen dazed, Ashu'ral whirled on Adam and Xani, as Morgan's voice shouted from the living room: "They're in one of the kids' rooms!"

"The 'kids.' I had forgotten about the children. Now, where could they be hiding?" Ashu'ral chuckled, taking a deep sniff of the air. His attention was diverted, then, by Cindy's rush into the room. "The Emancipator, herself. And she comes prepared," he said, noting the heavy metal knuckles adorning Cindy's fists. "The little ones must be close, then."

Ashu'ral turned and peered at his portal, then looked at the defenders around him. "I tire of this. I give you a last chance to surrender my property."

"They are not property," Adam said.

"You understand my speech, human," Ashu'ral grinned. "That would be helpful for your training."

"Guys, clear the room!" Cindy cried, pulling Adam's arm, which was closest to her.

"I will take a souvenir for my efforts," Ashu'ral said, whipping his tail forward and sweeping it around Xani's midriff, yanking her out of Adam's reach. "As recompense for my lost investment, and for my personal enjoyment."

Xani kicked and shoved but knew to stay away from the vicious-looking black barbs and spines that encrusted the tail. She began to hyperventilate, as the tail began to crush her body, and Ashu'ral dragged her with him towards the portal.

Galen was back in the air, his hands full with Ashu'ral's minions who were starting to swarm into the room again. Cindy and Adam both charged forward, with Cindy smashing her armored fists into Ashu'ral's swiping claws to keep him back, and Adam slashing at the massive tail coiled around Xani, to no avail.

"I recognize you," Ashu'ral said to Adam. "My witch has spoken of you."

In an instant, the tail coiled completely in reverse, releasing Xani but catching one of its barbs directly in Adam's chest. Xani shrieked, as she tumbled to the floor, and Cindy drove her metal knuckles into the tail with a furious yell, but Adam barely heard either of them. His limbs seemed to lose their strength and melt away, and as Mina's dagger tumbled to the floor, Ashu'ral's tail wrapped around him, almost swaddling him with its gentleness.

The bright whiteness of the room yielded to darkness, as Adam felt and saw himself carried through the closing portal, away from the anguished shouts of his friends, the warmth and relative safety of the apartment, into... *What the fuck is this place?* His eyes closed shut despite his efforts to stay awake, and then there was only silence.

149

Chapter 11

The hotel suite was too quiet and empty without Mina to share it, so Jonah packed his few belongings and checked out. He tossed his bag in the back of the Charger when the valet brought it around, and decided to pay a visit to Aunt Connie and Uncle Teddy.

To satisfy his morbid curiosity, Jonah took a detour to Brookline first, to see what remained of his aunt and uncle's old house. Thanks to Aciré Hart's summary of the insurance assessment and current state, he wasn't entirely surprised to see that the old clapboard house had already been reduced to rubble, with a half-filled construction dumpster in the driveway where he had last seen his truck in smoldering ruin. However, it was still jarring to see a pile of debris where he had spent his past several years.

He got out of the car to get a better view, although there wasn't much to see with the sky darkening overhead, which was perhaps for the best.

Where will you go now?

Jonah didn't turn to look, but he sensed Maggie White's pale, petite apparition by his elbow, not quite touching him but close enough that he could feel her chill. "I'm not sure, but I may go to New York, where Mina is." He knew that Maggie wasn't affixed to a location and was already hundreds of years old, but to him, she was child-like, so he was concerned for her welfare. "And you? Do you have a place?"

Not yet. We have other common relations, but they don't see me, as you do. Some of them fear what they don't see or understand, while others would seek to silence me or banish me from this realm.

Maggie's turn of phrase struck him. "'Other common relations'? We're related to each other?"

I thought that was clear, Maggie said. *My brother and I fell to the pox, but we had another brother who survived. Gideon White's line endures, and you are part of it.*

"Gideon is my family name," Jonah said, shaking his head. "It has been for hundreds of years."

One of my brother's descendants—and your ancestor—was James Gideon White, who was orphaned as a child. His records were poorly kept, and he was raised under the name James Gideon.

Jonah noticed that Maggie no longer spoke like a young child, but possessed an older individual's poise. "You seem different today."

Your friend Mina helped me to become 'unstuck' so that I could wander and listen, and learn how I am to move on from this world. Everything is so complicated and moves so quickly in this era. This is not for me.

She seemed melancholy but peaceful, and Jonah recalled Mina's emotion after she and Maggie had first spoken. "Do you know what you need to do?"

I must help you find the answers you need. She crossed in front of Jonah and looked up at him. *What you seek can be found in the lair of the demon Ashu'ral.*

"You say it like I should know where that is," he said, then recalled that Galen and his children had been enslaved by a demon: "You mean the warehouse where Mina and Galen were held?"

Maggie looked thoughtful. *Yes, that is it. The lair is underneath the floor.*

"How do you know about the demon?"

He is Miranda White's current master, she said. *The demon Ashu'ral is the reason that she disavows me and wishes me silenced.*

Jonah leaned back against the car, astounded. "Wait a minute, Maggie! This demon that you named—"

Ashu'ral.

"Asshole, whatever, with the lair under the warehouse. He's *Miranda's* master? And Miranda is related to you?"

Maggie nodded. *She is blood to us, both. Mina sees your tie to Miranda and hoped to keep you safe, but there are costs that she did not foresee.*

Jonah frowned, setting aside the fact that he was related to Miranda, and that Mina was aware of it, for the moment. "I don't understand. I thought Mina had reached a truce with her."

Our family will not be harmed, but at the cost of others, she said.

"What others?" She shook her head. "Maggie, please."

There is always a cost, a sacrifice. She saw the frustration on Jonah's face. *I think I have done something wrong. If I had not said so much, you would not be so upset, and you would not be so reckless. You will endanger yourself—*

"The danger doesn't matter." Jonah crouched and looked into her face. "I need to know who it is, Maggie. Who's the sacrifice?"

I do not know his name. She bowed her head sadly. *Soon, he will not, either.*

Adam was awoken by the pain in his chest and soreness in his leg. The recollection returned to him of how his thigh had been injured, and how the black spike had pierced his ribcage… Looking down at himself, propped in a chair, he saw a thin bandage over his chest, and another on his leg, but neither was stained. He caught a glint of his father's white gold chain and carved white jade pendant that still hung around his neck, much to his relief. He briefly looked around in a panic, recalling that he had used Mina's dagger at one point, but then remembered that he had dropped it back in the duplex.

Adam ventured a look around the dark space. He sensed that it was evening or night, although the lack of windows in the dank, chilled chamber gave no clue as to the actual time or where he was. Neither did the silent figures, looming in the shadows, as he tested his rope restraints.

Out of the shadows stepped a familiar figure: the gigantic, crimson-skinned demon with a black-spined tail snaking behind him. "You are a quick healer, or very lucky, or both," Ashu'ral said, standing over Adam. "You helped to hide something that belonged to me."

"They are not anyone's property," Adam said, watching a white-robed figure approach him with a syringe held aloft. He was bound too tightly to move any measurable distance away from the needle, so instead, he distracted himself from the pinprick by studying the embroidered symbols along the edges and around the sash of the hooded robe; this was one of Miranda's followers, now also in Ashu'ral's service? *My witch has spoken of you,* the demon had said.

Adam felt a peculiar numbness overtake his extremities and his spine, caused presumably by whatever had been injected into him. It had the more pleasant side effect of preventing him from feeling the tightness of his bindings or the lingering pains in his leg and chest.

"Ownership is a matter of perspective," Ashu'ral said patiently, his nostrils flaring as he hovered over Adam's head. "I would be willing to trade in my fae stock for a substitution of equal value. The girl would

153

have amused me, for a time, but you could actually be worthwhile to keep." He grabbed Adam's jaw to force his eyes up, and Adam fought not to flinch or scream at the scalding heat spreading into his head.

"You are human, but also, not," the demon commented with interest and released Adam's chin. "You heal easily, you understand my words, and my witch tells me that you can interact with spirits. You are more of a curiosity than either common fae or normal human, so you'll do as compensation."

Adam felt the pain dissipate slowly from his burned skin. "I'm not anyone's property, either."

"Not yet, not with your will intact," the demon said, flashing his razor-like teeth in a superior grimace. "Are you familiar with the work of Walter Freeman? Or Egas Moniz?"

The names sounded remotely familiar to Adam, but he had little interest in pondering their significance or engaging his demonic captor in any conversation.

"Moniz was recognized as one of the earliest practitioners of leucotomy in humans," the demon said, swinging his barbed tail forward, with each of its spines moving independently, like tools on a Swiss army knife. "Freeman refined the concept later, into the method I favor, using something like this."

One of the tail spines extended and pointed directly at Adam, who suddenly remembered the name Walter Freeman as the "inventor" of transorbital lobotomy, otherwise known as the "icepick lobotomy." Adam stared at the giant needle-like barb aimed at his head, as transfixed as he was horrified by the thought of something like that entering his head.

"I don't want my property damaged more than absolutely necessary, so I will be very precise," the demon said, examining Adam's face closely from different angles, his tail hovering close by. "No reaction?

Other creatures are usually crying for mercy or defecating themselves at this point."

"I don't see that either would help my situation," Adam said, more calmly than he felt. He was bound, and also anesthetized, he realized, as he felt the numbness spreading up his neck, into his head. More than the pain or horror of having something driven through his eye sockets to poke inside his brain, he despaired at the unknown effects awaiting him—he could just die during the procedure, which would be a greater mercy than a permanent vegetative state, or losing his mind, literally.

Adam felt his head become as numbed and disconnected as the rest of his body, and his thoughts slowed as he drifted towards semi-consciousness. He was aware of what was going to happen, as he watched the needle approaching his eye, but he was unable to move away from it.

"I like you, so I think I may keep you," Ashu'ral said admiringly, "and I won't think any less of you, should you scream, but try to keep your head still. The discomfort will be brief, then you will know eternal contentment."

Mina was never patient on planes rides, ever since she was a child, and especially when the plane wasn't moving. The plane in question was being held at the gate, with everyone already boarded, not technically delayed but yet queued for departure either.

Mina took a slow sip of her drink, thankful that her flight wasn't filled with justifiably fussy infants or unruly, tantrum-prone adults, and her business-class seat was more comfortable than most.

So, half an hour to reach the terminal, then another thirty minutes to clear security and pre-boarding check-in, and twenty minutes to board, now almost twenty minutes and counting to wait for air traffic clearance—

all for a forty-minute flight. Then she was going to deal with the congestion around Newark Airport before finally crossing the Hudson River to get home. Mina liked not having to stay awake and concentrate for traveling the same distance by car, but sometimes she wondered if it was really worth it.

Jonah's worth it. She played with the string of Jonah's gray hoodie and the ruby ring on her finger, mulling over Jonah's proposal, now that she had an idle moment. *He's worth the time, and my effort.* He had demonstrated his valor, his devotion and his love, and he had told her more than once that he wouldn't hurt her. He knew how important that promise was to her; he knew her history and understood her damage and wanted her anyway. *Am I ready to be someone's partner again?*

"Yes," she said tentatively under her breath, trying out the word on her lips. It wasn't as daunting as it had sounded in her head. Once she heard her own voice, she felt a sense of satisfaction, like when a puzzle piece falls into place. The thought of Jonah made her smile, and the idea of becoming his wife brightened her mood further. She felt almost giddy with happy relief, knowing that she was ready with her answer, for the next time that she saw him.

Her phone chimed with an incoming call, reminding Mina that she had forgotten to turn it off or switch it to an airplane mode. Since the call was from Cindy, Mina answered promptly.

"Hi, I'm on the plane, waiting for take-off," Mina said.

"You're still on the ground?" Cindy asked, an edge to her voice.

"Yeah, we're held at the gate," Mina said. "What's going on?"

"Your building was attacked, and Adam was taken."

Mina straightened in her seat. "What do you mean by 'taken'? How?"

"He was at the duplex with the twins, and Galen and the children. It happened too quickly, and none of us expected him to be…"

Mina's head was reeling. Here, she thought everyone was safe and sound, away from her, and now to hear that Adam was captured… "Who took him?" she demanded, keeping her voice low. If it was on Miranda's order, Mina swore, that would be the end of that deceitful witch.

"Galen's former master, Ashu'ral," Cindy said. "He recognized that Adam is special and could be more valuable, so he took him, rather than try recapturing Galen and the children."

Mina tried to stay calm, finishing her drink and passing the glass to a flight attendant with a polite smile. "Everyone else is alright?"

"Yes, Xani's a mess, and Morgan is too busy repairing and shoring up the breaches to talk, but Galen and the children are fine. Mina, I'm sorry—"

"Galen's master is in New York?" Mina asked, refusing to get caught up in her emotions. "I thought he and Miranda were here in Boston." She considered the timing of the attack, and how it was only by chance that she wasn't already in the air or on the road en route home.

"Galen confirms that Ashu'ral's lair is there, beneath the warehouse from where you had freed him, but Ashu'ral minions were able to open a portal for their master, once a few of them slipped through our defenses. I don't think the demon intended a prolonged, punishing siege, just a brief excursion," Cindy said. "The portal was only open for a few minutes, and large enough for him to get in and out, but not an army."

Mina recalled some of the warehouse layout, but hadn't had time to explore it independently, between her escorted entry and her rushed escape. "I don't like the idea of our enemies slipping through so easily."

"It wasn't easy for them. Your wards kept the majority out, and they suffered heavy losses. It's not your fault; no one could have anticipated that a demon like Ashu'ral would ever pay a sanctuary a personal visit."

There's a first time for everything, she mused. Mina had been overconfident about her own skills, and now others were paying for her hubris. "Will you be able to keep the building secure while I'm gone?"

"I think so," Cindy said. "There are just a couple of broken windows downstairs, and I have someone fixing them now. But given their casualties, and that Ashu'ral left with what he wanted, I don't expect them to return. Xani and Morgan will have this place like a fortress, just in case, now that we know what we're dealing with. I can also ask some of the Lotus regulars cast some protection spells or keep watch, if needed."

"Good, because I think I'll be delayed again coming home," Mina said, unbuckling her seat belt and bolting from her seat.

"Ma'am," said the flight attendant, rushing forward. "Can you please stay seated? We're getting ready to close the door."

"Mina, honey, don't do anything rash, okay? Wait for me to get there, or take Jonah with you for backup."

"No, there's no time," Mina said, to both the flight attendant and Cindy, as she grabbed her sling bag from the front seat pocket. "I have to leave, *now*."

Mina disconnected with Cindy and ignored the dirty looks and harsh comments from fellow passengers, as she rushed off the plane. She left the gate and jogged through the terminal, calling Aciré on the way.

"You can't be home already," Aciré answered. "Your flight's showing as delayed."

"Nope. I haven't even left Logan. I need a lift."

❖❖❖

Jonah was awake but dazed, conscious but unresponsive, so he plenty of time to regret his missteps from the time he arrived at Miranda's warehouse—the lair of Ashu'ral. The drive over had been uneventful, aside from Maggie's ghost riding shotgun with him. Once Jonah parked down the street and continued on foot, she had accompanied him silently, like an extra set of eyes and ears. He had moved quickly and kept to the shadows, but it wasn't enough.

By the time Maggie had warned him to duck, it was already too late. Once the first dart struck him, the rest found him easily. Jonah counted four strikes before he became too disoriented to focus, and he landed hard against the concrete ground, before he was even within fifty yards of the warehouse entrance. He had apparently made enough of an impression on Miranda's retinue during his last visit that they had prepared for his possible return.

Jonah had heard Maggie's frantic voice trying to rouse him, but he was unable to respond, his tongue feeling thick and heavy in his mouth. Clumsily, he waved his hand to shoo her away before his arms fell limp at his sides, as his fading eyes recognized the jerky, nimble dark shapes skittering towards him from the shadows. *Get away from here, Maggie*, he tried to shout, but only managed a noise like: "Gugth-meh," before he was hauled through the familiar sliding steel warehouse door, back into that horrible place of torture and suffering.

Except that on this visit, he received a more extensive tour, as he felt himself carried and dragged precariously down stone and concrete steps, deep below the ground level of the warehouse. Jonah fell onto a cold stone floor, landing on his side, and he nudged himself just enough to let gravity roll him onto his back, so that he could see where he had been taken.

The chamber was taller than he had expected of an underground room, with an elaborate, vaulted stone-lined ceiling that reminded him more of a subway train station than a basement. In fact, the chamber did seem to extend longer in one direction, past his line of sight. Whatever this chamber was, it was built to accommodate something—or someone—very large.

He heard the soft clicks of heels on the stone tiles, and he lolled his head to see the figure of Miranda approaching, with several of her acolytes in tow. She stopped a couple of yards away from him, wary of him, even as he lay almost immobilized at her feet.

"What am I to do with you?" Miranda asked. "Even when you're free, you persist in interfering where you shouldn't."

Jonah laughed weakly. "Must run in the family. What do I call you: aunt, cousin…grandma?"

Miranda simpered with annoyance. "Did your little witch tell you of our ties?"

"No, a little girl named 'Maggie,'" Jonah said. "She told me you took someone." That wasn't exactly what she had said, but to conserve his energy, he would be pithy.

"*I* did not, but our master did, as restitution for what was stolen." Miranda leaned over. "This is not your concern, little cousin. There was no reason for you to come."

"Who is it?"

Miranda laughed. "You came all the way here, and you don't even know for whom? He is not family to you, not any longer."

Not any longer. He was, at one time. "Adam? Let him go, and I'll stay in his place, willingly."

"You can't rescue him, as you did his sister, so now you're trying to negotiate a trade?" Miranda shook her head. "It's an interesting offer, but it's not a very compelling one. You see, he doesn't want to leave, so you've wasted your time in coming here," she said, waving one of her white-hooded acolytes forward. "Would you like to see for yourself?"

Miranda pulled back the tall figure's hood, like dropping a curtain, and Adam's blank, neutral smile greeted Jonah.

Jonah stared at Adam in bewilderment, then noticed the emptiness in his friend's expression. He mustered some strength to try to sit up. "What did they do to you?"

Adam's visage remained vapid, and his eyes were dull. "I am content."

"What the fuck does that mean?"

Jonah felt another dart strike his neck, keeping him subdued and weakened. As he sank back to the floor, he couldn't understand why Adam was just standing there, watching impassively, his hands hanging at his sides.

"Whatever they did to you, you have to snap out of it!" Jonah pleaded, as he was hauled to his feet and bound.

Miranda smiled. "That would require a regrowth and repair of his brain, which is very unlikely."

Oh, shit. "You crazy bitch! You lobotomized him?"

Miranda slapped him, hard. "Family or not, you need to learn some manners, or you'll get the same treatment. For your information, *I* didn't touch him. His new master did, to make him more complacent."

Jonah noticed her displeasure. "It wasn't your idea."

"No," she said sharply. "Look at him. He's a shell of what he was," she said disdainfully. "But he's an effective lure, whatever his condition. Wherever he is, his sister is sure to follow, eventually. For his sake, he'll need to demonstrate some usefulness soon, or the master will just send him down to the harem, or the larder."

"This goes against your agreement with Mina," Jonah said. "You promised that you wouldn't harm me or my family, or any of Mina's friends in New York."

"Sorry," Miranda pouted, "but as I said, *I* didn't go to New York to capture Mister Xing or do this to him—Ashu'ral did. And *you're* not harmed, just temporarily restrained until we can decide what to do with you. Technically, you're trespassing on private property, so we could have you arrested for destruction of property and any number of other offenses."

"I'm not leaving without Adam," he said.

"Mister Xing may have other thoughts about that. Or, maybe not," she giggled. She nodded to her acolytes. "Take my little cousin to the Pit, while I return Mister Xing to our master. I'll deal with Mister Gideon myself, when I return."

Adam followed Miranda from the hall to the servants' barracks without comment or complaint. He went into his barred cell unquestioningly and watched Miranda leave the barracks. He welcomed the time to himself, the first moment of solitude since his arrival, that he could recall.

Adam had observed the interaction between Miranda and the new arrival—she called him "Mister Gideon"—with interest but refrained from interrupting or interjecting. What had Miranda said, when the man yelled at him to "snap out of it"? *That would require a regrowth and repair of his brain...*

Was he broken, or damaged, then? He didn't feel any pain, either physical or mental, except when he thought too hard or too long about something, such as when he started thinking about a sister that Miranda mentioned. Mister Gideon had called her "Mina"? If he had a sister, wouldn't he remember that?

Unless I am broken, but I don't know it because that's the part of my brain that would notice. He thought about the pain, how it came and went, and it made his head feel hot and busy, but it was less now than when he had started before.

Started what? When he had arrived… Where was he before this place? He forced himself to unearth his buried memories, pushing through the pain until his head felt like it was going to burst, until he remembered *the* pain, the procedure that had reduced him to this state of absolute submissiveness.

And before that? That was still foggy, but he remembered Mister Gideon's face more clearly now. He had been his friend and fought at his side, and there had been someone else…a brother? No, a cousin. *Gideon. Malcolm and Jonah.* The man outside was Jonah, and he called his sister by name. *Mina.*

He remembered her now. First, more recent memories, of Mina in black, with a dagger in hand, then going backwards through his recollections: Mina in a pearl-spangled wedding gown, then as a child in his borrowed sweatshirt…soaking wet, shivering and crying with her face buried against his shoulder, after he had pulled her from the lake.

How could Adam have forgotten his own baby sister? *Wherever he is, his sister is sure to follow, eventually,* Miranda had said. He couldn't allow that to happen. He'd rather die than endanger Mina.

Jonah can help. If he could get to Jonah, maybe they could figure something out together. Adam was frustrated with himself at how sluggish he was feeling, mentally. As he pulled together the pieces that he still remembered about how he used to be, he knew he was quicker and smarter than this.

He didn't have much time to think about it, as he heard Miranda and their master come to his cell. It was considered a rare honor for the masters to visit the servant quarters, and Adam and the others knelt on the dusty concrete floor to show their respect to their lords.

Ashu'ral came directly to Adam's cell. "Someone came for you."

"Yes…Master," Adam said and winced at his halting response.

"Do you wish to leave with him?" Miranda asked.

Not yet, Adam thought and answered instead: "No."

"I don't believe him," Miranda said, taking a spear from one of the guards and driving it between the bars of an adjoining cell, impaling and killing one of the demon's other slaves.

Adam controlled his outrage at her sudden barbarity, staying on his knees with his head lowered, but Miranda saw through his false docility. "He's recovering," she said. "The procedure didn't take, despite your skillful technique. You could try it again, I suppose, but he's probably blessed in some way that allows him to heal."

You fucking bitch. Adam stole a peek and caught Miranda's knowing smirk down at him.

"If he isn't trustworthy enough to be useful, he's more trouble than he's worth," Ashu'ral growled with disgust. "He can be sent to the kitchen for a quick dispatch, then fed to the pigs and guards."

"If I may, Master," Miranda said deferentially. "I may have a use for him, as a trap for the rogue witch."

"You owe me two replacement slaves," the demon said. "This one, and the one you killed," he said, pointing his tail to the impaled demon corpse, oozing a growing pool of black blood that was seeping towards Adam's cell.

"Once we deal with the witch, I will gladly go to New York and personally oversee the recovery of your fugitive fae's whole family," Miranda said, motioning to the guards to remove Adam from his cell. As he was pulled to his feet, she smiled at him. "And we'll kill anyone and anything who resists or gets in our way."

Chapter 12

Aciré Hart was a trusted counsel to the Xing family, but the title belied the scope of the functions she performed for the family, as well as her personal connections to its members. She managed Selina's East Coast vault, the family's communications with external interests and parties, and she had served as Mina's lawyer during her divorce from Malcolm Gideon.

As a result of the last, she had spent more time with Mina than any of her own family during that period. Aciré watched Mina's emotions shift from sentimental, wistful love to cold indifference, settling eventually into a nostalgic resignation, when all the papers were signed, and all the parties went their separate ways. Very rarely did she ever see Mina disgusted or frazzled; in that way, she had taken after Selina.

So, when Iago pulled the town car up to the curb at Logan's Terminal C and rolled down the rear passenger-side window, Aciré respected Mina's glower of frustration and incredulous disdain and knew not to take it personally.

"We're always happy to see you, but I'm sorry you had to put off going home, again," Aciré said, as Mina waved to Iago to stay in the driver's seat and slipped into the back unassisted . "I had to let your mother know, of course; she's pissed, as you can imagine."

Mina winced. "I figured she would be."

"Not at you, just at your situation," Aciré clarified. "So, I just called Jonah before you came out, but he's still not picking up. We dropped him off at the hotel some time ago, before Iago and I returned to the office. We just checked with the concierge, and apparently he took the car and checked out about an hour ago. "

"Shit, he knows something's wrong, and he went ahead," Mina said, calling out the address to Iago to plot the route. "What the hell is Jonah thinking?"

"Probably that your family needs help, and he should pitch in where he can," Aciré said. "Can he handle himself in a fight?"

"Most of the time, but Jonah's still recovering from his last bout with them yesterday. If they're onto him, he may get seriously hurt, or worse."

Aciré recognized Mina's look of deep concern. "You really like him, don't you?"

Mina looked at her sideways. "I wouldn't fool around in the back of a limo with someone I didn't like."

Aciré shrugged. "You know I don't judge. He's into you, and he's kind of hot, if you like the dark, broody, chiseled type." Aciré, herself, preferred curvy, freckled blonde girls, but she could appreciate attractive men from an aesthetic vantage point.

Mina flashed the modest, but very pretty ruby bauble on the ring finger of her left hand. "Yes, I like him. He wants me to marry him, and I think I might."

"Mazel tov, 'Missus Gideon'," Aciré smiled. "This makes things easier; I don't even have to draft any paperwork to change your legal name," she joked.

"Five minutes out," the driver called from the front.

"Thank you, Iago," Aciré said, pulling out a weathered black canvas tool bag from behind one of the seat cushions. "Your luggage is back at the office, Mina, possibly en route to New York, already, but you may find something useful in here."

Mina stowed the heavy bag next to her on the seat and sifted through the selection of tools, which served for a variety of scenarios: oak and silver stakes, more lockpicks, boxes of silver ammunition, of different calibers... even a plain, long-sleeved black t-shirt, with the tags still on it.

"I picked that up for you, just in case you want to avoid getting blood and guts on your boyfriend's clothes," Aciré said. "Sorry, fiancé's clothes."

"You think of everything." Mina took off Jonah's hoodie and started changing shirts.

"It's part of the job. Plus, it gives me a chance to see you in lingerie for a few seconds. Eyes on the road, Iago," she teased, then smiled at Mina's chastising frown, as Mina pulled on the new shirt over her head and amply-filled black lace bralette. "Totally worth it."

Mina ignored her flirty tone and continued to rummage through the tool bag.

"What do you know about this demon?" Aciré asked.

"From what Cindy and Galen said, it sounds like a stone-skin demon," Mina said. "Non-porous skin, can't be cut or pierced by anything other than something from its own body. Cindy uses enchanted brass knuckles that seem to sting him a little, since they hit the tissue below the surface."

"Okay. Try this one, then," Aciré said, reaching into the bag to search for the hammer she had stowed earlier. It looked like a brick-sized, toothed chunk of dark metal, on a hefty, reinforced handle. "It's lightweight and compact, and if your aim is good, you can probably get around two thousand PSI on a direct strike. Farrier uses it for cracking black walnuts."

Mina grasped and held it easily. "This is Erik Farrier's? Did you swipe this from your partner's stash? He's not going to be happy about that."

"Erik had it mounted behind his desk on State Street; he's not going to miss it, as long as you get it back to me soon," Aciré said smartly. "Anyway, he's personally used it to take down some stone-skins and others, so it's field-tested."

"So, their skin's impervious to damage," Mina realized, "but the bones aren't."

Aciré nodded. "Bullfinch always said you were a quick study. Two thousand PSI is like a full-on alligator bite, so it packs a bigger wallop than it looks and feels. You can just imagine what Erik can do with it."

Mina noticed the runes etched into the handle. "My ancient Norse is a little rusty."

"It's the hammer's name: 'Troll-Hobbler.' Erik said one of his Viking ancestors would run circles around bigger and slower enemies and smash their ankles with it."

"Yikes, so this is a family heirloom?" Mina said. "I can't take this from Farrier."

"Mina, you know I'm useless in a fight," Aciré said regretfully. "I'd feel better if you had a good weapon with you, at least. Don't worry about Erik; he still has a *huge* crush on your mother and won't mind you borrowing 'Trobler' for the evening."

"We've arrived," Iago announced, as the car slowed to a stop.

"Thanks, Iago," Mina said. "And thank you, Aciré. You've done plenty, already. If you could just keep an eye on Connie and Teddy, that's one less worry for me."

"Consider it done," Aciré nodded. "Good luck, Mina, and God speed."

Jonah knew that something had gone wrong during the time that he had been waiting in the Pit chamber, from the look of the procession into the round room. In the minutes since he had last seen Adam, Jonah had mostly recovered from the sedatives and tranquilizers that had been pumped into him; once he was shackled around his wrists and ankles, the drugs were unnecessary, so his mind had time to clear, and the day-old flesh wound in his side started to sting again. His hands were cuffed together behind him, while there was enough give to his leg constraints to allow him to stand and take small steps, but not much more. Not that there was much space for him to move, anyway.

While he had still been sedated, Jonah had been hoisted onto a small steel mesh panel, about the size of a door, suspended by long, heavy chains over a deep, empty black pit. While there was nothing ominous or threatening about the eponymous Pit itself, the threat of broken bones was enough to discourage him from jumping down, especially without his hands and legs free to cushion his fall. The edges of the Pit were too far away for him to try to jump across.

Jonah read the expressions on Miranda and Adam's faces and noted that they both looked equally annoyed, albeit for different reasons. Miranda led the procession with a look of aggravation, while Adam walked behind her with an air of grim defiance, flanked by two of the ubiquitous, burly demonic guards.

"Plan's gone awry again, cousin?" Jonah cracked.

"Not at all," Miranda said, visibly forcing her jaw to unclench. "You overestimate the abilities of your little witch to save you."

Mina's coming for us. He tried not to react, but something in his face must have betrayed his concern, as a satisfied smile crossed Miranda's face.

"She is skilled, but predictable," Miranda said, cueing Adam's guards to shove him towards Jonah's mesh platform, setting down a wooden plank for him to walk across. Adam shoved his guards back roughly, but Miranda cautioned him: "Watch your step, Mister Xing.

A fall seems like such an ignominious end for such a promising young man."

Jonah watched the guards force Adam into the same types of shackles, and prod him across the walkway with their spears, removing the plank once he was on the platform next to him. Jonah couldn't see the fulcrum or rigging that held their chains, but he felt the platform sag a couple of inches with the extra weight. He tested his shackles again, and once again deliberated on the odds of surviving a jump or fall.

"You have so much potential, Jonah," Miranda said. "I could use someone with your determination, always analyzing and thinking in order to find a solution. I'm sorry to tell you, however: not every problem can be solved, and not every solution may turn out in your favor."

A slim, white-robed acolyte rushed into the Pit room, and lowered her hood to address Miranda in hushed whispers. Jonah recognized her as the blonde who had masqueraded as a caterer at Malcolm's repass. That was what...almost three days ago? It felt like much longer.

"The witch is near the gates," Miranda said. "Let's not keep her waiting, then," she said to her entourage, then turned to Jonah and Adam briefly, as she exited. "Don't worry, gentlemen—you'll see her soon enough."

Mina?

"What the—" Mina half-turned and saw Maggie White's wispy white form hovering behind her. "Maggie! What are you doing here?"

I came with Jonah. He told me to leave, but I didn't want to abandon him here.

If Mina had harbored any lingering doubts about Jonah's whereabouts, Maggie's presence erased them. Mina took a moment to survey the warehouse from her vantage around the corner. She was fairly certain that she had been spotted already, if she hadn't been trailed from the time she left Iago and Aciré down the block. When she had seen Malcolm's Charger parked on the street, she had texted Aciré its location and told her to check under the rear seat floormat on the passenger side for the key; it was where Malcolm had always left it when he didn't want to carry it around.

"There's not much else that you can do," Mina said. "You already told Jonah about your family? About Miranda?"

Maggie nodded. *He did not react much. Instead, he wanted to come save the one that was taken by Ashu'ral.*

Mina scowled. "I would've preferred that Jonah stay far away."

As do I, but his fate is his own to decide. Maggie floated up the side of the building and dropped back down to Mina's side. *There are three guards on the roof, aiming at this corner.*

"Can they see you?"

No, but they will see you, if you are not careful. They sense that you are close.

"My arrival is no surprise, I'm sure," Mina said. "Still, I'd like to avoid bumbling and battling my way into the lair, especially without knowing what Miranda has planned for Jonah and Adam."

Maggie seemed surprised. *You know the other one? You share a resemblance, but I did not want to assume a relation.*

"He's my brother," Mina said. "We frustrate and confound each other sometimes, but I don't know what I would do without him. I'm not leaving without him."

My brother and I never had the opportunity to grow so close, Maggie said sadly, *but I can see how we might have become that way, given enough time. I will return.*

As Maggie vanished, Mina checked her sling bag a last time. The hammer looked a little ridiculous with its

171

handle jutting out the opening of the bag, but it was better than carrying it around in her hand. A first-aid kit, a set of lockpicks and her phone, with one missed call and a text. Mina glanced at the text, which had come from her mother: *Be careful and thorough.*

Maggie returned shortly. *Miranda and her master's minions wait for you.*

"I expected as much," Mina said.

No, I mean that they are posted at every entrance to await your arrival. Jonah and your brother are being held in a chamber below the ground. They say that they are fine, but they know that they are in danger. Maggie paused. *Your brother can see me, also. Can everyone in your family see ghosts?*

"It's possible." Mina hadn't really thought about it. She knew that both of her parents were as attuned to spirits as she and Adam were, and she had always attributed the sensitivity to having near-death experiences, but perhaps there was something more. "How is Adam? How does he look?"

He looks well, but this was the first interaction we have had, Maggie reminded. *However, Jonah seemed curt and irritated during their exchange. Not directly at your brother, but at his general condition. Is he usually so terse with him?*

"No, they usually get along very well," Mina said, trusting Jonah's assessment of Adam's wellness.

Your brother seems confused and slow to react, compared to you. Is he slow?

"Absolutely not!" Mina exclaimed in alarm. "He's one of the brightest people I know."

Then something has happened to him, because he did not seem very bright when we were speaking.

It stung to hear a small child disparaging her big brother's intellect, but frankly, if Maggie had noticed it during such a brief encounter, then he probably was impaired in some way. *Shit.*

"I'm going to take a gamble," Mina swallowed. "I don't have time to guess at what's happened, so I'll have to see it for myself." She took a deep breath and began to step out from behind the corner, with her hands raised to show that she was unarmed.

You're going to surrender? Maggie cried. *You don't know what they'll do to you.*

"I have no choice," Mina whispered, averting her eyes from the blinding floodlights focused on her. "Whatever Miranda or Ashu'ral choose to do to me, I still have a better chance of walking away from this than Adam does, without me."

She was still taking a risk, that she would soon be in Miranda's company, and therefore still protected enough by Lucifer's order to remain unharmed, but she couldn't speak to Maggie's safety. As she heard the noises of creatures skittering through the shadows towards her, she said, "You should go, Maggie. There's nothing else for you to do here."

I will stay until this is finished, she said resolutely.

Mina wasn't sure what Maggie meant, but she didn't have time to think about it, as she was roughly prodded with the blunted ends of spears that encircled her and escorted towards the nearest warehouse entrance.

Maggie stayed alongside, and as the warehouse door slid open, the guards were able to see her and tried to corral the spirit inside.

"No!" Mina said. "She's a protected member of the Gideon family, so you're not allowed to hurt her."

Miranda's laughter greeted her from inside the door. "Theoretically, she's dead, so she's not really part of the family anymore," Miranda said, "but we'll allow it. It's the least we could do, since Miss Xing has surrendered so peacefully." Miranda looked at Mina's closed, flaccid sling bag. "And without weapons?"

Mina glanced down and saw the handle of the Troll-Hobbler dangling from her bag obtrusively, but evidently no one else did. "I'm just here to talk and negotiate."

Miranda smiled and gestured for Mina to enter, accompanied by four of the guards, while the rest remained outside. Miranda stepped around Mina into the open doorway, cutting between Mina and Maggie. "No spirits allowed, family or not."

Miranda waved her hand, and a ripple of energy glimmered around the door, extending to the walls around it and beyond. "The building is now restricted to you, Margaret White. You've been in and out of here enough tonight; now you *stay* out."

Maggie reached out her small, ethereal hand and jerked it back with a whimper, as if she had been shocked by an invisible barrier. *Mina!*

"It's okay. We'll be out soon," Mina said with forced ebullience. As the heavy door slid shut, her smile faded, as she faced Miranda. "Now, tell me: what have you done to Adam and Jonah?"

Adam had never felt such an intense headache in his life, and there was nothing he could do to alleviate the pain and pressure inside his skull. He had tried talking to Jonah, but somehow, that seemed to actually make the pain worse. Jonah's comments and questions only served to remind Adam of how fragmented his mind really was, as there were references to prior discussions and situations of which Adam recalled nothing.

What seemed to help, oddly enough, was focusing on the molten sludge that was slowly filling the pit under their mesh platform. Trying to figure out whether the steaming, smoking substance was made of tar, lava, molten metal or some combination, was an intellectual exercise that helped to distract him from the churning inside his head.

"Feeling better or worse?" Jonah ventured.

"I can't tell," Adam said. "I want to throw up, but I'm trying to figure out: does burning vomit smell better or worse than the regular stuff? Either way, I'll be sure to aim it away from you."

Jonah smiled. "At least you still have your sense of humor. Or, did that have to grow back, too?"

"I don't know. Was I funny before?"

"Sometimes," Jonah said. "As long as we've known each other, you've always had a very dry sense of humor, so it's hard to tell when you're serious, like when you give me advice about Mina."

"There are no hard and fast rules about dealing with her," he said. "Just go with your gut."

"What if my gut completely botched it?" Jonah frowned.

Adam wondered what had transpired between him and Mina, and he rationalized that it was none of his business, and it was better for him not to know the details. "I wouldn't worry about it. She has a great capacity to forgive almost anything."

The door to the Pit's chamber yawned open, as the chains seemed to slacken, dropping the platform another couple of inches closer to the sludge. Jonah and Adam both got to their feet at noticing Mina entering a step behind Miranda.

"There," Miranda said, with a flourish. "Unharmed, both of them, as I promised."

"You shouldn't have come," Adam said to Mina.

His sister gave him a wilting glower. "I couldn't *not* come. I'd end up as an only child, and that would suck, for everyone." She gave an apologetic smile to Jonah. "I'm sorry that you keep getting into trouble for me."

"You're worth it, baby," Jonah said soothingly. "I'm sorry my relatives are such assholes," he said, shooting a glare at Miranda.

175

"Not all, just some cousins," Mina said, then turned to Miranda. "So, what do you want? You're going to truss me up and frog march me out there, too?"

Miranda shook her head. "No, little witch. I still can't risk causing you any bodily harm, and as I've told you before, your behavior intrigues me."

The platform dropped again with a groan, and Mina jumped at the sudden noise, to Miranda's amusement. "I've set up a game, a puzzle for you to solve. That mesh plate will touch the top of Ashu'ral's bathing pool very soon and dissolve into it, and all you have to do is decide which of your men to save before it does."

"You want me to pick one of them to sacrifice?" Mina asked incredulously. "What if I refuse to play your shitty game?"

"The platform will be gone, either way, along with anyone still on it, so you can either save one or let both of them die horribly," Miranda said, and a mesh plank materialized, connecting the platform to the solid stone floor where the women stood. "That plank is enchanted to be used only once, and will only support the weight of one of them." She pulled out her phone and set a digital timer, which she flashed at Mina. "You have thirty seconds to decide who gets to cross it."

"There has to be some way around this," Mina said, eyeing the chains, the platform and the plank.

"There isn't," Jonah said. "We've been looking."

"Twenty-five seconds," Miranda cajoled.

"This is an impossible choice," Mina said, looking at both Adam and Jonah in turn. "I'd rather sacrifice myself than either of you."

"I think that's the idea," Adam said, looking at Miranda, who was observing with great satisfaction.

"Miranda can't harm you directly," Jonah said, "but if you have to decide who dies, then you're choosing your own torture and guilt."

176

Miranda shrugged innocently. "Fifteen seconds," she said cheerfully, glancing at her phone. "Pick one, or lose them both."

Jonah took a step towards Mina but was still out of reach, as the platform dropped again, with the smoke and steam licking at their ankles through the mesh grate, inches beneath them. "You know I love you."

Mina held back her tears of frustration, refusing to break down in front of Miranda. "I know."

"Then you'll understand," Jonah grinned. "Maybe I'll see you around."

Before either Adam or Mina could act, Jonah stepped off the edge of the platform and plummeted into the pool of molten slurry, disappearing soundlessly into the black, boiling sludge. While the plank still held, Adam ran across and shoved Mina back from the edge of the pool, keeping her out of the splash range, as the platform plunged into the burbling Pit. The heavy, acrid sludge scorched everything it touched before hardening into obsidian-like chunks on the stone tiles by their feet.

Adam watched Miranda and her followers rush from the room, and he wanted nothing more than to chase her down and rip her apart, but his arms and legs were still bound, and his place was with Mina. His sister screamed and pushed against him to return to the Pit, and Adam did his best to intercept her, but she slipped past him anyway.

Mina wasn't stupid or mad with grief, as he had feared. She merely stood at the edge of the Pit and stared silently into its smoldering, opaque darkness, as if trying to make sense of what had happened and where Jonah had gone. As Adam watched the bubbling mire with her, he hoped for Jonah's sake that it was a quick death, as the thought of slowly drowning in that foul sludge seemed a far worse fate.

After a moment of stillness, Mina's infuriated, anguished shrieks erupted from deep inside, as though torn from her soul, and Adam let her lean into him until her despair consumed her, and she sagged to the floor, hanging onto him. She seemed to recover after a few seconds, and she looked at him. "You're not hugging me."

"I'm still shackled," he reminded gently. "I don't know if you brought lockpicks with you. No rush, or anything."

"Oh, yeah, sorry," she muttered, wiping the last tears from her eyes. She still seemed tremulous and unsettled, but she had more important shit to do now. She found her lockpicks easily and had Adam's wrists and ankles loose in seconds. "Are you good now?"

"Better, thanks," he said, getting to his feet and pulling her to hers. They were alone in the chamber, and he wondered if this was always going to be Miranda's pattern: cause trouble, cut and run when things get ugly, then start again somewhere else. With him and Mina always a step behind.

"She's going to pay for this," Mina said evenly, her eyes clear and cold, as she pulled a weapon from her seemingly empty bag. "I will send her to her master in pieces!" To Adam's relatively untrained eye, it looked like a toothed bush hammer, like a meat tenderizer crossed with a mini sledge hammer.

"Where did you get that?" he asked.

"I borrowed it from a friend," she said, jogging towards the door. "This way. Let's go find you a weapon."

Adam followed with an uncertain shake of the head. "I don't know how to use weapons."

Mina turned around and touched the white jade pendant that hung around Adam's neck. He wasn't sure that anyone else could see it but him, but it seemed obvious to her. "Trust me, *ge-ge*, it'll come back to you," she said.

Mina took a deep breath, and with a determined gleam in her dark eyes, screamed Miranda's name at the top of her voice. She raced ahead of Adam, almost bouncing off the stone walls in her dizzying pace to catch up to her enemy.

Shit, she's going to run into a trap. Adam charged after Mina, reminding himself of Jonah's words to him, when they were confined to the platform and Adam was trying to piece together his mind: Adam always had Mina's back, was always her champion when she needed one, and her support when she didn't. He replayed his last conversation with Jonah, and it was still jarring and baffling that Jonah was dead, so suddenly and so meaninglessly... Not meaningless—Jonah had sacrificed himself so that Mina wouldn't be forced to choose—

Adam jumped back, almost caught by surprise by a guard who jumped out at him and probably expected him to flee. Instead, Adam barreled into the guard, impaling him on a spiked door behind them. As Adam caught his breath, he grabbed the guard's saber. The violence wasn't pleasant, but it felt familiar and comfortable. *I can do this.*

He followed the sounds of Mina's angry, taunting wails but lagged purposefully to stalk the creatures that were drawn by her cries and planning to ambush her. Instead, he followed in their wake and slit their throats or disemboweled them with the pilfered sword. He dispatched the creatures as quickly as he could, but he was falling behind.

Mina was enraged, but not careless. She used her borrowed hammer with frightening speed and skill to dispatch the witches and demons that dared to cross her path, leaving a trail of disfigured, crushed limbs and howling, screeching wounded for Adam to follow.

Eventually, Mina's pace slowed enough for Adam to catch up, and her voice echoed through the empty halls, bloodless and eerie in its calm: "Get out of my way."

Adam reached the T-intersection in time to see a wall of flame erupt on either side of Mina, too far to singe her, but close enough to stop her advance. The flames dissipated, and a tall, elegant blond man stood in front of Mina to block her path.

"I can't do that," he said.

"Sure, you can, Lucifer," Mina cajoled. "You just have to take a half-step to one side or the other. About four inches, which—despite what you may have heard—isn't very much at all."

Lucifer. Adam cringed internally, wondering about Mina's wisdom in goading the devil, but Mina looked far too livid to care. She gestured to Adam to stay back and asked Lucifer, "Did all this happen on your order?"

The devil looked at Mina with seeming earnestness. "No, this was designed and executed as a collaboration between Miranda and her new supervisor. I would've dissuaded them, had I known beforehand."

"Then let me settle this with them, directly," Mina seethed. "Walk away."

Lucifer straightened, clearly surprised by Mina's nerve. "I don't take orders from you, Miss Xing, but I'll overlook your impertinence this once, as you seem upset." He stepped closer to Mina, and she did not yield, even as he loomed over her. "You're also not thinking clearly, so I'm giving you a chance to consider your choices."

"And what choices might those be?" Mina asked.

He folded his hands in front of him to avoid gesturing. "In one direction lies the exit; the path is clear and unguarded. In the other direction is Miranda and her master; if you face them, I can't intervene in your favor."

"That's fine with me," Mina shot back.

"Consider your brother, then, and the others who need you," Lucifer said quietly. "His mind is still splintered and incomplete, so if anything happens to you here, how does he get home? And for your friends in New York; if you fall here, there is no one to prevent them from being besieged and slaughtered."

"Miranda's actions can't go unanswered," Mina said. "What's to prevent her from doing this again?"

"You gave your word to her that you wouldn't threaten her," Lucifer reminded. "That was only this morning, so surely, you must remember."

"You know the bargain we made this morning?" Mina scowled. "I thought she didn't report to you anymore."

"She is still pledged directly to me, so if she negotiates with you, I am aware of it," he explained patiently.

"Then you're aware that she also swore that she wouldn't harm Jonah or his family, and that she would leave my friends in New York alone," she snarled.

Lucifer grimaced. "Technically, Miranda pledged not to *personally* harm any of your friends in New York, but what Ashu'ral chooses to do is, frankly, out of her span of control. As for Mister Gideon," he said, more delicately, "he actually caused his own demise."

Mina nodded. "Now, I see where Miranda's learned her negotiating skills. Well, you leave me no choice, then, than to destroy everyone who follows her, until she is left with nothing, and no one. But, she can keep her shitty title, and her fucking life—since I gave her my word."

Lucifer gave a conciliatory nod. "That would still adhere to the terms, that is true, but it seems a little extreme, even in your current state. What if I give my word, that I will deal with this matter personally?"

"Your word?" Mina hissed. "Your word means shit to me, because if Miranda is still pledged to you, then you are ultimately accountable for all this, and your ignorance and negligence has cost me Jonah." She stared into his face, as she avoided his hand as he reached towards her. "No! You swore to never cause me pain, and you've broken your oath, so you will never get to touch me. Ever."

Lucifer smiled stiffly. "And if I let you release your rage, try to thrash her to your heart's content, will that make you reconsider? What would that be worth to you?"

Mina seemed to consider it, but then she looked over her shoulder at Adam. He was shaking his head, silently beseeching her not to seek her vengeance then. Not out of fear for himself, but concern for how her wrath and grief were clouding her judgment; it was dangerous enough to bargain with devils. Any deal with Lucifer would cost more than she could afford to pay. "There will be another time, *mei-mei*. Let's just go."

Mina took a deep breath. "Deal with Miranda as you wish," she said to Lucifer, "but if I see her again, I *will* kill her. My truce with her is over, and I am finished with all of you, except one."

Lucifer looked at her. "Which one?"

"Ashu'ral," Mina said. "I have a specific grievance with him; since he's personally responsible for what's been done to my brother, I demand restitution."

Before Lucifer could respond, Ashu'ral appeared from the other end of the intersection, flashing his blackened teeth with a smug sneer. "I accept your challenge, little witch. When you lose, I'll add you to my harem. If you die, I'll keep you as a trophy, anyway."

Little witch. It was Miranda's term of belittlement for Mina, and Adam wondered if the demon's own judgment wasn't tainted by Miranda's influence. The more Adam watched Mina, the more he remembered about her, and the more he realized that the demon was in far greater danger than Mina appeared to pose.

"Are you sure you want to do this?" Lucifer asked.

"I think you should be warning Ashu'ral, not me," Mina mock-whispered to Lucifer, then looked at Adam. *"Duì bù duì, ge-ge?"* She was asking if he agreed.

"Duì le, mei-mei," Adam returned automatically. *Right.* He still had his languages, thank goodness. "No matter what, I'm with you."

"I'm not leaving until I do to 'Asshole' over there, what he did to my brother," Mina said to Lucifer, unflinchingly. "You don't have to stay and watch."

Ashu'ral laughed at her bravado and flexed his brawny limbs, as Lucifer vanished, taking Miranda with him. As the snarls and scratching noises of claws converged from the shadows on their position, Adam stood shoulder to shoulder with Mina.

"Any words of wisdom or advice?" he asked under his breath.

"Don't get killed," she whispered gruffly. "I've already lost Jonah; I can't lose you, too. It might not have come to this, if I had just listened to Mom at the start."

"What are you talking about?"

"She texted me a reminder tonight: to be careful and thorough," Mina scowled. "Time and again, with Miranda, I've been careless and have tried to be merciful, and now Jonah's gone." She twirled the hammer in her grasp and caught it firmly, as she stared up at Ashu'ral unblinkingly. "This time, I will be thorough."

Chapter 13

Selina had been walking for hours but still felt a restlessness and frustration that refused to be quieted by her meditative stroll through the streets of San Francisco. Without her husband home to distract and entertain her, Selina sought her recreation and amusement elsewhere. She had walked from the Presidio to the Embarcadero, stopping at Grace Cathedral along the way to partake in the calm tranquility of walking the church's indoor labyrinth, then down through the Dragon Gate of Chinatown, until she found herself staring up at the Embarcadero Ferry Building's clock tower.

From the waterfront, she watched the sun set behind the San Francisco skyline, the direction from which she had come, as the ferry boats passed by and underneath the Bay Bridge, carrying tourists and commuters to and from the bustling piers.

Selina checked her phone periodically, waiting for an update from Aciré Hart about Mina and Adam. The last text she had received from Aciré was an hour ago, to confirm that she had accompanied Mina to the warehouse where Adam was held and would be returning Malcolm Gideon's car to his parents' home, per Mina's request.

If Malcolm's car was at the warehouse, that meant that Jonah was there, as well. Selina worried for Jonah's welfare, for Mina's sake as well as Connie and Teddy's. She had observed the family's interactions enough to recognize that Jonah was like a son to the couple, and for anything to happen to him, so soon after losing Malcolm, would have destroyed them.

"They will be fine, Missus Xing," said a serene, resonant voice over Selina's shoulder.

"Who will be fine, angel?" Selina asked, spying the glint of Gabriel's pin on his lapel and the bright flecks of his hidden halo, before she focused her eyes on the rippling waves of the bay.

"Malcolm's parents, and the rest of the Gideon family," Gabriel said. "There are no stalkers following or threatening any of them now."

"Because my children's enemies no longer have a use for them," Selina said stonily. "It doesn't mean that my children are out of danger, themselves. I can feel when my children are in pain, and they are in terrible agony right now."

Gabriel raked back his long dark curls and leaned back against the railing next to Selina, observing the Ferry Building teeming with shoppers, diners and sightseers. "I did warn you that your son may be tested."

"My son," Selina said sharply. "Not my daughter."

"Your daughter is always tested," Gabriel said amiably. "It's a regular part of her vocation, which she executes admirably, with an even hand, on most days. It is why she has allies in the unlikeliest places, and why your children will persevere."

"I'm restless, but I still grow weary of your riddles," Selina growled. "I can sense that my children are no longer suffering physically, but they're certainly not content. If they're still undergoing a trial, then tell me when you expect it to be over, and when their lives may return to normal. Or, at least, a close semblance to normalcy."

"That would depend on your powers of intervention, not mine," Gabriel said knowingly. At her silent frown, he reminded, "You gave your son a piece of white jade,

185

on behalf of your husband, did you not? It's a protection charm, that helped to shield your son from worse injury. It also speeds his recovery, it appears—"

"Yes, I intervene in the affairs of my children, however and whenever I feel it's necessary," Selina interrupted. "So, I will take direct action to fix whatever damage had been done to my son this time, as well. Should I pace myself, or hold off for now, or are you nearly done with him?"

"I am afraid that I don't follow," Gabriel said.

"Did you save my son's life earlier, just so that you could torture him now?" she asked plainly. "I'm still unclear about your motives and involvement, as it comes to my children's lives."

"Ah, I see." Gabriel bowed his head. "Be at peace, Missus Xing. Believe it or not, this current trial that's caused your children such anguish, is not even theirs. If it eases your mind any, your children are superb judges of character, and their friends are as true and brave as they are, so they will endure and thrive, and be happy."

This trial is not even theirs? Selina considered the other individuals whose lives had become so intertwined with Mina and Adam's that they would be willing to suffer together… "Jonah Gideon is with them. He's the one being tried and tested."

"Alas, Mister Gideon is no longer in their company," Gabriel said quietly.

Selina narrowed her eyes. "What does that mean?" But the loss and grief that Mina and Adam were feeling could only mean one thing…

She was distracted by the buzz of her phone in her hand, and she smiled despite her dour mood, as it was a text from her husband to let her know that business had concluded, and that he would be home soon. She had missed his presence; her husband was not always physically affectionate or cloyingly sentimental, but

Selina was always more tranquil and less prone to anger when he was around.

She looked up from her phone, and of course, Gabriel was already gone.

In his place, a small boy was staring at her, open-mouthed, with some yellow cake crumbs and chocolate frosting edging his mouth. His half-eaten cupcake forgotten in his hand, he asked: "Were you talking to an angel?"

Selina raised her eyebrow haughtily. "What do you know about angels?"

"They have halos, like that man did," the boy gushed, "and they bring messages and gifts from God. I wish I could talk to an angel."

Selina looked behind the boy and saw an anxious young woman approaching quickly: either the boy's mother or his nanny, so hard to tell these days. "You don't need angels to tell you or give you anything. If you believe in God, everything you could ever need or want will be provided, if you know where and how to find it."

As the boy took his relieved guardian's hand, Selina reconsidered the cynicism of her words, even as her meaning was lost on the innocence of a child. She had never relied on the mercy or providence of omniscient beings, so she had never raised her children with such beliefs and dependencies, but it wasn't her place to ruin religion for those who wanted or needed it.

"Miss Lady," called the boy over his shoulder, as he walked away. "It doesn't matter if you don't trust in God. God trusts in you."

Mina filled her lungs with the chilly night air, thankful for the downpour on her skin as she turned her face to the sky. It was her first breath of fresh air, her first taste of fresh water, since stepping into that infernal warehouse. She and Adam were drenched to the skin in

sweat, blood and other nameless liquids, and the rain was
a welcome rinse. She heard Adam sliding the heavy steel
door shut behind them, but she kept her eyes forward.
She never wanted to set eyes on that hellish place again,
now that they were finally free of it.

Maggie's ghost appeared, in the exact same spot
where Mina had seen her last. *You're not hurt!* Her smile
faded when she saw only two of them. *I couldn't go
inside to see. What's happened to Jonah?*

Mina crouched to look directly at Maggie, who was
gazing back with concern. "He died, Maggie. I'm sorry."

Maggie lowered her eyes. *I see. I will look for his
spirit, then, and guide him, if he needs me. Then I will be
finished here and can finally join my family.*

Mina realized that it was what Maggie had meant
earlier: she was there for Jonah, to give him the answers
and guidance he needed, until everything was "finished."
Only Mina hadn't understood until it was too late, and
she missed her chance to chance to say good-bye to
Jonah.

Are *you all right?* Maggie asked uncertainly.

"I will be," Mina sniffed. "Thank you for
everything, Maggie."

Maggie nodded and leaned over to give Mina a hug,
only to pass through her with her ghostly limbs. Still,
Mina felt a lightness and warmth where Maggie passed
through her, and for a moment, she felt at peace. *Good-
bye, Mina.* She looked up at Adam and curtsied. *Good-
bye, Adam.*

As Maggie's pale form dissipated in the drizzle,
Adam wrapped his arm around Mina's shoulders, and
she leaned into him. It was the first hug they had shared
since leaving the Pit, and within the supportive embrace
of her brother, away from the eyes of enemies and
strangers, Mina finally let herself break.

She buried her face against Adam's chest,
shuddering with her sobs, as he cradled her and shielded

her from the frigid wind. He turned to face her away from the darkened edifice of the warehouse.

"Let's get back to New York," Adam suggested, and Mina nodded her agreement.

"There's nothing left for me here, anyway. I just need to call Aciré to get my stuff and maybe she can send a car over to pick us up. Hopefully, Malcolm's parents didn't ask her why Jonah didn't return the Charger himself."

The mention of Malcolm's name made the edge of Adam's lips twitch with fond familiarity, but he sobered. "God, what do we tell Malcolm and his parents about Jonah? They'll be devastated."

Mina took a step back and looked at him in alarm. "Adam, are you feeling okay?"

"I feel fine," Adam smiled, although he seemed puzzled about why he was smiling, and he stopped. "Well, you know my brain was scrambled a little, so maybe bits of my memory aren't quite right, but I remember everybody, like you, and our parents, and Jonah and Malcolm…"

"Malcolm's dead," Mina said. "We went to his funeral three days ago. You don't remember that, do you?"

She could tell from his face that he didn't, at all. "It'll come back, I'm sure," he said, his voice slightly quavering. "It's probably just a short-term memory issue."

"Okay," Mina said, dubiously, as she pulled out her phone. "Maybe things will come back once we get back to New York. It'll be good to see everyone," she said, as the phone started to ring at the other end. "And I'm sure Xani's been worried sick about you… Hi, Aciré," she greeted.

Mina kept the call brief, as Aciré was actually driving through downtown when they were talking, plus

Mina was concerned by Adam's continued look of confusion.

"Shit, you don't remember Xani," Mina said. "What about Morgan, or Cindy?"

"Is Xani my cat?" he guessed wildly. "Goldfish?"

"Fuck, no!" Mina cried. "Shit!" she yelled, with half a mind to charge back into the warehouse and end Ashu'ral's life, instead of leaving him the way she had. "This doesn't even make sense! Why should you seem so...*normal*, and still have such a fucked-up memory?" she said, more to herself than to Adam. There had to be a way to reverse or heal what had been done to him...

"The jade," Adam said quietly.

Mina looked at him. "What?"

"Dad's jade," Adam said, touching the pendant at his neck. "I think it kept me from staying broken, or breaking further. You saw some of Ashu'ral's servants: some of them could barely speak in sentences or remember their own names."

Mina turned at the distinctive grumble of a particular car engine, and she stared in disbelief as Malcolm's car rolled to a stop next to her.

The passenger side window lowered, and Aciré's smile greeted them from the driver's seat.

"What the fuck, Aciré?" Mina asked, gesturing to the Charger.

"What?" Aciré said innocently. "I was shopping for a car, and Connie and Teddy wanted to get rid of this one, so I bought it from them. In cash, on the spot." She looked past Mina and waved to Adam. "So, you want to get in, or just stand out there in the rain looking like an idiot?"

"I'm thinking about it," Mina muttered, then huffed and opened the doors, letting Adam ride shotgun, as she slipped into the back, on top of plastic sheeting that Aciré had thoughtfully laid out. "It looks like I'm never getting away from this fucking car." She then spotted the string of tri-color Mardi Gras beads hanging from the rear-view mirror. "Oh, Malcolm would've *hated* that."

"Too bad, it's my car now," Aciré smirked. "I'm thinking of getting it re-painted in metallic, grape candy-purple, with hot pink pinstriping. Maybe a little hibiscus stencil or a rainbow on the back, like a tramp stamp."

A bubble of laughter escaped Mina's throat, even though her brevity was fleeting. She appreciated Aciré's attempt to try to lighten her mood, but she wasn't ready for her mood to be lifted just yet. "Connie and Teddy are okay?"

"They seemed to be," Aciré said. "I kept my visit very brief, since it was late, and they had company. A cute little ginger, nicely stacked, husky voice."

"That sounds like Ellie, Jonah's ex," Mina said.

"Like I said, she was built like a Danish Red heifer, with a face and voice to match," Aciré corrected herself without a hitch. "Anyway, how did the Troll-Hobbler work for you?"

"It works great." Mina recalled the pulverizing, crushing carnage she had caused with the toothed hammer, as she unpacked it from her sling and set it atop Aciré's sturdy black tool satchel. "You were right—it hits harder than it looks. You didn't tell me that it turns invisible, too."

"Yeah, Trobler doesn't like being handled by demons and creatures it doesn't trust, so it goes turtle, when it wants to be ignored," Aciré smiled, then nodded towards Adam. "And how are you, Adam? How's your head?"

"I'm feeling a little better," he replied. "Thanks for all your help, Miss Hart."

"I'm just glad you're coherent and speaking in complete sentences," Aciré said. "These procedures don't usually end well, and stone-skin demons are not known for their surgical precision."

Aciré glanced into the backseat at Mina. "The penthouse is empty presently, so I took the liberty of taking your hoodie and the rest of your belongings there, that you had left in the town car. There are some other clean clothes for both of you; I figured that you would want to take a shower before you leave." She glanced at Adam's feet, clad in drenched socks. "We'll find you some shoes, too."

Mina looked at the far end of the back seat and recognized Jonah's messenger bag. "Jonah's things are still here."

"It seems that he left everything in here before he went to face Miranda," Aciré said quietly. "He never passed by Connie and Teddy's, and he never picked up our calls or texts because his phone's still in the side pocket of his bag. Anyway, I think we'll keep it at State Street for now."

Mina nodded, then realized that Aciré's eyes were focused on the road.

"That may be easier," Adam said, "until we figure out what to say to his family."

"We'll discuss it later," Aciré agreed. "Right now, let's get you both cleaned up and ready to go home. You two look like you just came off a Tarantino movie set."

Cindy was a businesswoman, so she needed to keep a balance between her personal and professional responsibilities. As much as she wanted to remain in the duplex to console Xani and Morgan after losing Adam, she also needed to maintain a semblance of normality for her employees and her more curious and watchful clientele, so she returned to the Red Lotus to socialize with the evening crowd. Above all, she needed to keep attention away from the family of fae living in Mina's building, or Adam's sacrifice would have been for nothing.

Get a grip, she rebuked herself. *Adam's not dead, just captured.*

Cindy kept her phone in her snug front jeans pocket, anxiously awaiting Mina's text or call that everything was fine, that they had freed Adam from Ashu'ral's lair, and that they were coming home soon.

"Hey, boss," called one of the waiters, approaching the bar with a tray of plates from the kitchen. "The elves said you looked like you needed a pick-me-up." He set down one of the plates with a respectful nod and a flash of his fangs before he delivered a vegan samosa platter to the beautiful, bejeweled rakshesha at one of his tables.

The kitchen staff had prepared for Cindy a plate of finger-sized churros, freshly fried and generously tossed with the elves' own cinnamon-sugar blend, which also contained a dash of allspice and nutmeg, just like Cindy's mother mixed hers. A steaming bowl of espresso-dusted dipping chocolate was served alongside.

Cindy was touched by the thoughtfulness of her team, who felt like her extended family, more often than not. Regardless of her own opinions and leanings, she had always held to her belief that everyone deserved a chance at the Red Lotus, unless they were so disgustingly vile and reprehensible that their presence drove her customers away. She had experienced her share of exclusion and ostracism at other establishments and institutions, both before and after her transition, usually based in part on the color of her skin, so she had pledged to always keep an open mind, both in her hiring and her service.

She reminded herself of her pledge, as Lucifer entered the Lotus. Despite his nature and his reputation, she never felt threatened or endangered in his presence, so she reserved comment, as he was greeted by Micah with cordial indifference and took a seat at the bar. The devil was neatly and handsomely dressed in a bespoke suit, as always, but he was less glib and engaging than his usual charming self.

"What can I get you?" Cindy asked, setting down a napkin.

"Whatever you care to serve me, Cin," he said with uncharacteristic humility. "I wasn't sure if I had already been barred from entering the Red Lotus."

Cindy set a glass of cranberry and vodka on the bar for him, the vibrant red hue matching his tie and pocket square. "Not yet. I don't like you very much, right now, but I don't have to."

"Thank you," he said, to both the drink and her cool professionalism. "Do you want to chastise me now, or later, for my lack of foresight in dealing with my underlings?"

"That's not my place, Luci, but thank you for offering," Cindy said unsmilingly. "Honestly, I haven't heard from Mina since earlier tonight, so if you have news to share, I'd be willing to listen."

"I've just come from surveying her handiwork tonight in Boston," Lucifer said, and it was hard to tell whether his tone was gleeful or blasé. "It's been some time since I've seen the wrathful vengeance Miss Xing can deliver—it's impressive work."

"I don't think Mina cares about your opinion," Cindy said, wondering what had caused Mina to unleash her ire. Had something happened to Adam?

"Clearly, she doesn't, otherwise, she might have shown *some* restraint," Lucifer said, looking over his glass at Cindy, his cool blue eyes assessing and thoughtful. "Miss Xing and her brother are both fine, by the way. Not a scratch on either of them. Well," he amended, "they did sustain a few boo-boos here and there, but they're physically unharmed now."

Cindy propped her lean, mahogany-tan limbs on the counter to hold Lucifer's gaze. "You wanted her to do this, didn't you? You gave up your underling for Mina to demolish and execute—"

"Not execute," Lucifer corrected. "Miss Xing's sense of justice is whimsical, so she left the fool in arguably a far worse state than death. It's what he deserves, for listening to his subordinates' advice instead of doing his own research, just like a typical middle manager." He shook his head disappointedly. "Hopefully, his replacement is a little brighter."

"You could've warned Ashu'ral about Mina," Cindy said. "He did report to you."

Lucifer finished his cranberry and vodka with a wry smirk. "I'm a devil, sweet Cin. I'm not known for my veracity. Besides, if he had been paying attention at all, he would've known to follow my example and show Miss Xing some respect. She still would've lobotomized him, but she might have done it more mercifully."

Cindy had spoken to Galen on several occasions since his arrival in New York, and he had shared his tales of what his fellow slaves had suffered under Ashu'ral, but she had hoped that he had exaggerated some of his claims of the demon's cruelty. "Was that what he had done to Adam, too?"

"If you must know, yes," Lucifer said. "Ashu'ral attempted to break Mister Xing's mind and failed dismally, but Miss Xing is more meticulous with her technique."

"Ashu'ral's ineptitude doesn't exempt him from punishment," Cindy said, set a chilled glass of ice-cold vodka in front of Lucifer. "I thought he was a stone-skin demon, impervious to attack, so how did Mina manage to defeat him?"

"You needn't be coy," Lucifer said slyly. "I know you keep a set of knucklers on hand for dealing with these types."

"I do have a set for emergencies," Cindy admitted, "but Mina doesn't, so what did she use?"

"I just saw the fallout, not the event," Lucifer reminded, taking an initial sip. "From what I can tell, Miss Xing managed to get her hands on a bone-crushing weapon, which she used to pulverize every large bone she could find on Ashu'ral, through his unbroken skin, systematically and methodically. She broke off his longest tail barb—I imagine her brother informed her that it was Ashu'ral's favored orbitoclast—and used it to perform the same procedure on the demon that he was so fond of performing on others.

"I found the spike still wedged in his eye socket," Lucifer said, and drank more deeply. "And since the bones of all his extremities were crushed beforehand, he had been helpless to stop her. His jaw was shattered, too, so he couldn't even properly scream, just drool copiously, but that may be a permanent side effect of his new mental state."

"*Dios mío*," Cindy muttered. It was the kind of wanton savagery she would've expected from a fellow fae, not Mina.

"What's wrong, dear Cin? Your friend gets her revenge, and the villain got his comeuppance. Whose side are you on, anyway?" he asked flippantly.

"Mina's," Cindy said easily. "Always Mina's. And I think in some veiled way, you are, too, which is one of the reasons that Micah still deems you worthy enough to come sit at my bar."

"I didn't make her do anything that she didn't want to," Lucifer said.

"No, I'm sure you didn't, which makes it more disconcerting," Cindy said. "I've seen Mina do terrible things, but never without reason, without first being pushed past her tolerance. So, what happened in Ashu'ral's lair that made her snap?"

"Aside from having her brother mentally and physically tortured, you mean?" Lucifer said lightly, getting to his feet. "You say 'snap,' but I call it meeting her potential. Either way, you'll have all the answers you want soon enough. They're on their way back, and should be in New York before closing time."

"You're not going to tell me what happened," Cindy said.

Lucifer shrugged, as he slid his empty glass to her. "I can't. I wasn't there."

"You know what I mean."

"I do, and I'm being entirely truthful, for once. There are events in flux, so you'll have to ask your friends for their perspective, when they return. In the meantime," he said, "I have an appointment with my former employee, Miranda White, on the matter of her habitual underperformance and subordination, and subsequently, her immediate dissolution."

He paused and looked at Cindy. "You may tell your friends that they will not be troubled by her again. I'll concede that you may have been right on your earlier point."

"And which point would that be, Luci?" she asked, taking the glass.

"That prevention is sometimes the more prudent course," he said. "Some things cannot be fixed or made better, once they are broken."

With that, he bowed his head to Cindy and vanished.

The drive from Boston to New York was uneventful, given the late hour, except for the occasional construction zone traffic from the overnight road work crews. From the highway, each city looked the same as the next, with urban streetlights illuminating malls and office buildings visible from afar, when the highway wasn't bordered by woods or farmland.

Mina imagined that the scenery was prettier during the day, although most of the deciduous trees in the New

England area had already dropped most of their autumn leaves, but at night, there was only darkness beyond the shoulder and railings of the road. She glanced at the passenger side, thinking that Adam was asleep, but he was wide awake, even as they passed the halfway point somewhere in Connecticut. He simply stared out the window in silence, not even bothering with the radio.

"Let me know if you need to take a break," she said. She was prepared to drive straight through to New York. She would probably sleep late, but at least she'd be in her own bed. It was easier that way; it was always easier to be alone, and she had been foolish to hope for more.

"I'm okay for now," Adam said quietly. "I'll feel better once we're home."

"I'm with you." They both felt broken and battered, in their own way, each feeling their own kind of loss and guilt.

Gripping the steering wheel, she felt the gold of the ruby ring bite into her finger, but she didn't want to take it off. Not yet. Jonah hadn't even been gone hours, and she hadn't even worn the ring for a day. "I was going to say 'yes' to him," she said, keeping her eyes fixed on the road ahead. "He asked me to marry him, and I hesitated, but I was going to tell him when he got to New York."

"I think he asked me for my blessing, over the phone," Adam said. "I don't recall the conversation exactly, but I remember his mood. He sounded serious and committed. He was ready to do anything and give up everything to see you happy."

Because he loved me. "I think I need a moment," she said hoarsely, signaling to pull over to the side. Given the emptiness of the road, Mina was able to execute a sharp, possibly illegal, two-lane switch to get the rental onto the rumble strips on the right shoulder. By the time she had stopped and parked, her torrential tears had all but blinded her, streaming down her cheeks unabated. She unbuckled her seat belt and got out to get some air; she was in no condition to drive like that.

"Want me to take over?" Adam offered, joining her outside the car. "I do remember how to drive. I know that much."

"You don't have your license on you, in case anything happens." Mina shook her head. "No, I can do this. It was just a mistake to bring up Jonah; clearly, I'm not ready to talk about him."

"Alright. When we get back to New York, we'll sit down and have some drinks when you're ready."

Mina smiled, looking forward to returning to familiar surroundings. "A round of drinks at the Red Lotus sounds wonderful." The blankness on Adam's face reminded her that there was plenty of work ahead. "You don't remember the Lotus, do you?"

"Is that a bar?" he hazarded.

"You got so much more fucked-up than you even realize. Get in the car," Mina said, with renewed resolve. "I'm not going to sleep tonight until we get some answers."

In the car, Mina checked the time. It was well past midnight on the East Coast, but California was three hours behind. As she started the car, she set her phone on speaker and called their parents' home.

Their mother picked up on the second ring. "Min-Min," Selina greeted, and her clear, serene voice immediately settled Mina's nerves.

"Adam's here, too, Mom," Mina said. "We're in a rental, driving back to New York."

"I know," Selina said. " I just got off the phone with Aciré. She called me after she saw you off."

"So, you know what's happened," Adam said quietly. Jonah's fate didn't have to be mentioned.

"I do. I presume that Mina is driving, so we can keep this conversation brief, and we will talk more when you're back in New York."

In case their mother was planning to hang up, Adam asked in a rush, "Mom, what happened to me?" At the silent air, Mina and Adam could almost envision their mother's imperious, inquiring gaze upon them. "The demon stirred a spike around in my head to sever connections in my brain, and now it feels like my brain is trying to repair itself."

"It is, and it will continue to do whatever it can," Selina answered. "This demon... What's happened to him?" she asked, almost casually.

"He's been dealt with," Mina said coolly. "What do you mean by 'whatever it can'?"

"The flesh will heal, but memories are always transient," Selina said. "I will discuss this with your father when he returns, and he may have some additional insight, but be prepared for the possibility that your memories may remain incomplete."

"It could be far worse," Adam said. "It's just some memories, and there will always be more to fill the space."

Mina was silent, glancing at her ring. Memories were now all she had left of Jonah, and there would be no more.

Chapter 14

By the time Mina stopped the car on Fifth Avenue near his building, Adam was feeling more positive about his outlook. He recognized the streets of Manhattan and Greenwich Village with an instinctive sense of direction and place, and the looming, illuminated arch presiding over Washing Square Park resembled a "Welcome Home" banner, to herald his return. Maybe his head wasn't in as bad a state as he had feared.

"You'll call if you need anything?" Mina said, as Adam shut the car door behind himself.

"I will," he promised. "You, too."

Mina chuckled tiredly. "As long as you remember to pick up your land line. Your cell phone's dead, so we'll have to track it down tomorrow. I'll call your apartment in the morning. Good night."

"Good night. Love you, *mei-mei,*" he said, automatically.

"Love you, too," she smiled and drove away.

Adam walked into the lobby of his building with a spring in his step, feeling at home in the identifiable surroundings. He waved to the night doorman, whose name he recalled was "Dave"—just like the older gentleman who covered the day shift, so everyone in the building called him "Junior" despite the lack of relationship or resemblance to the more senior doorman. Adam counted twenty long strides across the marble tiles to the elevator bank, as he had done hundreds of times over the years.

His memories weren't all gone, after all, he thought hopefully, as he pushed the button for his floor, almost automatically. Upon exiting the elevator, he counted the twenty-three steps to the right, landing him on his doormat in front of his apartment. He tapped the seven-digit alphanumeric code to unlock the front door and stepped into the apartment, reaching for the light switch instinctively.

Except that the lights were already on. Adam looked around at the elegant, modern glass and metal furniture and smelled a woman's perfume in the air: a breezy mix of freesias, daisies and cut grass. It was elusively, hauntingly recognizable, as something that had enveloped and filled him with love and desire...

"Hey, Adam," greeted a warm, sultry voice from across the granite kitchen counter.

It was a gorgeous woman with jade-green eyes, porcelain skin and a riot of bright red curls like flames around her head and shoulders, dressed in an oversized white shirt. She looked very much at home, as she cradled a mug of tea.

"Hey...you." Adam struggled to recall the names that Mina had thrown at him over the course of the four-hour drive from Boston.

The woman set down her tea and stepped out from the kitchen, and Adam realized that the oversized shirt was one of his own monogrammed, tailored dress shirts, and that it was all that she was wearing, unbuttoned to her navel.

"Xani?" he hazarded. *Not a cat.*

"Lucky guess," she smiled, facing him directly. "It's okay. I was warned that this might happen. I'm just glad you're back, and that you're okay."

Xani gestured to a pile on his counter. "Anyway, I brought back everything you left at the duplex: your keys, your wallet, your phone—that's completely dead, so I plugged it in for you."

"That was very thoughtful of you," he said. "Thanks."

"It was the least I could do." She wrapped her hands around his neck and gave him a gentle peck. "I had to do something, instead of just sitting around and waiting."

As she rested her head against his shoulder, he kept his hands to himself. He was uncertain about the liberties he could take, as he had no recollection of their past relationship, if they even had one.

After a moment, she whispered, "You don't remember me, do you?"

Adam shook his head regretfully. "I'm sorry, I really wish I did."

She faced him again with a patient smile. "My name is Alexandra Crain, but I go by Xani."

Alexandra Crain. That did ring a bell, but he associated the name with a slightly-awkward co-ed from his college years, with wiry, frizzy copper-red hair... *Oh.*

"You remember me now?" she asked hopefully.

"Not like this," he admitted. *There must be something seriously wrong with me.* Maybe he could have bluffed his way through it and pretended that he remembered, to make her feel better and enjoy her attention while he could, but that didn't feel right. He couldn't see himself lying to her, ever. "I'm *so* sorry. I wish I could tell you otherwise."

"It's fine," she said, looking disappointed but doggedly optimistic. "It's an honest answer, and that's better than a pretty lie." She leaned into him and kissed him more deeply.

That felt familiar, too, and natural. "Were we together?" he asked.

"You could say that," she said, as she took his hand and rested her cheek against his palm. As his thumb brushed against her downy skin, he struggled to understand how he could have no recollection of the feel of her. "It's alright," she said. "The memories will come back to you."

"There's a chance that they may not," he said, trying futilely to at least recall his emotions, if not the details, of their time together. It seemed that they had been very close, probably intimate. "If they don't, would you really want to start over from the beginning with me?"

"We haven't been together very long, so maybe that's the reason you don't remember me," Xani said. "We slept together before we had our first date, and you only started calling me your girlfriend this weekend." She took his hand and laid it on her breast with an alluring smile. "We kind of went about this relationship thing a little backwards, honestly."

Adam was relieved that she was being so accommodating, but his pulse still raced at the feel of her warm, supple skin under his fingers, and her mouth against his. Even if his mind didn't recall her, it seemed that his body certainly did. "I guess we could try this again, if you're up for it."

She looked him over with an expectant glint in her jade-green eyes. "I can see that *you're* up for it. Come on," she said, leading him by the hand to his bedroom. "How often do couples get to experience their first time together, a second time?"

Adam grinned, following Xani's lead. "Did I mess up anything the first time, that requires a do-over?"

"Not at all. Even with a bullet hole in your side and a taped-up finger, you were pretty damned good," she simpered, pulling him towards the bed. "I wouldn't have stuck around, if you were disappointing."

Galen awoke at the sound of the front door of the building opening and closing with muffled clacks, followed by hushed voices and light, quick-footed steps rushing up the stairs. It certainly wasn't Mrs Krantz, who had retired to bed hours ago. The footsteps continued to the top floor, where Mina Gideon's apartment was located.

Listening to make sure the children were asleep in their rooms, Galen arose from the armchair and flitted to the alcove, staying above the floorboards to avoid stirring anyone with accidental creaks. He opened the door and listened for any noises in the stairwell, before he shut the door quietly behind himself and flew up the center of the stairs to the top floor.

On his ascent, he discerned Cindy and Mina's voices, exchanging urgent whispers before the door of the upstairs apartment clicked shut. They didn't sound particularly happy, but they weren't belligerent towards each other, either. More than anything, they just sounded tired—

The door to Mina's apartment opened suddenly. She didn't look surprised to see him in her hallway, but nor did she look welcoming. "Dawa told me you were still awake," she said, gesturing to her snow-white *ruishi* bouncing on her couch, swishing his tail around Cindy. "Did you want to come in?"

"I don't want to interrupt," he said, waving to Cindy through the door. "I just heard voices and wanted to make sure everything was alright."

Mina nodded. "It's good to see you again. Maybe we can catch up in the morning?"

"That would be nice," he said. "You could come down, meet the children and join us for breakfast."

"I may have to," she said dryly. "All my pans and cooking utensils seem to have disappeared from my kitchen over the weekend."

"Oh, sorry. We'll have everything washed and returned to you right afterwards," he said sheepishly.

"I'm kidding," Mina said. "They've probably seen more use downstairs these past days than they have up here in weeks. Keep them as long as you want." She opened the door wider. "Are you sure you don't want to come in?"

Galen shook his head. "It's late, and you probably want to get some rest. You've had a long and arduous day, from what little I've heard."

"Thanks, Galen," Mina said. "Not everyone is as considerate as you," she said pointedly, with a glance over her shoulder at Cindy.

"Just talk to me, *chica*. The sooner you give me some straight answers, the sooner I'll leave and let you sleep," Cindy pledged. "Otherwise, I'm fine with sitting on your sofa for the rest of the night."

Mina flashed Galen a weary smile. "Good night."

Galen leapt over the railing and dropped down to ground floor, landing softly before returning to the duplex. Back in the warm security of the spacious apartment, he was overwhelmed by the generosity of the humans he had met. Despite not personally knowing him or his family, Mina and her associates had risked her home and their lives to protect Galen and his children. With chagrin, he thought back to his initial meeting with Mina days earlier, and how suspicious and harsh he had been with her and Jonah, not yet understanding the extent of their graciousness and support to secure his family's safety.

"Papa, are you out here?" Gia's voice called.

"Here, my girl," Galen called back, perching on the edge of the sofa seat to avoid pinching his wings. "Why are you awake at this hour?"

"I heard voices outside," Gia said, playing with the end of her plaited hair. "Was that Miss Xing speaking with Cindy? Has she returned, with Adam?"

"Yes, Miss Xing is home, and Mister Xing is back in his own apartment, as well, presumably," Galen said, hearing the excitement in his daughter's voice. "They deserve to get some sleep, after everything they've been through, so let's not bother Miss Xing until morning."

"I know that," Gia beamed. "I'm just excited to finally have the chance to meet her."

All night, Galen had been receiving messages through Cindy and her father Dan from their friends who had been liberated from Ashu'ral's lair in Boston. Once Mina and Adam had incapacitated the demon and killed or maimed most of his guards, the servants' quarters and harem were unlocked to enable Ashu'ral's slaves and captives to escape, but everyone seemed to have a different account of how the Xing siblings actually looked. Over the past hours, their legend had grown and been embellished until they had become almost folkloric heroes.

As someone who had met and spent time with both of them, Galen found the accounts laughably inaccurate, especially the ones where Mina somehow resembled a sleek red fox and Adam was a seven-foot tall deaf-mute giant.

A quiet knock sounded at the door, and Gia burst from the living room to answer it. "Cindy! Are you staying with us tonight?"

"No, thanks, I'm on my way home. Galen," Cindy called, her voice quietly subdued, "Mina told me something, that I think you should know, before you speak to her again."

Galen went to the door, as he heard the emotion in Cindy's voice. "What is it?"

"Jonah Gideon is dead," Cindy said. "He died in Ashu'ral's lair, swallowed by the Pit."

Galen was stunned into speechlessness, as the last time he had seen Jonah had been little more than a day ago, and the man had been in good spirits and fine health, with no greater concern weighing on him than not making a fool of himself in front of Mina. For her part, Mina had spoken effusively of Jonah's qualities and charms when she had been drugged, but she was clearly attracted to Jonah, even when she had recovered her senses and cooler head.

"Who's Jonah?" Gia looked back and forth at Cindy and Galen in puzzlement.

"He was a good man," Galen said, holding his arms out to Cindy to offer an embrace. "He was our friend."

"He was a great friend," Cindy said, sinking into Galen's arms. "He deserved a better fate. He and Mina deserved a chance to be together."

Gia was moved by the adults' show of grief, and she joined them in the embrace, wrapping her arms and wings around both of them. "Is there anything I can do?" she asked quietly.

Cindy straightened and stroked Gia's cheek, touched by the girl's offer. "No, honey, I think Mina just needs some time and some space. Maybe she'll feel better in the morning, after she's had some sleep."

As she turned to go, Galen called after her: "Anything we can do for you?"

Cindy smiled gratefully and shook her head. "I'll just need some time, too. I think we all will."

Xani became slowly awake when she realized that Adam was no longer in bed with her. She heard the low whistle of the tea kettle and urgent bubbling of the coffee maker coming from the kitchen, as well as noises from the drawers and dish cabinets, signaling that Adam was up and about, but she was tempted to stay in bed.

She rolled onto her back and stretched out on Adam's bed, with a prolonged, feline languor, feeling the silky sheets slippery and warm under her skin. She sighed, remembering the hours she had spent with Adam becoming entangled in them, tugging and clutching them, as she and Adam rediscovered one another.

It hadn't been that long ago since they had last had sex, but Adam's abduction and the subsequent hours of uncertainty had reminded Xani not to take her good fortune for granted. Once Cindy had gotten Mina's text that they were on their way home, Xani had gone to Adam's apartment and waited anxiously for his return, to give him a proper hero's welcome home.

Unfortunately, it hadn't worked out exactly the way she had envisioned. She hadn't expected his initial blank politeness, or the profundity of his lack of memory of her, but then she remembered that they really hadn't known each other that long. She had thought about him often over the past years, but she was a recent acquaintance, in his eyes. She had decided that she would take the lead, then, and show him how close they had been. She didn't expect to jar his memory, or anything close, but it was important to her that he knew the extent of her commitment, that he knew what had already existed between them and would still be waiting for him, when he was ready.

On the primal and physical level, Adam seemed to have forgotten nothing. He had an innate, intimate awareness of her body, of what she liked, and what she *really* liked, without any guidance from her, and when he whispered her name, he didn't appear to have to think about it. On some subconscious level, he still remembered her.

Feeling the sheets getting cold, Xani finally rose from the bed and pulled on Adam's t-shirt that he had worn home, and half-staggered to the kitchen, with her legs still feeling loose and wobbly from the evening's fun. Adam watched her unsteady stance with an amused smile, but there was still a lingering sadness in his eyes.

She couldn't begrudge him that. As they had remained in bed in the small hours, nestled together, Adam had shared with Xani what had happened in the demon's lair, of what had actually been done to him, and

209

what had happened to Jonah—or rather, what Jonah had chosen to do. While Mina had unleashed her righteous fury with ferocious, animal rage, Adam was silently dealing with something closer to survivor's guilt: why didn't he think of throwing himself into the Pit, before Jonah? Did Mina resent him for being the reason for Jonah's sacrifice?

She imagined those questions were still floating through his mind, judging by the solemnity in his eyes, as he poured her a cup of coffee.

"You didn't sleep much," she said, taking the cup from him.

"I couldn't," he said, clinking his cup of tea against hers. "Milk or sugar?" he offered.

Xani mixed in the milk and scant teaspoon of sugar into her coffee without comment. Adam used to know exactly how she liked her coffee, and have it ready for her without her even asking, as though he had read her mind. She had taken for granted how much he had learned about her, just from observing her habits and quirks.

"You remembered that I drink coffee," she noted, noticing her forgotten mug of tea on the counter from the night before.

"Don't most people drink coffee in the morning?" Adam said dismissively, taking her cold mug of tea to the sink.

"You don't," she said.

He paused and looked at her. "I have a coffee maker on the counter and coffee in the pantry, so I took a guess that you might want some. Is that a problem?"

"No, it's just... forget it," she said, sipping from the cup. The brew strength of the coffee was perfect, with an extra scoop to boost the caffeine and intensity of flavor. "The coffee's great, thank you."

Adam seemed to notice the shift in her mood. "I don't know what to tell you, Xani," he sighed. "Some things come to me, naturally, and other things I can't recall, no matter how hard I focus, so I'm trying to piece it together like a puzzle, figuring things out by context. As long as I'm stuck like this, I'm useless to everyone."

"Stop!" Xani snapped. "You're not useless—"

The apartment phone rang, and Xani stared at it, having rarely heard Adam take any calls on it, but he went readily to it.

"Mina said she might call in the morning," he said, reaching for the phone, but he stopped and frowned at it. "That's not Mina's number."

"Who else would be calling you? It's too early for telemarketers and robo-calls," Xani remarked.

"It's a local number," he said, reading the slow crawl of the caller ID. "What the fuck..." His eyes widened in recognition, and he pushed the button to answer on speakerphone. "Good morning?"

Xani looked at the caller ID. *Global Pacific Trust.* "Wasn't that your company?" she mouthed to Adam silently.

Adam nodded, as an older man's voice greeted: "Good morning, this is Stan Sobol, from Global Pacific Trust. Am I speaking with Adam Xing?"

Adam raised his eyebrow. "I'm sorry, I'm not interested in investing right now—"

"No, I'm not calling for that," Sobol answered, half-chuckling. "I don't know if you remember me. I'm the senior vice president for Global Pacific's research division—"

Adam mouthed to Xani: "My old boss's boss's boss."

"—and I wanted to speak with you personally, on the matter of your premature severance. Is this a good time, Adam?"

Adam gave Xani a dubious glance and ignored Sobol's question. "I do remember you, Mister Sobol. I'm not sure what more there is to discuss, though. I thought

211

Human Resources and my manager had everything squared away."

Xani gave him a silent kiss on the cheek and ducked into the bedroom to get dressed. As she pulled on her jeans and sweatshirt, she listened a little to the conversation, as Adam had felt no need to take the call off speakerphone, with nothing secret about the discussion.

It sounded like Adam was being offered his job back, or even a promotion, with a commensurate pay raise. Apparently, upper management had determined that they had been overzealous in their cost-cutting measures, especially with their overseas operations, and were looking for an experienced analyst like Adam to take over significant portions of their private equity research division...

It sounded like a lot of corporate jargon to Xani, but Adam seemed to be listening politely, even attentively, to Sobol's re-recruitment pitch.

By the time Xani had emerged from the bathroom after brushing her teeth and washing her face, the call had ended, and Adam sat at the counter, thoughtfully staring at the phone.

"They want to hire you back?" Xani asked.

"That's how it sounds," Adam said. "Twice my old salary, plus I get to pick my team, and I don't have to deal with my old supervisor anymore."

"That's great!" Xani said, trying to sound supportive.

"I told him I have to think about it," Adam said, taking a sip of his tea. "I have a few days to consider the offer and make a counteroffer, just to be a pain in the ass," he said with a gleam.

"Wait, I thought you loved that job," Xani said. "It let you travel around the world, and stay and do wherever you wanted, all on the company's expense account."

"That was before I realized the kind of mischief my sister gets herself into, here," he quipped, "and before Global Pacific decided to drop-kick me to the curb. Something is definitely peculiar about this whole deal—I call shenanigans."

Xani folded her arms. "So, what are you going to do? This could be a great opportunity for you."

Adam stepped closer to Xani. "We already have something great here, unless I've totally misread the signals."

"We do," she said quietly, "but you know what I mean. Honestly, I might feel better if you had a safer job." Adam chuckled, but she was serious. "I mean it, I was a mess when you were gone, and I didn't know if you had gotten hurt or killed—"

He held her and kissed her tenderly. "I'm sorry you had to go through that, but I want to be someplace where I can help Mina and make a difference, not just write reports to help some billion-dollar company make even more money for their global investors in..." He stopped with an "ah-ha" kind of look. "Malaysia."

"What? Malaysia?"

"My father was in Malaysia last week and just finished up some business meetings," Adam said. "Now I have to wonder what he said, and to whom."

Xani stepped back from his arms. "You're suggesting that your dad talked to someone at Global Pacific to offer you your job back?" Xani knew that the Xings were well-off and well-connected, but this still seemed like a bit of a stretch.

"Not just a job, but a promotion," Adam said. "Sobol could've picked someone from within his group, but he picked up the phone and called me, hat in hand."

"Maybe it was an honest screw-up on their part, and they really want you back," Xani said. She couldn't believe that she was debating the sincerity of the company that had effectively fired Adam, but she also wanted to make sure that he had no regrets, regardless of his choice.

Adam laughed cynically. "No, Stanislav Sobol does not call *anyone* unless he absolutely must—he's paranoid about people hearing his voice whom he can't see. Even his wife and mistress have gotten used to just receiving texts from him; if he called me, then he was ordered to do so."

"That's why you kept him on speakerphone?" Xani smiled. "To make him squirm about who else could be listening in?"

"He's a two-timing motherfucker, and a shithead of a boss. I don't want to go back to that," he said, reaching for her hand. "I'd rather stay here, with you."

"Shit, and here I was hoping that I could quit my job, travel the world with you, and do some sightseeing and shopping while you're toiling away at the office," Xani said with an annoyed pout.

Adam laughed. "Bullshit, you love working with your brother," he said. "Morgan couldn't manage..." He stopped with an enlightened grin. "Holy shit."

"You remember Morgan!" Xani beamed, throwing her arms around Adam. "It's coming back to you!"

Adam seemed cautiously optimistic. "Not everything, but I can picture his face and his crazy red hair, and I remember letting him beat me up?" He gave Xani a quick kiss, since she was pressed against him, already. "Either way, I think I need to talk this out with my parents: about my head, and about this job offer."

From his tone, it didn't sound like a quick phone conversation. "In person?"

"I think it needs to be," Adam said quietly. "I owe them a visit, anyway."

"How long would you be gone?"

"It depends on what my parents say, and how long things will take to resolve," he said. "Could be a day, could be a week. Might even be longer."

"Should I come with you?" she offered, leaning her head against his shoulder.

"It's probably better if you don't," he said, kissing her forehead. "Mina and I thought we were just flying to Boston for a day-trip on Friday, and we all know how that turned out."

Chapter 15

Jonah looked around and just saw sand, in every direction, all the way to the horizon. Despite the darkened, star-filled sky suggesting that it was evening in the desert, Jonah didn't feel cold. He just felt...lost. Without any idea of where he was before that moment, or how he had arrived there. He was utterly alone.

Not alone, Jonah. I am here for you, for the moment.

Jonah looked down and saw Maggie White's small figure standing with him, her delicate fist wrapped firmly around his fingers. For the first time, she looked solid and real, and not just some projection or ghost. "If you feel this real to me, this must mean I'm actually dead."

Are you afraid? Maggie asked, her pale, colorless hair now shiny and almost glowing in the starlight. *You don't have to be scared of being dead.*

"Not scared, Maggie. Just sad, because there was more that I wanted to do."

Maggie nodded sagely. *That was why I stayed, to make sure they would let you go back. Now that I know they will, I can be with my family again, and meet my baby brother Gideon for the first time.*

"Wait, I don't understand," Jonah said. "Go back? Who's letting me go back?"

Maggie shrugged with a carefree smile. *You don't need me for answers anymore. Just ask around.*

Maggie vanished before Jonah could ask anything else. There was still so much that confused him, and no one to help clarify matters. "'Just ask around'?" he shouted to the empty desert surrounding him. "Ask whom?"

"Ugh, children," came a voice over his shoulder, and Jonah spun around in his surprise, nearly throwing himself off-balance. "I presume she meant me, Mister Gideon."

"Lucifer," he said, recognizing the devil's blond hair and his overall glow. "Where am I?"

"You are in between," Lucifer said, sounding bored. "You were alive, then dead, and now you are somewhere in the middle."

Jonah felt his own body as unbroken and solid, and cold, but not uncomfortably. "Is this purgatory, then?"

"No, this realm is more tedious and featureless," Lucifer said, gesturing for Jonah to turn around.

Behind them was a small wicker table with two matching chairs, under a marketplace canopy strewn with tiny lights. Lucifer seemed to notice Jonah's distrust and said, "Please join me, Mister Gideon. I'd hate to look up at you, as we speak."

Cautiously, Jonah took the seat across from Lucifer. "How did I get here?"

"My angelic counterpart and I brought you," Lucifer said, his lips twisted with annoyance. "It was not a simple task, as you were in small bits, and some parts of you had already been liquified and incorporated into the slurry, but for this modern, technological world, it was important that we restore your original body, rather than create a facsimile, which would have been the norm in simpler times. Perhaps, you could explain it more clearly to him, Gabriel."

A swarthy, tan-suited figure joined them at the table, sitting in a third chair that had suddenly appeared. "That is to say: your scars, enchantments and other experiences that were memorialized on your mortal body prior to your death had to be retained, so that you are still recognized as Jonah Gideon when you return. That includes your recent gunshot wound, but we healed that—too much effort to maintain a festering hole, when a scar will serve as a marker just as well. One must be thorough; identity theft was less of a concern in your ancestors' age."

Jonah resisted the temptation to make sure that *everything* had been restored to its prior state and heard Gabriel's stifled chuckle. "Yes, all of your features were recreated to their original dimensions, Mister Gideon."

Jonah opened his mouth and closed it again, glancing between Lucifer and Gabriel, and resting his eyes on Lucifer. "But you didn't like me, as I recall."

"I *still* don't like you," the devil said distastefully. "But I am bound to honor my word: as you are aware, I've pledged that I wouldn't cause Mina Xing any discomfort or grief. For some reason I can't fathom, your loss has left her inconsolably bereft, so Gabriel has suggested that I remedy the situation in the only way I can: by restoring your life."

"Lucifer has left out an important detail," Gabriel said, knitting his dark manicured fingers under his chin. "Had the plot unfolded the way that his followers expected, your fate would be significantly different. The sacrificial decision was intended for Miss Xing to make, and her involvement in choosing her grief would have left Lucifer blameless in the matter. However, your distant cousin Miss White miscalculated your resolve, and the removal of choice returned the accountability back to her, and ultimately, to my counterpart."

"Technically, your act could be argued as a suicide," Lucifer said pithily.

"Mister Gideon wouldn't have killed himself, if he had seen another option," Gabriel reminded, then returned his attention to Jonah. "Self-sacrificial death is different, otherwise, we'd all be elsewhere, not here in the void, discussing your return. You *do* want to go back, we presume?"

"Yes, absolutely!" Jonah said, automatically. He thought back to what Maggie had said. "Maggie said something about my being 'allowed' to go back. Is this why you're letting me return: because I sacrificed myself?"

"That little brat cheated," Lucifer grumbled.

"That precious child did not cheat," Gabriel retorted. "She saw an opportunity to help her descendent and took it, and freed herself in the process."

"She gave him information that he wouldn't otherwise have," Lucifer said.

"But she didn't tell him how to use it," Gabriel said, then turned to Jonah. "Maggie gave you the answers you needed, but the decision to save Mister Xing was your own, was it not?"

"Of course," Jonah said. "Maggie didn't want me to go to the warehouse at all."

"So, there you are, Luci," said Gabriel. "You are simply upset that your followers misjudged Mister Gideon's character, and so have embarrassed you in the process. It is neither Maggie's nor Mister Gideon's fault."

"So, is Miranda being punished for making you look bad?" Jonah asked Lucifer.

"After a fashion," Lucifer sniffed. "She is no longer in my service. I have no use for followers who defy or try to circumvent my orders, or sheep who will not be herded."

Gabriel cleared his throat quietly. "Miranda White was banished from the earthly realm and unmade, and her energy was harvested to restore you, and fill in your gaps, so to speak. All things remain in balance: one life given in place for another."

"'Unmade'?" Jonah asked.

Lucifer rolled his eyes impatiently. "Ripped asunder, broken down into her component atoms and recycled and reconstituted into...*you*," he said testily. "She no longer exists in the universe, not even as a soul."

"Oh, my God," Jonah said, feeling a little queasy.

"Miss White wouldn't have cared as much about your annihilation," Gabriel said.

"Miranda was an awful human being, as far as I knew her," Jonah acknowledged, "but I liked to think that there was some possibility of redemption for her, even if it was after she had died, like with Malcolm."

"You've spent too much time with Mina," Lucifer said sharply, and Jonah caught his slip of the tongue. He had called her "Mina," not "Miss Xing" or "Missus Gideon."

"Your compassion serves you well, Mister Gideon," Gabriel said, with a cautionary sideways glance at Lucifer.

Jonah looked around at the bleak, empty desert landscape. "How do I get back?"

"We will leave you wherever you wish to be, once you're completed," Gabriel said. "We needed to confirm that you indeed wanted to return, before our crafters continue their reconstructive work."

Lucifer snorted. "It won't be an overlong process, Mister Gideon. You're not that complex, so you should be done in a few more hours. Time has passed concurrently, so you've been gone for less than a day. The local authorities won't recognize you as missing until more time has passed."

He recalled his last moments. "But Mina and Adam... what did they tell my family about what happened to me?"

Gabriel looked at his nails. "They haven't said anything, yet. Given your tendencies to wander off and disappear for days at a time, no one will think anything of your absence."

220

"Miss Hart was also at the home of your aunt and uncle recently," Lucifer said. "To leave with them whatever items could be recovered from your apartment before this week's demolition, as well as a substantial check from Garrison Brothers, made out to Constance and Theodore Gideon, for their insurance settlement." He glowered at Jonah's surprise. "I believe Miss Hart had discussed the matter with you, and she has a generous hand when writing checks from Garrison's accounts. That was the final portion of the agreement between the witches: compensation for your family's time, loss of property and 'mental anguish.' Not my idea."

Gabriel held up a thick, hefty envelope. "Your passport and all your official documents, including *your* disbursement from Garrison," he said wryly. "They will be returned to you when you are remade, then we can return you to any place you wish to go in the world: Maui, Paris, Singapore... or New York, perhaps?"

"Back to Boston, first," Jonah said and noticed Gabriel's bemused smile. "I want to get my shit together, say a proper good-bye to my aunt and uncle, *then* I'll go home to New York." *To Mina.*

Morgan was flushed and panting from his rush over from Crain Private Security's Flatiron office to the First Avenue greasy-spoon diner where Catherine Crain was having breakfast, from where she had texted him: *Breakfast with Cindy.*

Crap, he thought to himself as he spotted Cindy seated at a window table across from his mother, seemingly engaged in congenial, friendly conversation. His mother was a creature of habit, always having breakfast at the same diner and finished before eight o'clock, whenever she was in New York, so he knew exactly where to find them. Morgan was less sure about how his mom had gotten hold of Cindy's number to set up their morning get-together, then realized that she probably gotten it from Xani.

Morgan had been deliberately nebulous and tight-lipped with his mother about his relationship with Cindy, uncertain about how easily it would be accepted, given Xani's prior involvement with Cindy: the one-time Cyril McManus. Honestly, he wasn't sure how long the relationship would last, given his own insecurities about what Cindy could possibly see and want in him.

Cindy spotted him through the window and waved to him, and he felt a little better at the sight of her warm, assuring smile. He steeled himself, as he went inside and directly to their table.

To his dismay, their dishes had been cleared, with tell-tale stray toast crumbs and coffee rings on the table, which meant that they had been there for a while, already. A waiter came promptly and offered to bring a third chair.

"No, thank you, I was just getting ready to go," his mother said, rising to her feet. She brushed off some lint from her slender-cut designer jeans and tailored camel-hair blazer and placed a twenty-dollar bill on the table. "Why don't you take my seat, dear, and stay with Cindy at least until she finishes her coffee?"

Cindy rose to her feet deferentially. "This was very nice, Missus Crain. I hope we'll have a chance to talk again soon."

His mother smiled inscrutably. "I'm sure we will, Miss McManus." She gave Morgan a gentle hug and kiss on the cheek. "We'll talk later."

Morgan watched his mother leave, as he and Cindy took the empty seats. His mother was harder to read than usual, but Cindy seemed nonplussed, as she sipped her coffee.

"You didn't tell her who I was?" Cindy asked. "Who I *really* was?"

"She knows your last name," Morgan said.

"Not through you," Cindy said, shaking her head. "Xani didn't say anything, either, when she gave your mom my number, but she didn't have to. Your mom recognized my number, and when she saw me, it was pretty obvious."

Morgan stared at his folded hands. "I'm sorry. I didn't even know how to start explaining you to my mom." *That sounds really bad*, he realized belatedly.

Cindy caught the eye of the waiter and gestured for a cup of coffee for Morgan. "Which part of me: the fae aspect, my history with Xani, my skin color or that I used to be a boy?"

Morgan shrugged helplessly. "All of it. There's a lot to go through."

"I know. I just went through all of it with your mother over eggs and kielbasa," Cindy said. "She was already aware of some things, of course, but some of it was news. I know we haven't been together long, and we haven't even discussed whether we want to be exclusive, but your mother apparently noticed something different about you, so she reached out to me to share her concerns."

Morgan rolled his eyes at his mother's protectiveness, and Cindy smiled, as she reached across the table for his hand. "She loves you, and she wants the best for you. She wants you to have a happy, easy life."

Something in Cindy's voice was off. "What did she say to you?"

"She thinks we should give each other some space," Cindy said.

"And what did *you* say?" he asked, grasping her hand.

"I said it's your choice," she said. "It has to be. After how I treated Xani, your mother doesn't trust me, for good reason."

"Well, I want us to stay together," he said resolutely. "I don't care about what's happened in the

223

past; if we're happy, my mother will get used to the idea, sooner or later." He saw the hesitation in her face. "What?"

"You need to assure your mother that she's not going to lose you to me," Cindy said, in earnest. "You have to convince her in your own words, because my words don't carry the same weight.

Morgan recalled the friendly rapport that the women seemed to have. "She seems to like you."

Cindy flashed a pretty, patient smile at him. "Of course, she likes me—I'm partly fae and ravishing, but that doesn't mean she likes me for *you*. As far as she's concerned, I already seduced one of her children, and now I'm after the other. *I* wouldn't trust me, if I were in her shoes."

"I'll talk to my mother," Morgan said, "and I'll figure out what to say." He picked up Cindy's hand and kissed her slender, tan fingers. He had never been happier in a relationship, and he didn't want to screw it up. He certainly didn't want to give it up. "So, going back to this exclusivity thing…"

Cindy looked at him expectantly. "Yes?"

"Are we?"

"You're asking if I'm seeing anybody else?"

"I guess I'm asking if you want to keep your options open," he said apprehensively. He had been too busy working to even look at anyone else, but Cindy met new people every day.

She didn't answer right away, which made him more nervous, but he noticed the sly glimmer in her dark eyes that told him that she was playing with him. "I think I can limit myself to one partner," she said, finally. "What about you?"

"I haven't thought of anyone else since we've been together," he said.

"That's so sweet," she smiled.

"No, I've just been too busy with all the setups and upgrade work on Mina's building, and the repairs on the duplex after Ashu'ral's attack ate up the rest of my time," he said.

"That's sweet, too, for other reasons," she said. "That you're putting in all this time and work, to help protect people that you don't even know… that's pretty special, and enough to make me want to stick around." She leaned over and kissed him.

"It's worth the effort, just for that," he smiled, feeling warmed and sated by her simple touch.

Cindy sat back in her seat and flagged down the waiter for the check. "Come by the Lotus after work," she winked, "and I'll throw in something extra.

From the time she climbed out of bed on Monday morning, barely hours after she had returned to her apartment, Mina threw herself into her work. Despite succumbing to Cindy's prodding to share her burdens and tears, and finding some comfort in the effort to unload, sleep had eluded Mina for the night, so she chose to distract herself, instead.

She visited the duplex downstairs and met Galen's three beautiful, spirited children, who greeted and bowed to her as though she were royalty. She let the eldest, Gia, follow and observe her, as she replaced the wards and protections that had been weakened by Ashu'ral's siege.

Mina was surprised that the apartment wasn't in worse condition, considering what had transpired the evening before. Even the windows that Cindy had ordered repaired and replaced had already been repainted to match the original sills and sashes.

"We swept and cleaned what we could," Gia said. "Papa will pay you back for the broken furniture."

"There's no need for that," Mina said, spraying her own blend of lavender and sage oils onto the curtains and area rugs. "Cindy's already compensated me, more than enough. I'll tell your father, myself—if he tries to pay me, I will refuse it."

"Thank you, Miss Xing," Gia said. "We will always be indebted to you."

"I don't believe in life debts," Mina said mildly. "Just be happy, and share whatever good fortune befalls you with others, and that'll be enough."

After she finished at the duplex, sampling a leftover lemon and blueberry muffin that Gia had made with Adam, she looked in on Mrs Krantz to make sure that everything was fine. The older tenant seemed to enjoy having the family downstairs, as Gia liked to visit with homemade treats and listen to the widow's accounts of her younger, simpler days, and the children's raucous play and laughter enlivened the building with a joyful energy that had been lacking for some time.

The rest of the morning and afternoon passed with relative ease, punctuated with brief phone conversations with Adam and their mother, and a quick stop in at the Lotus to check that the protection wards were still holding. As she worked, she kept her ring turned around and out of sight to avoid well-meaning comments and questions from others. She said little to her friends, and they knew her situation well enough to understand her need for privacy.

Mina's overnight travel satchel was waiting outside the front door of her building when she returned. It was carried by a tall, broad-shouldered man with light blond hair and a healthy tan, looking something like a Nordic surf enthusiast.

"Bullfinch," she greeted, unlocking the front door. "You should've texted me that you were here."

Jacob Bullfinch bowed his head. "No worries, Mina. I just got here. You got back okay?"

Mina nodded, holding the door open for her parents' regular counselor. "No traffic that late at night," she said

226

idly, just for the sake of conversation. "Did you want to come up, have some tea?"

Bullfinch smiled, as if he realized that she was just being polite, and didn't bother coming inside. "No, I just wanted to drop this off in person," he said, holding out her satchel. "I have to get back to the office for a client meeting, anyway."

"Thanks," she said, for hand-delivering the bag, as well as for his consideration. "How's Izzy's ghost-dog, by the way?"

Jacob grinned that Mina recalled his girlfriend's spectral chihuahua. "Taquito's awesome. He's enjoying the biscuits you made him—Isabel wants the recipe, whenever you have a chance."

As Mina took the bag, Jacob passed her a folded note. "Your mother says you'll need this: the details for tonight. I'll have the car here to pick you up at six."

Mina glanced at the note. "Bullfinch, that gives me less than an hour to get ready."

Jacob smiled mischievously. "Then you'd better get started."

Mina sprinted up the stairs to her apartment and pulled everything together that she needed, almost unconsciously. Once she was focused on the urgency of what needed to be done, she forgot about everything that was beyond her power to control and change. Unthinkingly, she pulled on Jonah's black sleeveless U2 shirt and gray hoodie, wearing them like a second skin, or armor.

Temporarily freed of troubled thoughts, Mina was able to catch a quick nap in the back of the black town car that Jacob had sent to ferry her, so she unwittingly avoided the aggravation of sitting in New York rush hour traffic and the crowded, serpentine roads on the Jersey side of the Hudson. Mina only stirred when her driver called Jacob to let him know that she had arrived at the appointed terminal at Newark Liberty.

Adam stopped reading and looked up from his airport kiosk copy of *Scientific American*, at the sound of a familiar, chastising voice calling his name.

"You were going to ditch me?" Mina was channeling their mother's imperious glower, as she glared at Adam with clear disapproval.

"No?" Adam said evasively, casting a glance around, wondering how Mina had managed to track him down, directly to his departure gate. "We just got home last night, this morning. I didn't think you'd want to come. Don't you want to take a couple of days to rest and recharge?"

"And do what, exactly? I'm caught up with work, so I could either sit in the apartment and cry my eyes out, or drink myself into a stupor at the Lotus."

Mina sat down heavily in the seat next to his, setting her sling bag on her lap, and her overnight satchel on the seat next to her. "Mom texted me your flight details and had Yumi book my seat. You didn't even tell me you were leaving, you jerk!" she said, slapping his arm.

"Mom wants you to tag along to babysit me?" he asked.

"And to keep my mind off my own shit," she returned.

Adam nodded. "Multi-tasking."

"What else is new?" Mina shrugged. "Where are you sitting?"

"Coach," he said, just as he heard his name called by the gate attendant.

"Mom wants us to sit together," Mina said, watching Adam go to the gate.

"Mister Xing, good evening," smiled the attendant blandly, with almost mechanical politeness, befitting the plastic-like perfection of her chestnut curls. "There seems to have been a mix-up with your seat. *This* is your actual seat assignment," she said, handing Adam a new boarding pass. "Our apologies for the confusion, Sir."

Adam glanced at his new boarding pass and returned to his seat, flashing his upgraded ticket at Mina with a cynical shake of the head. "First class. Really?"

Mina threw her hands up. "It's Mom, and she's set in her ways. If we're heading all the way across the continent to visit, she wants us to be comfortable. What are you going to do?" she asked rhetorically.

Adam settled back into his seat next to Mina. "What *are* we going to do, when we get to San Francisco?"

"We do what we always do. We figure out what's wrong, and we fix it," she said casually. "Before that, Mom and Dad will feed us, take us shopping and offer us an exorbitant bribe to stay on the West Coast—as always."

"Speaking of exorbitant offers, what do you think about this Global Pacific package?" he asked. He had outlined the basic details over the phone with Mina, and she had agreed that it resembled their father's handiwork. "A cushy, six-figure position with hardly any responsibilities?"

"I think Mom and Dad love you and want you to stay out of trouble," she said. "This last situation was too close of a call, and far more than they're willing to risk again."

"But you've been doing stuff like this for years, by yourself," he said. "You need support."

"It shouldn't have to be you," Mina said. "You're the first-born, and the son." At Adam's eye roll, she said quietly, "I know our parents aren't that old-fashioned, but there is a reason that Dad gave you his jade, and not me."

Adam looked at her inquiringly.

"I take more after Mom, and you take more after Dad, so I'm not the one who needs guarding and protection. Do you remember what I am?"

"You're *huli jing,* but only partly," Adam said, wary of fellow passengers eavesdropping on their conversation. "And Mom's had a lot more experience than you with dealing with supernatural forces, so I really doubt that Mom and Dad expect you to watch over me, in the same way that she used to watch over him."

"And that's why you're being offered a shitload of money to be a corporate drone, so you can be safe," Mina smiled. "Look, maybe there's more to it than that. We'll just have to ask Mom and Dad what they're expecting, when we finally see them in person."

The more he saw her smile and heard her voice, the more he felt his old self returning. He wasn't at a hundred percent, yet, but given what he had endured, his recovery so far was nothing short of miraculous. "I guess so."

They picked their heads up as the activity picked up at the gate exit, as the gate and flight attendants took their stations.

"Whatever happens, I'm glad you're here with me for moral support," Adam said.

"Me, too," Mina said. "Maybe Mom's right, and I need this break, too."

Adam caught her glance down at the ruby ring on her left hand, and her face looked pained, as though an old wound had just reopened. He took her hand and looked at the ring. "Are you sure you want to keep wearing it?"

She frowned. "Right now, I can't bear the thought of taking it off. I've only had it on for a day."

"We are now boarding our first class passengers and platinum members," the gate attendant announced cheerily.

"That's us," Adam said, getting to his feet and pulling her up with him. "You ready for this, *mei-mei?*"

She squeezed his hand. "As long as you're with me, *ge-ge,* I'm ready for anything."

✧✧✧

Monday nights were usually light at the Red Lotus, due to some of the nearby Broadway shows going dark on Mondays and generating less pre and post-show business, but Cindy didn't mind. It was her night to catch up on bookkeeping, usually, which she usually did with Xani, and inventory, which she did with her staff.

It was a good night to provide Gia some experience with the lounge business, without overwhelming her with the usual, more colorful clientele. Gia had expressed some interest in perhaps working some day at the Lotus, so Galen gave his permission for her to shadow Cindy for the night. Cindy had the young fae bussing tables and delivering drinks, and it was an unspoken rule in the Red Lotus that no harassment would be tolerated, especially towards younger staff and customers, so Gia felt safe and respected in the protected space.

Cindy's phone was having a slow night, too. She only had one text message, earlier, from Mina: *Heading to SF with Adam. Turning phone off. Text you when we land.*

Cindy had spoken to Xani earlier in the day and knew that Adam had booked a flight to visit his parents, but Cindy hadn't realized that Mina would be going, too. *It'll be good for her to get away.* The reminders of Jonah would still be waiting in her apartment, and even at the Lotus, when Mina returned, but maybe they wouldn't be as painful for her by the time she returned.

After the dinner rush was mostly over, Cindy stepped out from behind the bar and waved to Gia. "Come with me."

She turned briefly at Morgan and Xani's arrival at the door, and she called over, "Give me two minutes."

As Morgan and Xani helped themselves at the bar, Cindy led Gia to the kitchen, where the young woman *really* wanted to be. "You may give the elves a hand

231

tonight, but only if they ask," Cindy directed, as the elves stopped working their stations, and even the salamanders looked over from their stoves and grills. "They are trained masters, and you are not, so observe, stay out of their way, and do not offer comments."

The elves nodded in unison, grateful for Cindy's support. "If you're asked to assist, keep your hair covered, your wings tucked, and your hands scrupulously clean." She called over her shoulder to the staff, on the way out: "And if *any* of you ask her to handle meat of any sort, you're dead!"

Morgan caught her outside of the kitchen and pulled her into the office, kissing her deeply once the door was closed behind them. "You're so sexy when you take charge," he whispered.

"I'm the boss here, so I'm always in charge," she smiled, brushing back one of his unruly red locks.

"I know," he grinned, leaning in for another kiss.

She set her finger briefly on his lips. "Did you speak with your mother?"

"As a matter of fact, I did," Morgan said solemnly. "Like you said, she expressed some doubts, but I told her that I love you—"

Cindy's eyes widened. "You told her *what*?"

"I told her what I felt," he said. "And what I feel, is that I can't bear the thought of not having you in my life." He noticed Cindy's surprise and dropped his eyes. "I know, it was probably weird and premature to say, but after what happened to Jonah… I don't know, I just didn't want to miss the chance to say it."

"You said that to your mom?" she asked.

"Just the first part," he said, shaking his head. "She has no idea who Jonah is, but yeah. That's how I feel."

Cindy kissed him, touched by his sincerity and his willingness to actually stand up for himself before a formidable figure like Catherine Crain. She thought also of the time and effort he had dedicated for her benefit and causes, without questioning her reasons or resolve, and sometimes without her even having to ask—if that wasn't a show of love, what was?

"This morning, at the diner, I had promised to have something extra for you tonight," she reminded.

"That's the only reason I'm here," he joked, letting her lead him to the door.

"Let's go into the spare room, and we'll let Xani watch the bar for a little bit," she enticed, nodding her head towards her erstwhile boudoir.

Xani was in the hall waiting for them, with her jade-green eyes wide, and the color drained from her face.

"Honey, what's wrong?" Cindy asked. "You look like you've just seen a ghost."

"Both of you, come out with me," Xani said shakily.

Seated at the bar, nursing a glass of plain ice water, was the very solid and alive-looking Jonah Gideon. He wore a scruffy black beard over his chiseled jaw, but it was unquestionably Jonah, with the same ice-blue eyes and threads of silver shot through his black hair. He hadn't noticed them yet, so he was looking around the Lotus with rapturous wonder.

When he finally spotted them, he smiled warmly— same handsome, boyish grin, as always. "There you all are!"

"Holy fuck," Cindy said under her breath.

"You're alive," Morgan said, with the same astonishment.

"It's a surprise to me, too," Jonah said, pensively. "It's been a long, strange journey."

"But Mina and Adam watched you die," Xani said.

"Yes, they did," Jonah said, brightening, with a glance around. "Speaking of Mina and Adam, are they here?"

233

You know the story can't end there…

If you've enjoyed this story, and the series so far,
please connect with me or leave me a review!
It's always great to hear from fans and readers!

Ande Li

About the Author

Ande has lived in Hong Kong, China, and the various boroughs of NYC, and has settled in the NJ suburbs with her husband and occasional collaborator Maurice X. Alvarez, their children, their free-range budgie and incredibly forgiving and patient rescue dog.

Discover other titles by Ande Li

The Gideon Files
Book One: Red Lotus
Book Three: Gold Peony
Book Four: Black Rose *(Upcoming Release)*

The Xonen Archives
Book One: The Healer's Girl
Book Two: The Children of Xon
Book Three: The Second Life of Cyrus Ex
Book Four: The Trickster's Game
Book Five: The Souls of Stars *(Upcoming Release)*

Team Spirits *(as Anne deLys)*
Art Appreciation
My Husband's Best Friend
Ever Faithful

co-written with Maurice X. Alvarez
The Trouble with Thieves
Book One: Return to Averia
Book Two: Trials of Halgarin
Book Three: Elmar of Tranquility

Connect with Me!
On Twitter: ***twitter.com/andeliauthor***
On Amazon: search **"Ande Li"**
On Facebook: ***facebook.com/Room808Press***

On the Web: *room808press.alvarezli.com/*